"So, you wanted to talk?"

That voice was the definition of sultry. Tori swayed to the music, her pelvis bumping against Dante's every few seconds, her fingers stroking the hair at his nape.

There were too many people on the crowded dance floor to talk about what he wanted to. Plus he wasn't sure he could keep his mind focused on the conversation while she was plastered against him like she was. "Not here," he murmured close to her ear.

Dante felt the shiver that went through her. She turned her face so that their lips were less than an inch apart. Amber flickered in her eyes and her breath tickled across his cheek. The slight curve of her belly brushed against his groin again, eliciting a resulting hardness to his lower body.

Before he could talk himself out of it, he dropped his mouth onto hers. His entire focus centered on the woman in his arms. Everything else—all the noise, the smells of the club—faded away. His heart thundered in his ears. Her tongue, tasting slightly of chocolate and amaretto and wholly of hot, sensual woman, twined with his...

ACCLAIM FOR
KISS OF THE VAMPIRE

"An inventive spin on supernatural mythos draws readers into this fast-paced paranormal series launch...Garner shows promise with great characters, constant action, and steamy sex."
—*Publishers Weekly*

"Intriguing...Garner provides both a cool premise and interesting characters. One to watch!"
—*RT Book Reviews*

"A deliciously dark and scorchingly sexy treat for fans of paranormal romances."
—*Chicago Tribune*

"With interesting back stories and even more interesting futures ahead, Garner keeps the readers wanting more...Tobias and Nix's relationship is passion-filled with hot lovemaking and even hotter story lines. I will eagerly be awaiting the next addition in this new series."
—*GoodReads.com*

"Various characters in the story have complex, yet compelling, backgrounds . . . As for the ending—*awesome*!...I closed the cover of this book while wishing that the second title was available for me to dive immediately into."
—*HuntressReviews.com*

"A refreshing look at the origin of vampires, werewolves,

and other myths. Fast-paced, the romantic and police procedural subplots deftly balance a strong storyline...never slows down as Cynthia Garner provides a fascinating take on the supernatural."

—GenreGoRoundReviews.blogspot.com

"I cannot wait for this series to continue...Garner seamlessly combines paranormal romance and romantic suspense that has you on the edge of your seat."

—-ANovelAddiction.wordpress.com

Secret of the Wolf

Also by Cynthia Garner

Kiss of the Vampire

Secret of the Wolf

Cynthia Garner

FOREVER

NEW YORK   BOSTON

Copyright © 2012 by Cindy Somerville
Excerpt from *Heart of the Demon* copyright © 2013 by Cindy Somerville
All rights reserved. In accordance with the U.S. Copyright Act of 1976, the scanning, uploading, and electronic sharing of any part of this book without the permission of the publisher is unlawful piracy and theft of the author's intellectual property. If you would like to use material from the book (other than for review purposes), prior written permission must be obtained by contacting the publisher at permissions@hbgusa.com. Thank you for your support of the author's rights.

Forever
Hachette Book Group
237 Park Avenue
New York, NY 10017
www.HachetteBookGroup.com

Printed in the United States of America

OPM

First Edition: June 2012

10 9 8 7 6 5 4 3 2 1

Forever is an imprint of Grand Central Publishing.
The Forever name and logo are trademarks of Hachette Book Group, Inc.

The Hachette Speakers Bureau provides a wide range of authors for speaking events. To find out more, go to www.hachettespeakersbureau.com or call (866) 376-6591.

The publisher is not responsible for websites (or their content) that are not owned by the publisher.

I'd like to dedicate this book to my sister,
my most stalwart fan.

Secret of the Wolf

Chapter One

Hard muscles rippled beneath skin and fur. Sharp teeth reformed themselves. Bones crunched, shifted, and re-aligned. Glossy brown fur receded, leaving behind only silken, tanned skin as wolf became human.

Became woman.

Hugging her knees to her chest, Victoria Joseph took several shuddering breaths and fought her way back from the mind of the wolf. Perspiration dotted her skin. Her body ached, muscles flexed and quivered, recovering from the shock and pain of transformation. As the last of the wolf retreated inside, giving her one final slash of pain through her midsection, a soft moan escaped her. She took another deep breath, the humidity of the August morning traveling deep into her lungs. The rain overnight had cleared out, but not before it had tamped down the pollen and dust that ordinarily floated in the air. It was monsoon season in the Sonoran Desert. Even with the rise in humidity, unbearable with the hundred degree temperatures, she loved this time of year. Monsoon storms were wild, swift, and deadly yet they spoke to her soul.

She skirted a large saguaro and, with arms that still

trembled, shoved aside a large rock to retrieve the plastic bag she'd stashed there earlier. She pulled out a bottle of water and took a long drink, then another and another until she'd downed it all. She'd learned a long time ago to rehydrate as soon as possible after a shift. Otherwise she'd be in real danger of passing out from the strain of the metamorphosis.

Dropping the bottle back into the bag, Tori drew out clean clothing and shoes. Once dressed, she tucked her cell phone into the front pocket of her jeans and plaited her long hair in a French braid. She hiked the mile back through the desert to the trailhead where she'd left her car. Whenever she went wolf, she wanted to get out where she'd have some degree of solitude, and the McDowell Sonoran Preserve afforded that, especially at night.

As she steered the Mini Cooper into her driveway, the sun began to rise over the eastern mountains, sending alternating shafts of light and shadow across the valley floor. She shut off the engine and sat there a moment, enjoying the stillness of the dawn, and wondered if her brother was awake yet. Randall had shown up four days prior without warning. The last time she'd seen him had been just before they were stripped of their bodies and put in a holding cell for decades. Their souls had then been sent through a rift between dimensions as punishment for a horrific crime committed by their cousin. As incorporeal entities they'd been drawn to Earth, to the bounty of human bodies available for the taking, for instinctively they'd known if they didn't take a host they'd die. She'd ended up in London in the body of a woman making her living on the streets of the East End. Through the years, she'd managed to get away from that kind of lifestyle, and the new Victoria Joseph had made her way to the United States at the turn of the twentieth century.

Rand, she'd found out just recently, had gone into a man in a small village outside of Manchester. It might as well have been the other side of the world. In 1866, it had been impossible to even begin to try to find him. She'd been alone, a stranger in a borrowed body, overcoming the guilt at displacing the rightful owner while trying to find her way in a primitive world. Staying alive was about all she could do for a long time.

She and her brother hadn't seen each other in nearly a hundred and fifty years until he'd shown up on her doorstep, a familiar spirit in a stranger's body. She'd known him instantly. He was the same sweet brother she remembered, yet he was different in some ways. More withdrawn and evasive with a chaser of surly. But even with the newfound secrecy, she would take what she could get. He was family. She was willing to overlook a few eccentricities and irritating behaviors to have him with her again.

Tori just wished she knew what to do to make him more at ease. He'd had some predisposition toward obsessive-compulsive behavior before the Influx of 1866, but those tendencies seemed to be exacerbated here. Perhaps the human he'd ended up inhabiting, Randall Langston, had also had such predilections.

With a sigh she got out of the car and let herself into her small two-bedroom rental. Smells of lavender and vanilla assailed her from the various bowls of potpourri she had scattered around the house. Her job as werewolf liaison to the Council of Preternaturals was more often than not dark and full of violence, and as a werewolf she was predisposed to be more aggressive in nature than an ordinary human woman. So when she came home she wanted calm and tranquility. She needed it in order to slough off the stress of the day.

Tori drew in a breath and held it a moment, letting the tranquil setting of her home seep into her spirit. Neutral beige and cream furniture was piled with blue and green pillows, and the same color scheme played out on the walls. The wooden wind chimes on the back patio clinked, the sound coming to her as clearly as if she were standing beside them.

She didn't need to use her keen werewolf hearing to pick up the snores coming from Rand's bedroom. He rarely arose much before noon, preferring to stay up until the wee hours of morning and run as a wolf as much as possible.

She tried to get over his choosing to run alone instead of with her. After all, he'd been on his own just like she had, and he was much more of a loner than she'd ever been. But it bothered her. Why had he gone to the trouble of locating her if he didn't want to spend any time with her? It was as natural for werewolves to run as a pack, even a small pack of two, as it was to breathe.

Tori moved quietly through the house, not wanting to wake him. She undressed in her bedroom, putting her cell phone on the nightstand. After she took a quick shower, she slipped into a robe and padded barefoot into the kitchen. She was starving, which wasn't unusual after a shift. She pulled some raw hamburger meat out of the fridge and gulped down a couple of handfuls—just enough to satisfy her inner wolf. She'd long ago gotten over the gross factor of eating raw meat.

That first time, she'd been half asleep and had come wide awake when she realized she was chowing down on raw liver. She'd soon discovered that the longer she denied the wolf its meal, the more violent it became when it finally got out. As long as she fed it regularly, she could shift without worrying that she'd kill someone.

She dumped some granola into a bowl and added a few diced strawberries. She poured herself a cup of coffee and went into her bedroom, closing the door with a soft *snick* behind her. She placed the cup and bowl on the end table and went over to her bookshelf. Reaching for a well-worn paperback, she pulled it off the shelf and went back to her queen-sized bed. She perched on the edge and opened the book in the middle, staring down at the pages before her.

She spooned cereal into her mouth and slipped a finger into the book to retrieve the small black device nestled into the area she'd cut out. The size of a cell phone, it was about half an inch thick with a couple of small knobs and two retractable antennae at one end. Tobias Caine, former vampire liaison to the preternatural council and now a member of the same, had given it to her two weeks ago. Apparently, he and his wife, Nix, had acquired it months ago but held onto it in secret, waiting for a safe moment to hand it off to her.

As Tobias had put it, he'd chosen Tori because she had two things he needed: a background in radio communications and the ability to keep her mouth shut. Discretion was most important until they figured out the gadget's purpose. She'd been honored that he trusted her with such a task.

He'd also given her the schematics, though they weren't very useful in getting the thing to work. Oh, she'd managed to turn it on, but within minutes a voice had spoken in the standard language of the other dimension, asking for a password. She'd quickly turned the device off. Now, as she studied the thing, turning it over and over in her hands, she tried to figure out how to activate it without having someone on the other side know. The schematics didn't seem to indicate that, at least not that she could tell. Perhaps it wasn't possible.

She wouldn't know until she tried. As far as she knew, only three other people knew she was in possession of this little doohickey—Tobias, his wife, Nix, and Dante MacMillan, a human detective who'd been right in the middle of the action when the device had come to light. Her resources were limited.

Tori finished her cereal and set the bowl back down on the nightstand. Grabbing her coffee, she took a sip and carried the cup as she went to her dresser. She opened her lingerie drawer and lifted her panties out of the way so she could pick up the folded schematics. She shoved the drawer closed with her hip. Going back to the bed, she spread out the plans and stared down at them while she sipped her coffee.

There were drawings of gears and lines and sections for a first amplifier and a second amplifier, R-F output, a resonator, and at least two doublers. Mostly though, it was a lot of letters and numbers that must have meant something to the person who'd drawn them up, but she couldn't decipher it. Not yet, anyway.

She placed her empty cup on the table and folded the paper up again. Sitting on the edge of the bed, she slid the schematics under her pillow for the time being and stared down at the device. The idea that this little thing could open up a mini rift amazed and frightened her. What was the purpose? Oh, she knew enough to figure that right now it was used to communicate from one dimension to the other. But there had to be more to it than that. What nefarious plans were being hatched, and by whom? Tobias hadn't told her from whom he'd gotten the device, just that the person had been mad with ambition.

Tori picked up the black apparatus and brought it closer to peer at the small knobs. She couldn't discern any labels or hash marks on the casing, nothing to indicate what function each knob had. She needed to get a magnifying glass to tell for sure.

The more she studied this thing, the more intrigued she became. It really was an ingenious contraption created by an imaginative and clever inventor. What had been his intention behind building it? Had he meant to make mischief? Or had his plans been more altruistic than that?

A quick rap on her bedroom door was followed by the door swinging open. Rand poked his head around the edge. "Good morning. You went out early. Or is it that you came in late?" His head tipped to one side as if he were considering a complicated brain teaser. "Oh well, no matter. What's that?" he asked, his gaze on the device in her hand. He came into the room wearing jeans, his chest and feet bare.

"Rand!" Tori closed her fist around the object in question and fought the urge to hide it behind her back. She wanted to deflect him from the device, not call attention to it, and putting her hand behind her back would make him all the more curious.

Lifting a hand, he lazily scratched his chest. His mouth opened wide in a huge yawn.

"You can't just barge in here. You need to wait for me to tell you to come in." She scowled at him. "What if I'd been getting dressed?"

"Then I'd have seen bits of you I don't necessarily want to see," he said. Tori had lost her East End accent long ago, but even after all these decades, Rand's tones still held the flavor of his British human host. He stuck his fingers into the front pockets of his jeans and hunched his shoulders. "I dare say I'd have recovered from the shock eventually." He glanced at her hand. "So, what *is* that?"

Though she was certain she could trust her brother, she was duty-bound not to divulge the secret. She liked Tobias. More than that, she admired him. She wouldn't betray his trust in her. As nonchalantly as she could, she replied, "It's just an MP3 player a friend asked me to try to fix for him."

Rand raised his brows, skepticism shadowing his eyes. "And why would he think you could fix it?"

"I was a radio communications technician back in the day. I've kept up with all the new gadgets as a hobby," was all she offered. She didn't want to talk to him about serving as a communications officer in the American Army during World War II. If he was as pacifistic as he'd been before their Influx, he wouldn't approve. She was sure he'd felt right at home during the sixties. Hell, he probably started the whole "Make Love Not War" movement. He would overlook the nobility of the cause, and right now she didn't want to get into an argument with him. Not when they'd just found each other again.

It was time for a change of subject. "So, what do you think of Arizona?" She kept her eyes on him and her hand wrapped around the device. It wouldn't do for him to get too close a look or he'd see it wasn't an MP3 player. She kept her voice cheery, hoping to distract him. "I mean, I know you've been here only a few days, but how do you like it so far?"

Her brother looked like he wanted to pursue the other topic, but for now he let it drop, for which she was grateful. While ordinarily she had no problems discussing her job or, in this case, a special assignment, this situation was different. He was her brother, and she didn't like being deceitful with him. She wanted him to feel like he could trust her because maybe, just maybe, he'd be more inclined to stay. But if he thought she was being disingenuous with him, it could be all the encouragement he needed to leave.

"I don't know," Rand said. His shoulders hunched further. "I like it well enough, I suppose. I don't believe I'll be staying here for the long term, though." He grimaced. "It's hotter than hell, for one thing. I mean, who the hell lives where it's a hundred and ten degrees, for crying out loud?"

"Right now it's hot, yeah. But it's perfect in the winter months." Tori bit back her disappointment. Rand didn't have to stay in Scottsdale with her, but she'd like him to be close. "And of course I want you to stay here, but wherever you end up, we have to stay in touch."

"Absolutely." He walked over to her dresser, making her stiffen for a moment. Not that there was anything he could get into—the schematics to the device were under her pillow. When all he did was stick a finger into the glass bowl of potpourri, she relaxed. He stirred the fragrant mixture around, making the scent of lavender and vanilla permeate the room. "It's been great to finally find you," he said without glancing her way, his tone one of a stranger making small talk. They might as well go back to discussing the weather.

He sounded less enthused about being with her than she'd like. It befuddled her. What was going on beneath that brush cut? She'd thought they had been on their way toward rebuilding the relationship that had been put on hold by their trip through the rift all those years ago, yet he seemed remarkably disinterested.

Before she could delve into it further, her cell phone rang. With a murmured apology, she slipped the rift device under her pillow and then grabbed her phone from the nightstand. She noticed her brother's sharp eyes hadn't missed the fact that she'd hidden the alleged MP3 player. She'd have to make sure to find a better hiding place than a book and her underwear drawer. She answered the phone on the second ring. "Hello?"

"Got a brouhaha over on Chaparral, just east of Hayden," the council dispatcher said without any formal greeting. He was an irascible werebear who didn't put up with a lot of crap, though he sure could dish it out. "Local LEOs have things in hand at the moment, but you need to get your furry self over there."

"What happened?" All business, she rose from the bed and headed toward her closet. For now, at least, the Scottsdale police had things under control. She paused as she reached for a blouse and wondered if Dante MacMillan was already at the scene. A sensual shiver worked its way through her. There was something about that man, something that, even though he was human, called to everything feminine and primal within her.

"Some kind of skirmish between a werewolf and a

vamp," the dispatcher answered, drawing her back to the conversation, "with a human bystander caught between 'em. Think the human's okay, though. Well, mostly okay." The werebear gave a little growl. "As okay as one of 'em can be in the middle of a fight between two prets, I suppose. But you need to get over there pronto."

"Ten-four." She grinned at the dispatcher's disgruntled snarl. He really hated it when she used police codes. Tori rang off and looked at her brother. She shoved the phone into the pocket of her robe. As she pulled the blouse from its hanger, she started, "Rand, I—"

"Let me guess," her brother said. His voice held a hint of sarcasm that dismayed her. "You have to go."

She nodded and went to her dresser to pull out a clean pair of jeans. "Rand, we really—"

He slashed a hand through the air. His face darkened, glittering gaze meeting hers. "Just forget it, Tori. It's always been this way with you. Job first, family second." He sounded like a sulky child.

She tamped down a surge of irritation even as she felt the need to defend herself and her choices. "That's not true!" She dropped her clothing on the bed and went over to him. She put her hand on his shoulder and gave it a squeeze. "I love you, you know that. And I love having you here. It's just like old times. With you around, it makes this place, this planet, feel like home." For the first time since she'd arrived in this strange, new world it felt... comfortable. Family made all the difference.

She was surprised to see a film of tears make his blue eyes shine. "It's not that I don't like being here with you," he said, his voice low, a little hoarse. "It's just..."

He shook his head with a sigh. "I've always felt like I existed in your shadow. 'Why can't you be more like your sister?'" he mimicked in an excellent approximation of their father's bellicose tones. "'Your sister never disappoints us.'" He went back to his normal voice. "I knew he was disappointed in me. Always disappointed. And I'm just not sure that, if I stay, things will be any different. I'll be known as Tori's little brother, the inept one. The loser."

"Rand, no you won't." Tori felt much more compelled to build up Rand's self-esteem than to defend her father. He had been strict, demanding perfection from a son who was too emotionally fragile to withstand the pressure. She gave her brother's shoulder another squeeze. "You're not inept. And Father loved you. You know he did."

"Did he?" Rand shrugged. His fingers started tapping against his thigh. "Whatever." He wore the same churlish expression he had when he'd been a teen. She felt momentary dismay that he could still be so immature. Hadn't he learned anything from his trip through the rift? Had he not grown at all in the century and a half they'd been on Earth? He seemed to shake his mood, because a slight smile tilted his lips. He lifted his hands, spreading them in a sheepish gesture. "Listen, I'm just being..." He shook his head. "Don't pay any attention to me. Go. Get to work. Save the day," he said in an approximation of a superhero's voice.

She returned his smile, though she couldn't get rid of the worry niggling at the back of her mind. He was lost and alone and resisting her attempts to make him part of her life again. If she pushed too hard she might lose him again. On impulse, she hugged him and quickly released his thin but firm body. Anyone who made the mistake of thinking he'd be physically weak might make the last mistake of their lives. She pressed a kiss to his cheek and tried to ignore the sour-milk scent of his sullen discontent. "I'll see you later, all right? We'll have dinner together. Think about what you'd like, and I'll stop by the grocery store on my way home." She searched his eyes, looking for a sign, any sign, of what he might be thinking, what he was feeling. "We'll talk. Catch up some more."

"Yeah. Sure." He gave another smile, though this one was definitely forced. With a nod he left the room, pulling the door closed behind him.

Tori grabbed the device and schematics from beneath her pillow. She slipped the folded paper into the pocket of a fleece jacket she hardly ever wore and tucked the device into the toe of one of her boots. The jeans she shimmied into were formfitting, and the blouse was frothy in various shades of turquoise. Her women's athletic shoes were serviceable with bright purple along the edge of the sole. Being a werewolf was so much a part of what she was, she needed to find ways to feel like a woman. To be feminine. To be more than the beast. Purple shoes and filmy blouses helped.

She brushed her still-damp hair and braided it, then slipped her brush into the fanny pack she usually wore instead of carrying a purse. After shrugging into her shoulder holster, she retrieved her Magnum from the gun safe. It was a requirement of the council that all liaisons, in essence law enforcement officers for preternaturals, had to carry guns. Tori didn't usually mind, but sometimes the gun was the least favorite part of her job.

While it often made her feel sexy, it rarely made her feel feminine.

Besides, when it came to defending herself or running down a suspect, all she really needed were her claws and fangs.

Chapter Two

Tori parked her Mini behind a Scottsdale squad car and hopped out. She gave a nod to one of the uniforms standing at the perimeter of the scene, keeping the crowd at bay. Several squad cars with lights flashing marked the area of the grocery store parking lot where the action was taking place.

As she approached the police van near the group of black-and-whites, the acrid scent of drying blood wafted to her. Quickly, she scanned the scene, seeing patches of blood on the pavement and a lump of bloody material lying near the entrance to the store. Never far from her thoughts, she wondered if Dante had arrived yet, and she glanced around again, this time to suss out something, someone, entirely different. Her stomach bottomed with disappointment when she didn't see him. Maybe because there wasn't a human fatality he wouldn't be dispatched. It's not like he covered all the cases. There were several members of the Special Case squad that could be sent to work an active crime scene, but the extent of their involvement, if at all, depended on whether humans were embroiled in the action. If Dante had too much on his plate, another detective would be sent here. At that thought, her disappointment grew.

She blew out a breath and put her attention on the police van. A man sat in the back, huddled in a blanket, his hands clutching the edges in front of him to cover his nudity. Since he was naked, she had to assume he'd tangled with the vampire in his werewolf form. She grimaced. That was easier to picture than him just cavorting around in the buff. "Well, there's the werewolf," she murmured to herself. "Where's the vampire?"

Glancing around, she spotted him off to one side, a couple of uniformed officers standing beside him. Their hands rested on the butts of their weapons; their eyes shifted from one another to the vampire. Tori made a mental note to keep the van between her and them in case those itchy trigger fingers weren't held in check. The vampire liaison, Aldis Knox, was already there, taking the vamp's statement. She lifted a hand in greeting and stopped next to another uniformed officer. "What's the status of the human?" she asked the young cop.

"EMTs took him over to County."

If he was taken to the hospital, it meant he'd probably gotten in the way of somebody's teeth. "Was he bitten?" she asked.

"Looks like." The officer gave a quick shrug. "They weren't sure which of the EDs did it, so they'll keep him in the secure wing until they know whether or not he's going to turn."

"We prefer to be called preternaturals. Or prets if it's easier." Tori held his gaze.

A slight flush darkened his cheeks. "Sorry?"

She couldn't tell if his confusion was genuine or put on. "You called them"—she gestured toward the werewolf and the vampire with a swoop of one arm—"EDs.

Extra-dimensionals. Most of us prefer to be called preternaturals," she repeated, just in case he was missing her point.

"Oh." He stared at her for a few seconds, then offered a muttered apology. "I didn't know."

"No problem," she responded easily. "Now you do." She glanced around the scene again, unable to keep from searching for Dante. She didn't see tall and sexy anywhere. "Has Detective MacMillan arrived yet?"

"No, ma'am."

She gave a brief nod and, as she started to move off, the officer said, "Ah, ma'am?"

Tori stopped and looked back at him.

"How does that work, exactly? Turning someone, I mean." He gave a sheepish smile. "They explained it to us in the academy, but I didn't really understand it."

She was glad to educate him, figuring the more informed humans were the less they might let their imaginations overtake them. "The pret releases a little bit of their essence—a piece of their soul, if you will—into the victim's blood. For a vampire, the timing is critical. It has to happen right before the person dies." She remembered the first time she'd seen someone "come back" after being bitten by a vampire. The poor thing hadn't been expecting it, and it had taken all of Knox's considerable strength to hold the woman down while he explained what had happened. Only the sound of Tori's voice had finally calmed the new vampire enough so that she could actually hear what Knox was telling her. Tori looked at the officer. "A shapeshifter can do it at any point during the attack. And the victim doesn't necessarily die. But at the next full moon they will transform."

"Okay." He glanced over his shoulder at the vampire. He seemed much more nervous of the vamp than the shapeshifter.

Tori decided to disabuse him of any illusions he might have that werewolves weren't a threat. He'd live longer if he learned this lesson now instead of while being maimed by teeth and claws. She leaned in and let the wolf come to life in her eyes, just a little. "We're all just as dangerous, officer."

His face paled and he jerked back a couple of steps. "Right. Yeah."

She'd meant to get her point across, not scare the crap out of him. She sighed and held up a hand. "Look, I'm sorry. That was a little heavy-handed." She put some space between them and heard his breathing even out. "Just...don't underestimate any pret, okay? You'll live a lot longer," she added in a dry tone.

"Right." He swallowed and then dipped his chin. "Thanks."

Tori nodded and walked over to the werewolf in the blanket, unzipping her portfolio as she went. She drew a breath and frowned as she stopped at the back of the van. "Barry," she greeted the werewolf in a calm voice. She'd discovered over the years that having such a melodious tone was at odds with her being a wolf, and it kept people off guard long enough for her to worm out more information than she might otherwise ordinarily get. She drew out her pen and jotted down the date and location on the incident report form.

"Ms. Joseph." He briefly met her gaze and then ducked his head. She hadn't thought it possible but his shoulders hunched even more. A definite odor of tequila and rum poured off him, though it lessened with each passing second. The smoky mixture of chagrin and irritation only grew.

"You want to tell me what happened here?" she asked.

"Not really." At her sharp look, he cowered as if expecting a blow. When one didn't come, he lifted his head slightly and looked up at her. Well, looked in her general direction, because he didn't make eye contact.

"Barry," she said. "I'm not part of your pack." She wasn't part of anyone's pack, not really, unless you counted the other werewolf liaisons in the region. "I'm not going to hold you to your Omega status, okay?" It was obvious to her from his subservient demeanor that he was the lowest ranking member of his pack, one that treated him roughly, if his cowering was anything to go by.

His eyes darted to hers but he didn't say anything.

"Now, tell me what happened."

"He started it." His expression turning mutinous, Barry pointed at the vampire. "He called me a mutt." His words came out a little slurred, but she knew any intoxication he currently suffered would soon dissipate. The incredible metabolism of a werewolf made it impossible to maintain a drunken stupor for long.

She knew that from firsthand experience.

"And calling you a mutt started the fight?" She made a few notes.

"Well, no." He shifted and pulled the blanket tighter. "He said my mother was a real bitch." His mouth tightened. "I loved my mother."

"I'm sure you did." Tori held her pen at the ready. "So that's what started the fight? Him insulting your mom?"

"No." Barry straightened. "He said my Wilma was a shitmobile. A shitmobile!"

That seemed a strange insult to deliver to a wife or girl-friend. "I take it Wilma is your…"

"She's a 1965 Mustang convertible." He gave a low growl. "Shitmobile." His face darkened. His gaze on the vamp, he started to get up.

"Barry, sit down. Now." Shooting him a look but not changing the calm tenor of her voice, Tori jotted a few more notes on the incident report. Once Barry had sunk back down onto the seat, she looked at him. "So you let this guy insult you, insult your mom, but when he dissed your car, that's when you let him have it?" She lifted her eyebrows. It made no sense to her, but then she didn't have testicles.

"Wilma can't stand up for herself. He had no business insulting her. I had to make him pay for it." He sent a glare the vampire's way.

Tori glanced over her shoulder to see the vampire completely ignore Barry, though she could tell by the smirk on his face he was well aware the werewolf was glowering at him. The vamp said something and then shook Knox's hand before he walked off.

"They're just letting him leave?" Barry jumped down out of the van, leaving the blanket behind. "What the hell!"

Shocked gasps and then titters from the crowd drifted to Tori. "Oh, for the love of…Barry!" she barked, dropping her calm voice. Barry flashing his junk was not going to garner any points with the locals. "Get your ass back in the van. And cover it up, for crying out loud." When he started past her, she grabbed his arm and whirled him around with a snarl. She held his gaze, the wolf clawing to get out. She was determined to maintain her professionalism, despite the fact that her inner wolf wanted to let loose with teeth and claws. It always wanted to rumble. "You do not want to start something with me. Do you?"

Her voice was no longer the soothing tones she'd been using. It was low with the growl of the wolf. And he took note of it.

"No, ma'am." He climbed back into the van and draped the blanket over his lap. "Sorry."

Tori drew in a deep, cleansing breath. She made a few more notes on the incident report and then closed her portfolio and tucked it under her arm. She looked at Barry. "You'll have to spend the night at the council jail, and go before the council tomorrow. They'll decide what your punishment will be." The western region Council of Preternaturals, made up of thirteen members representing most of the major clans of prets, handed out swift justice. It wasn't always merciful, though, and Tori hoped Barry got a break.

"Why do I have to spend the night in the pokey but he gets to walk away?" He sat there, shoulders hunched, blanket bunched over his lap, looking like a recalcitrant child, not the vicious killer he had the potential to be. The killer he probably was. Every werewolf she'd ever known had killed at least one person. Some on purpose, some by accident.

It was something you never forgot, that first kill.

Tori pushed back guilt over dark things she herself could never undo. "Pouting on a werewolf is never pretty, Barry." She narrowed her eyes. Referencing a popular board game, she said, "Do not pass Go, do not collect two hundred dollars. You started the fight. You're the one who lost control, not the vamp. Just pray you weren't the one who injured the human, or your punishment will be worse. And if you turned him, against his will..."

Barry heaved a sigh and leaned his elbows on his knees, scrubbing his face with his palms. "Oh, God," he moaned, his voice muffled by his hands. "I am in so much trouble."

"You very well might be." Tori reached in and touched his arm. She remembered a time when she hadn't made the best of choices, so she could certainly feel for him in his current situation. Faced with what he'd done, she knew he'd do anything to turn back the clock, to undo what had happened. "I'll do what I can for you," she murmured.

"Thanks." He rubbed his hands over his face again and then turned his head to look at her. "I won't cause any more trouble." He sounded weary. Defeated.

Sooner or later the wolf broke them all. Then you learned to live with what you were, learned to accept your darker side and the atrocities it was capable of committing.

Tori lifted her chin in acknowledgment and pulled her cell phone out of her pocket. After making transportation arrangements for Barry, she put her phone away. Struck by a thought, she looked at the disheartened werewolf. "Barry, you've heard about the attacks in the north quadrant?"

He held up his hands. "Hey, it's not me. I'm not stupid."

She raised her eyebrows in unspoken disagreement. The idiot had taken on a vampire because of an insult to his car.

"Usually," he amended with a sigh. "I'm usually not stupid." He crossed his arms. "And I'm definitely not stupid enough to go turning people into wolves without council sanction."

An accidental turning now and then was usually forgiven, as was an unsanctioned turning out of necessity, done to save someone's life. But in most cases a rogue pret who willy-nilly started making other preternaturals was executed. And one who turned people against their will had no other option than to pay with his own life.

Preternatural law was efficient and deadly.

She studied Barry, saw the honesty in his eyes, smelled the light aroma of his sincerity, yet still, she had to be sure. She ripped a blank piece of paper out of her notebook and handed it to him. "Write down where you were on the fifth, sixth, ninth, and tenth. Account for every minute, Barry." Deciding she wanted the vamp's side of the story, Tori started toward Knox. "Sit tight," she said to Barry over her shoulder. "Transport should be here in about half an hour."

He gave a nod. Blowing out a breath, he leaned back against the inside of the van.

Tori's long strides covered the distance between her and the vampire liaison quickly, but when a spicy, woodsy scent wafted her way she faltered. She glanced around and saw Dante MacMillan standing at the perimeter of the parking lot, talking to one of the uniformed officers. As she stared at him, her heartbeat picked up speed, setting up a hard thump in the pulse at the base of her throat. Mutant butterflies began doing somersaults in her stomach. Her breathing quickened.

This is ridiculous. She was a hundred and seventy-six

years old, for crying out loud. Yet here she was, reacting like a schoolgirl with her first crush. But she'd have to be dead inside to not appreciate that walking advertisement for tall, dark, and sexy.

Dante's head was bent as he listened to the officer, and the sun glinted off his dark hair. As usual, it was brushed back from his forehead, but stubborn strands insisted on falling forward. They made Tori's fingers itch to stroke them off his face just so she could watch them flop down again. He gestured, and her attention was caught by his masculine hands. Long, square-tipped fingers and broad palms.

She'd love to feel those hands on her skin.

Dante must have felt her gaze on him, because he lifted his head and looked right at her. Sexual interest flared in his brown eyes before he turned back to the man beside him.

"Uh, Tori?"

She jerked back to awareness and looked at Knox.

"You okay?" the vampire asked. Blue eyes stared at her with a mixture of concern and bewilderment. "You're just standing there, in the middle of the lot, staring..." His gaze drifted to Dante and he gave a soft grunt. "Ah. Never mind."

Tori felt her cheeks heat. She'd been caught gawking at Dante like a teenager. It was mortifying. She cleared her throat and deliberately turned her back so she wouldn't be tempted to start watching him again. "So, what did your guy have to say? What was he doing here?"

"Picking up a bottle of red wine." Knox pointed toward a broken bottle and the spill of wine near the front door. "He said your wolf-boy attacked him without provocation."

"Oh, come on." She put one hand on her hip. "Barry may be a little impetuous, but even he wouldn't go around jumping vampires without cause. Your guy definitely provoked him."

Knox shrugged lazily. "Eh. A few words about a car. If your wolf got all riled up over a guy with a big mouth, well..." His gaze dared her to defend that. "Besides, wolfie's the one who injured the human."

"You're sure about that?" Tori glanced over at the van to where Barry sat slumped on the seat, blanket still modestly covering his privates. He met her gaze for a second and then looked away. Tori faced Knox again. "It could have been your vamp."

Knox shook his head. "Nope. Wolf-boy is the one who took the human down in his hurry to get to the vampire. Who, by the way, kept his fangs to himself."

Tori sighed and rubbed her forehead. This did not bode well for Barry. "All right. Hopefully, Barry didn't release any pret essence when he hurt the guy. That'll make things easier for him."

"Hmm." Knox glanced over her shoulder. "Heads up. Here comes your boyfriend."

"He's not my..." Tori scowled at Knox's easy grin. "Shut up. What are you, like, twelve?"

"Four hundred and sixty-seven, actually."

"Well, you're acting like a twelve-year-old." She put a smile on her face and turned to greet Dante. "How's it going? Any word on the vic?" She couldn't keep her eyes from drifting down the lean length of his body. This close, his scent was stronger, more enticing.

"Not yet." His smile was slow and lazy. "You're lookin' good."

As usual, Dante was charming and flirtatious, completely impossible to ignore and utterly not serious about her. But she could flirt with the best of them, especially when he so easily revved her engine. "You're looking mighty fine yourself." Her voice came out throaty. She couldn't help it. He did look fine. More than fine. Any finer and she might jump his bones.

Dante winked at her, then glanced at the vampire liaison. "Knox, you look well, too. Rested. Have a nice vacation?"

Knox grimaced. "I was reassigned to Yuma, MacMillan, not spending a week in Paris." He muttered something that sounded like "Teach me not to get on Caladh's bad side again."

Tori pressed her lips together against a grin. Caladh was a seal shapeshifter and one of the more powerful members of the council. "Yuma's the third largest city outside of Phoenix and Tucson," Tori defended. "It's got the territorial prison. That's kinda cool."

Knox just looked at her.

She liked Yuma, personally, but the fact that Knox, the consummate urban dweller, had been assigned there tickled her to no end. She couldn't resist giving him a few verbal jabs. "It's right next to California. You could go dune bashing in the Imperial Sand Dunes. And San Diego's not that far away. You can go whale watching," she offered. "Or check out the sea lions in La Jolla."

The vampire's look went even drier.

"Give it up, Tori." Dante never lost his grin. "I think Knox here is a city boy through and through." He lifted a brow. "It must be torture for you to be here with us instead of L.A. or New York."

"Tell me about it," Knox muttered.

"So, what'd you do to get stuck here?" Tori asked. She knew he'd been assigned to one of the Los Angeles quadrants a few years ago, and she also knew he'd never have left L.A. voluntarily.

The vampire's lips tightened. "Never mind." His gaze flicked to over her shoulder. "Here comes the poster girl for comic book heroines."

Tori turned to see the quadrant's new human liaison, Piper Peterson, coming their way. The young woman had a lilt in her step, her eyes covered by round, dark sunglasses, her mouth curved in its customary smile. She always seemed perky, and with a name like Piper Peterson...well, Tori understood how a guy like Knox could be a little snide about her. She just hoped he wouldn't give Piper a hard time to her face.

The human liaison stopped next to Dante and pushed the sunglasses up on top of her blonde head. Ignoring Knox, an action that interested Tori greatly, she looked at Dante and Tori and said, "So, I just got word that the guy who was hurt is going to be all right. He wasn't, ah, enhanced in any way."

Tori blew out a sigh. Barry was still in trouble, just not as much. She'd go break the news to him. "I'll be right back," she said and headed toward the police van where Barry still waited.

As she approached, he looked up and then stiffened. "What? You found something out?" he asked, his voice holding a slight tremble.

"The vic wasn't turned. You're off the hook, for that at least." Tori glanced around the parking lot and saw some of the crowd had dissipated.

Barry gave a nod and leaned forward, resting his elbows on his knees. Staring down at his hands, he murmured, "I really messed up this time, didn't I?"

She wasn't going to sugarcoat anything for him. "Yeah, you did. But they'll go easier on you since you didn't accidentally turn the guy." She kept one ear on the conversation going on behind her and heard Piper talking about another case involving a distant relative of hers. A car pulling into the lot caught Tori's eye. She recognized the two council guards who got out. "Looks like your ride is here," she told Barry.

He exhaled and climbed out of the van, keeping the blanket securely around him. He paused and looked at Tori. "Thanks."

She tipped her chin. "Take care of yourself."

"Right." He walked toward the guards and got into the back of the car.

As the vehicle pulled out of the lot, Tori returned to Dante and the other two liaisons.

"If anything," Piper was saying, "I think the council treated him more harshly because of me."

"Oh, no doubt," Knox said. "Family members of liaisons are supposed to conduct themselves with the utmost comportment."

Piper rolled her eyes. "There aren't too many prets that I know of who can manage to comport themselves utmostly." She made quote marks in the air, and her glance at Knox suggested he had little room to talk about proper behavior.

Tori frowned. Man, she must have missed something between these two. The tension was almost to the point of animosity.

The vampire scowled. "I'm done here," he stated and walked off.

With another roll of her eyes, Piper said, "Good riddance to bad garbage."

"I heard that," Knox called out.

Piper shrugged. "It's not anything I wouldn't have said to his face." When Tori started to say something, Piper waved a hand with a muttered, "I'd really rather not talk about it." She looked at Dante. "So, I saw Nix last night, and she told me to tell you hello the next time I saw you. So... hello."

Dante's face softened with concern for Nix de la Fuente, the former human liaison. Well, Nix Caine now, since Nix and Tobias had gotten married a few months ago. Tori knew Nix and Dante had worked together for a short time but had formed a solid friendship, one that Tori would never admit out loud had made her envious.

Dante said, "I haven't talked to her in a couple of weeks. She doing okay?"

"I think she's having a harder time acclimating to being a vampire than she wants to admit. Plus her mom..." Piper shook her head and frowned. "Her mom isn't exactly thrilled to have a vampire daughter. And of course she blames Tobias."

"But Tobias had to turn her to keep her from dying." Tori planted one hand on her hip. "What, her mom has a problem with not having a dead daughter?"

"Apparently she has a real thing about vamps. You know how demons are." Dante hooked his thumbs over his belt, large hands framing his silver belt buckle.

That little action drew Tori's gaze to his midsection, then lower. He caught her looking, of course, his smirk knowing. She met his eyes and held them, challenging him. The man knew exactly what he was doing. So if he wanted her to look, she'd look. She deliberately dropped her gaze and saw the faintest twitch behind the placket of his zipper.

He cleared his throat and pulled his jacket closed, fastening one of the buttons. "So, I'll just take a look around the scene, do my job."

"I'm going to head over to the hospital and talk to the victim," Piper said. "I'll keep you two posted."

Tori murmured a good-bye to her and turned with Dante as he walked the parking lot. "So, how about a cup of coffee?" She rested one hand on his upper arm, able to feel the firmness of his biceps beneath the layers of clothing. "My treat."

The muscles beneath her fingers tensed. His tongue swept out to wet his lips, drawing her gaze to that sexy mouth. "I'd like to, Tori. I would. It's just…" He gestured with one arm. "I have a ton of cases right now. I should finish up here and get back to the station." Dislodging her hand, Dante rubbed the back of his neck. He looked as uncomfortable as a dog that had just gotten skunked.

"No problem," she said easily. "Tomorrow's Saturday. We could meet for breakfast."

His tongue swept across his lower lip, a gesture of nervousness that on him managed to look sexy. He gave a little wince and said, "Sorry. Weekends I'm tied up with my horses."

"I understand." But she didn't. Not really. He flirted, he teased, and then he turned skittish and shut down any time she made an approach. One of these days maybe she'd get it through her head that he just wasn't into her, and give up.

"Rain check?" he asked, his voice as polite as the expression on his face, though his eyes were awash with swirling emotions she had a hard time deciphering. Indecision crossed his face before his lids drooped, hiding his feelings even more.

"Of course." She should go back home and fiddle with that device, since Dante wasn't going to let her fiddle with him. Maybe she'd discover something new and see if she could reconnect with a brother who blew as hot and cold as a certain Special Case detective.

Chapter Three

Dante forced himself to focus on the job and not on how fresh and enticing Tori smelled, or how sexy she looked. He swore those damned jeans she wore were sprayed on, and the flimsy blouse accentuated the enticing curve of her breasts. But between building his career and taking care of a sister recovering from the double whammy of breast cancer and a divorce, he didn't have time for a relationship. So while he might flirt with Tori, because she was a beautiful woman even if she did go furry at least once a month, he wasn't ready for anything serious. Especially not with a pret. Not because he was prejudiced, but because simply being a pret meant she lived in a world even more dangerous than the one he did. Every day he fought back fear that he'd lose his sister to the cancer that had tried to ravage her body; he wasn't ready to go through a loss with someone else he cared for. If he had anything more with Tori than a working relationship, his admiration for her intelligence and abilities and, yes, his attraction to her would deepen to something he wasn't ready for. Because if he fell in love with her and lost her...

He blew out a breath and tracked bloody footprints

across the pavement, stopping next to a torn denim jacket lying a few feet away from the entrance to the now-closed grocery store. "This belong to the vic?" he asked her.

"I guess so." She glanced around. "The crime scene specialists are running late on this one."

Her sultry voice wrapped around him, tightening his gut and other parts that had no business getting tight on the job. He cleared his throat. "The CSS unit doesn't have the same sense of urgency for nonfatal incidents." He hunkered down and looked over the torn and stained jacket, careful not to disturb it. Criminalists would need to photograph it before anyone could move it. "From what I can see, there are holes in the shoulder area." He tilted his head to look closer. Parts of the jacket were shredded, he guessed from the werewolf's claws, but several holes had been punctured in the jacket as well. "More than two, which would support the supposition that it was the werewolf who bit the guy, not the vamp."

"Yes, well, until we get test results from the hospital, that part's still up for grabs as far as I'm concerned." Disgust dried Tori's tones. "I still wouldn't put it past that bloodsucker to have been the one to bite the vic. You know, just a slight slip of the fang for a quick snack."

Dante studied the ground around the jacket, noting the splashes of blood, then rose to his feet. "You got somethin' against vamps?" He shot a glance at her from the corner of his eye.

"Not at all." She raised her shoulders in a shrug. "Hey, some of my best friends are vampires. I just didn't like the looks of the guy Knox was talking to." She blew out a sigh hard enough to ruffle her bangs. "Though it probably was Barry who bit our vic. Poor guy."

"You talkin' about the vic or Barry?" Dante grinned, just a little, at the disgruntled look that crossed her face.

"Both, I suppose." She shoved her fingers into the back pockets of her jeans, an action that thrust out her breasts. She seemed completely unaware of her posture.

Dante was more conscious of it than he should have been.

"At some point I should head over to the council office to put in a good word or two...or three or four or five, for Barry." Defensiveness lit her gaze. "He's not a bad guy, you know."

Where'd that come from? He held up one hand in appeasement. "I didn't say he was."

Her sensual lips curved down. "Yeah, well, he attacked a human. I'd think in your book that'd make him a bad guy." Her arch look challenged him.

"In *my* book?"

She nodded. "In that how-to-be-a-by-the-book-detective handbook of yours."

"Me? A by-the-book guy?" His brows shot up. "I believe you have me confused with someone else. Maybe Tobias Caine?"

"When it comes to the rules, sure, you don't always follow 'em. But when it comes to bad guys, you're pretty much black and white on who's bad and who's not." Keeping her hands in her back pockets, she wiggled her elbows back and forth and sent him a look that was as dry as autumn leaves. "And, believe me, no one could confuse you for Tobias."

He wasn't sure whether he should be insulted or not. "And why would that be?"

She grinned. Her expression softened with sensuality.

"While you're both tall, dark, and handsome," she nearly purred as she stroked one slender finger down the middle of his chest, "Tobias has a bigger bite behind his bark."

"Can't argue with that." Dante eased back a step, putting himself out of her reach. Even that light, teasing touch fired his blood. He came into contact with his fair share of shapeshifters on the job, and one thing he'd noticed was that they all seemed to possess this earthy carnality that was impossible to ignore. Tori called to him on such a primal level it was all he could do to keep his distance. But she deserved respect from him even if all he wanted to do was take her with the raw fury of an animal.

He, at least, didn't go furry once a month. He was human. He had to remain true to himself, or what would he be left with?

He heard a couple of car doors slam and turned to see one of the crime scene vans parked nearby. "CSSU's here."

"'Bout time," Tori muttered, sounding a little cranky. Even so, her voice still held those dulcet tones that made everything male within him sit up and take notice.

Dante started toward the van, glancing around the gathered crowd out of habit. One man in particular caught his eye and Dante stopped, trying to get a better look.

Tori plowed into him, giving a little grunt of surprise, and he turned to grab her. He wrapped his fingers around her upper arms to steady her, and the feel of the firm muscles beneath his fingers—her strength wrapped in softness—scattered his thoughts.

"You need to give a gal some warning." She looked up at him, her gaze grass green in the sunlight. Her lips parted and those incredible eyes fixed on his mouth.

Before he could stop himself, Dante found his hand curled around her jaw, his thumb stroking over that provocative bottom lip. "Sorry," he rasped through a throat tight with desire. His chest constricted, his blood fired as need pulsed through him with every beat of his heart. "I thought I saw..." He dropped his hand and looked toward the crowd again. The man he'd thought he'd seen—Natchook, Tobias Caine's nemesis and the son of a bitch who was the reason his friend Nix was now a vampire—was gone.

"Thought you saw..." Tori prompted, her voice as husky as his had been.

"The bastard who attacked Nix and did his best to kill me and Tobias while he was at it."

She glanced around the scene. "Do you think he'd still be hanging around Scottsdale after what happened to Nix?"

Dante clenched his jaw. "Who knows? He's a crazy son of a bitch."

Again those luscious lips tightened before she murmured, "You're probably right, but still, I'd hardly think he'd take the chance of getting caught by staying in town."

Dante hooked his thumbs over his belt and rocked back on his heels. "Well, I know I'll feel a lot safer once he's behind bars."

"But he won't be behind bars, will he?" As she stared up at him, her eyes darkened. "Preternatural law is clear and concise on this matter. He drained Nix, knowing Tobias would turn her in order to save her. In doing so, the attacker has forfeited his life."

"Even though Tobias was the one who actually made

Nix a vampire?" Dante almost added something along the lines of "and he killed other prets" but remembered at the last second that Tori didn't know everything that transpired before that fateful day. She wasn't aware that Tobias had taken the rift device from the vampire who'd attacked Nix.

"Tobias carries no blame in this. He did what he had to in order to save her life." Her lips tightened a moment. "The responsibility lies with the vampire who attacked her."

For a second Dante mused about how much like the Old West the laws of the other dimension seemed, at least those he'd heard about. An eye for an eye. Deal fairly with other men and you'd have no worries. But cross someone and you'd have more trouble than you could safely navigate.

He looked at Tori. One of the things he liked so much about her was her strength of character. Her confidence. She was full steam ahead, no holds barred. He knew she'd be the same way in bed.

His cock jerked. Damn it. He had to get his mind off of sex and on the job. "I think I'm going to head back to the station and file my report."

"Okay." Tori took her hands out of her pockets. "I should probably head on over to the council and make my own report." A smile tipped up her lips. "I'll see you later."

He watched her leave, her hips swinging with long strides that really shouldn't look as feminine as they did, but there it was. Tori was a compilation of contradictions, soft yet strong, feminine yet brutally wild.

Dante walked over to his heavy-duty pickup and

climbed behind the wheel. As he started up the diesel engine, he noticed the fuel gauge hovered near the empty indicator. Damn. While he needed this truck to haul his horse trailer, he really should drive something else for work. And it wasn't as if the department offered unmarked vehicles for their Special Case detectives. The city felt it was the council's place to provide cars and the council had decided it wasn't, since the Special Case squad was made up of human detectives.

Meantime, said human detectives were left to their own devices. He could feed the citizenry of a small country with what he paid in gas every week. Mileage reimbursement from the department helped, but that still allowed him to recoup only half of his fuel expenditures.

Maybe it was time to buy that sweet little ride he'd had his eye on. He really couldn't afford it, but he couldn't afford to keep driving his truck, either. The car he was looking at needed some TLC, but once he fixed what needed fixing, put a modified engine in it so he'd get decent gas mileage, and got a new coat of paint on it, that '69 Charger would be ready to go.

He eyed Tori's small vehicle as she pulled away from the scene. He sure as hell wasn't going to drive a little matchbox car like she did. He wanted something with room, preferably a backseat.

Of course, thinking of Tori and a backseat led to thoughts of Tori *in* his backseat and sent his libido into overdrive. His randy cock flexed, aching for relief. "Down, boy," he muttered, and pulled out of the lot. By the time he reached the Downtown District's station, an inner recitation of the department's ten-codes had alleviated his problem.

As he walked into the patrol squad room he slipped his keys into his pocket. He headed toward the smaller room where the Special Case team was housed, only to be stopped by his boss.

"MacMillan. In my office." Captain Scott beckoned him with the waggle of two fingers.

"Whatcha do this time?" one of the uniforms muttered.

Dante shrugged and changed direction. He'd worked with Captain Scott for five years now, from the time he'd made detective. When Scott had volunteered to have the newly minted Special Case squad housed under him, he'd pushed for Dante to join the team. Now, as Dante walked into the captain's office, Scott motioned for him to close the door.

"Have a seat," the older man said as he sat down in his swivel chair.

Dante dropped into one of the god-awful straight-backed chairs in front of his boss's desk and clasped his hands over his stomach. "What's up?"

"You just come from the grocery store?"

Dante nodded. "Not much to report. Vic wasn't turned, and while it looks like it was the werewolf who attacked him and not the vamp, we won't know until the hospital files its final report with the pret council."

Captain Scott leaned back, the resulting squeaking an ominous indication of the rickety chair's ability to hold up his weight. He appeared to be considering something, working it over in his mind. Dante had seen him do this countless times before, and it usually meant whatever his captain was debating on telling him was nothing good. Finally Scott asked, "You hear about the pret attacks up in District Four?"

"No." Dante frowned. "What about 'em?"

"I just got word this morning. We've got some freak changing humans into werewolves." Scott shook his head and drilled the tip of one stubby finger onto his desk. "Like it's not bad enough that in another four months the Moore-Creasy-Devon comet is going to open a rift between dimensions and we're going to be hit with another influx of these damned EDs." His eyes held poorly disguised fear that Dante had seen in the general populace. No one was immune from being taken over by a preternatural when they came through the rift in December. Human scientists had yet to find a way to keep the rift from happening to begin with. They had no clue how to stop alien beings from squatting in their fellow men and women.

It was a bit unsettling to think you could be going about your business and then—*wham!*—you're no longer in control of your own body, rather, you had to share it with someone else, someone whose personality gets melded with yours.

All the prets he knew insisted that the soul or spirit, whatever you wanted to call it, of the human remained intact. The fact that the squatter had its host's memories seemed to support that, but Dante wasn't so sure. How could there possibly be room for more than one consciousness without the brain going into overload? And since there didn't seem to be a prevalent number of schizophrenic prets running around...

And what happened if he and Tori got involved and then he got taken over by a pret who hated her kind? What then? Would he have loved her only to lose her, as he feared?

He shook himself free from the anxiety that tickled

his gut. Instead of worrying about something that might never happen, he should focus on his job. "What do you want me to do?" Dante asked.

Scott leaned forward and rested his elbows on the desk. "Keep your eyes and ears open. Nobody on the council seems to know anything about this, but I'd wager a month's salary they have an idea who's behind it. They either don't care or..."

"Or?"

Scott's eyebrows climbed, furrowing his brow. "They support it."

Dante straightened out of his slouch. "I...No, I don't like to think they'd do that, sir."

"Well, who knows about them, right? They have their own agenda." Scott shook his head. "I'd like to think they wouldn't try to cover something up, but..."

"How many attacks have there been?" Dante asked. He'd have to remember to ask Tori what she knew about these attacks. Surely she'd been talking with the werewolf liaison of that quadrant. She might have more information than the council was releasing to its human counterparts.

"There was one each on Sunday and Monday, then again one on Thursday and one on Friday." Scott lifted a hand and scratched his head. "Four goddamned victims with just enough forensic evidence to get us nowhere. So far we've managed to keep a lid on it, but it's only a matter of time before it gets out."

"Shouldn't we warn people?"

"And tell them what? 'Be on the lookout for a rogue werewolf'?" He shook his head. "It won't do us any good to have people panicking. We'd be right back to the days before the Preternatural Protection Act was enacted.

Sons murdering their fathers, neighbors at each other's throats..." He swiveled his chair to look out the window. "Just keep your ear to the ground and let me know what you hear about these werewolf incidents."

Dante knew a dismissal when he heard one. "Will do." He pushed to his feet and left the captain's office. Once at his desk, he booted up his computer and sat back in his chair. He had his report typed up within fifteen minutes. He printed it off and added it to his folder of pending reports, intending to file it with the clerk later.

His cell buzzed. He pulled it out of his jacket pocket and glanced at the display. It was one of the Special Case detectives from District Four. Dante pressed the phone icon on the touch screen and put the device to his ear. "Hey, Manny," he greeted.

"Dante," Manuel Rivera responded. "I hear you had some werewolf trouble this morning."

"Good news travels fast." Dante put one hand on the back of his neck and rubbed the tense muscles there.

"Yeah. In some ways Scottsdale's still a small town. So?" The other detective's voice held hope.

Dante felt for the guy. Four werewolf attacks in a little under a week meant he was under the gun to produce results. Having the suspect handed to him would be a godsend. "I didn't talk to the guy, Manny. Sorry." Dante heard Rivera's sigh and added, "But I can check with our werewolf liaison and see what she thinks." He'd have to get over this lust thing he had going on for Tori. He had to keep things strictly professional between them so he could keep his emotional balance. For the time being, at least.

"Hey, man, I'd appreciate that. We got nothing so far.

No hair. Or fur as the case may be," Manny added, his voice deeper with sarcasm that quickly turned to frustration. "No fiber, no usable DNA, no nothing."

Dante frowned. "If he's biting people, how the hell can you not have DNA from his saliva?"

"Bastard washes the wounds with bleach. Whatever DNA's still present gets degraded, and subsequent tests are inconclusive." Rivera muttered a long string of expletives in Spanish, then said, "He's a clever mutt, I'll give him that."

"How are the victims connected?" Dante remembered the case he'd first met Tori on, where a group of vampires killed other vamps. At first, there had seemed to be no affiliation other than the obvious, but then deeper connections had surfaced.

"None that we can tell. First one is a twentysomething med student, the second one is a bricklayer, third one's a stay at home mom, and this last one..." He sighed. "He's a councilman from ward six."

Dante let out a low whistle. There'd be hell to pay on that one. And a local council seat to fill. Prets weren't allowed to serve in human governments at any level. *Equal but separate* was the motto of the day. "Well, I can see where a wolf might have thought he could use the councilman, but, still... He had to know as well as anyone else that the man would lose his seat."

"You'd think so." Manny sighed again. "Thanks anyway, *amigo*. Keep the faith," he said with his usual farewell.

"You, too." Dante ended the call. He slid his phone back into his jacket pocket and pondered what Rivera had said. At first blush it seemed the attacks by the werewolf were random. Maybe it was a pret who'd snapped and couldn't keep his fangs to himself. Maybe it went deeper than that. At the very least, Tori would have an idea if their guy from this morning's attack was involved. He pulled out his phone again and speed-dialed her.

"Hello." Her dulcet tones pulsed through him all the way to his toes, pausing to dance along his cock for much longer than was appropriate at work.

"It's Dante." His throat closed up. He cleared it and tried again. "Ah, it's Dante."

"What's up?" The rhythm of her voice didn't change, so he had no idea what her mood was. She seemed glad to hear from him, but considering the schizoid way he'd acted at the crime scene, he couldn't be sure.

"I just got a call from Rivera in District Four. He asked me about our guy from this morning. He's wondering if maybe he's the same one who's attacking people up north."

"I don't think so."

Dante heard voices in the background, then some snarling. What the hell? "Where are you?" he asked.

"At council headquarters, waiting my turn to file my report." She lowered her voice. "They're not too happy with the liaison from the north quadrant. They expect instant results and it's impossible in this case without viable forensic evidence. I feel sorry for him."

"So...he's the one who's snarling?"

"No, the snarlers are a couple of werecats being fined for drunken and disorderly conduct. They're not too happy, either."

Dante shook his head. If he lived to be ninety, he didn't think he'd ever get used to this new world he lived in. It was like being in a never-ending episode of *The Twilight Zone*. "So, about our guy this morning," he said, putting the conversation back on track. "Rivera tells me any DNA that's at the scene is too degraded for testing."

"I really don't think Barry is responsible for the attacks in District Four. He said he wasn't, and I believe him. He may be dumb, but he's not stupid. He attacked the man this morning unintentionally. The attacks in District Four are full of intention. And foresight, obviously, if the suspect is doing something to degrade his DNA." She sighed. "They're calling for me. Look, I'll talk to the other liaison." Voices filtered over the line, people walking close by her, and her voice went husky as she lowered it. "I'll let you know what I find out."

"Okay. See ya later." Dante disconnected the call and sat back in his chair. God, that voice of hers touched places in him he hadn't known existed. He knew things with Tori could get complicated fast. She was a pret, a werewolf. He couldn't ignore the fact that she could break his neck with the flick of a wrist. He supposed it would make having sex with her very interesting. All things considered, it might be worth the risk.

It was just...the timing sucked. He had to keep things platonic between them. At least for now, when his attention was needed elsewhere. Maybe down the line he could learn to follow his feelings.

Only today was not that day.

Chapter Four

Tori slipped her phone into the back pocket of her jeans and started toward the big double doors of the main chamber where the council members waited. She couldn't go in and face three of the most powerful preternaturals in the region with fantasies of Mr. Tall, Dark, and Sexy floating around in her head and playing havoc with her libido. She drew a deep breath and blew it out, trying to clear her mind of everything Dante. As she passed the liaison coming from the room, she murmured, "Ash, I need to talk to you. Can you hang around for a while?"

His normally blue eyes held flecks of amber. "Why the hell not? It's not like I'm actually doing a job or anything."

She scowled. She wasn't going to take any crap from him. From anyone. "Don't take your ass-chewing out on me."

He pinched the bridge of his nose and grimaced. "Sorry. Sure." When he looked at her again, his eyes were their usual hue. "I'll be in the kitchen. Come get me when you're done." He glanced inside the chamber. "Hopefully, they've gotten their nasty mood out of their system."

Tori watched him walk away. Her phone buzzed, and she dug it out to find an e-mail from the hospital. Opening the attached report, she read that they had indeed verified that the victim from this morning was bitten by a werewolf and not a vampire. She heaved a sigh. Poor Barry.

Her name was called again, this time with impatience, and she shoved her phone back into her pocket as she went into the cavernous room to report her initial findings. She gave a slight bow to signify her deference to them. *"Ati me peta babka?"* she asked in the common language from the other dimension. *How may I serve?*

The bright center light, recessed in the ceiling, clearly lit the front of the auditorium-sized room. She looked at the three men sitting in ornate, high-backed chairs on the other side of the long mahogany table. Deoul Arias, president of the council, was a high elf who'd come through the rift over five thousand years ago. There were only two other preternaturals in the region who were older than him, one a vampire and one a demon. But not just any demon. *The* demon. Lucifer. He was the oldest of them all, as far as anyone knew, and he had tremendous power and influence because of it.

And Deoul couldn't stand it, which meant it rather pleased Tori. She'd use any excuse she could to stick it to the snooty elf.

Sitting next to the president was Caladh MacLoch, a seal shapeshifter and frankly her favorite council member. She and Caladh had met in 1903 and soon thereafter developed a friendship that started as an apprenticeship of sorts, leaving her with a deep affection for the man who had helped make this world a little less lonely.

Next to him was the newest member of the council,

vampire Tobias Caine. He had been appointed to his seat as a replacement for the former vampire councilor who'd been killed. His murder was still officially unsolved, though Tori suspected it had something to do with the rift device she had secreted away at her house. Tobias hadn't told her where he'd gotten it or how he'd come by it, but she didn't believe in coincidence, especially where murder was concerned.

She gave him a smile of greeting. His gray eyes held welcome and a hint of suppressed humor. He probably could tell from the look on her face that she thought this greeting ritual was a bunch of crap. It was a stupid formality put in place to make the council members feel important. Not that she would ever say that out loud. She knew when to hold her tongue and toe the party line. If a little kowtowing was called for, she could bow and scrape with the best of them.

"Tori," Caladh said, his dark eyes shining with pleasure. "It is agreeable to see you."

"And you." Tori bit the inside of her cheek against a grin. Caladh had such a formal way of speaking, he always sounded like a Vulcan to her. "My lord Arias," she greeted the president. She met Tobias's gaze and inclined her head. "Tobias."

"What news do you bring us?" Deoul asked.

"I've just received confirmation from the hospital that our human victim this morning was bitten by a werewolf, not a vamp." She stood next to one of the folding wooden chairs that were there allegedly for liaisons to sit on while they made their reports, but she had never sat in the presence of the council, nor had any liaison she knew. She tried to put a positive spin on things by saying, "The great news is that Barry didn't release any preternatural essence into the wound, so the vic won't turn."

"That is your wolf's only saving grace." Deoul glanced at the other two council members and then turned his pale gaze upon Tori once more. "Our laws are clear on this. The werewolf will be chained in silver, restricting his ability to shift, for one full cycle of the moon."

Tori swallowed. To change into their animal form was as natural a thing to a shapeshifter as breathing. To be unable to shift at the full moon would be a torture she wasn't sure Barry's mind would be able to endure. "May I plead mercy?" She looked at all three councilors. "Barry didn't attack the human on purpose. He was provoked—"

"Only with words, as I understand it from Aldis Knox. We expect better control from the members of our community." Caladh sat forward and clasped his hands on top of the table. "We have been able to maintain calm among the human population only tenuously, especially as the next Influx draws near. If Barry were allowed to go unpunished..." He shook his head.

"Of course he shouldn't go unpunished," Tori said. "That's not what I'm suggesting. I'm asking for leniency, that's all. Please don't restrain him during the full moon. It would be torture."

"A fitting punishment, I'd say." Deoul's face creased in a smug smile as if the thought of a werewolf in agony somehow made him happy.

Tori clenched her fists against the urge to vault over the table and wipe that smirk off his face. Or just get rid of his face, period. But no matter how close she might be to Caladh and Tobias, even they wouldn't be able to save her if she ate the president of the council.

Tobias cleared his throat. "I agree with Tori. Binding him during the full moon is too harsh. Fit him with silver restraints for the next week, then remove them and let him shift during the full moon. Otherwise the strain—"

"He should have considered his actions first," Caladh broke in. He shook his head. "I must side with Deoul on this matter." He turned his gaze back to Tori. "I'm sorry, Tori, but as Deoul said, our laws are clear. Punishment would be even harsher had he turned the poor fellow."

"But he didn't," Tobias pressed. "Shifting from human to animal is an agony you're all too familiar with." He shot a glance at Caladh. "But from what I understand, *not* shifting is even worse."

"It is. Which would be the point." Caladh's gaze hardened. "On this I stand resolute. Actions have consequences. Preternaturals must be held to a high standard when it comes to our dealings with humans." He shared a glance with Deoul. "The decision stands. Barry will be restrained for thirty days, including the night of the full moon."

Tobias's lips tightened. He slumped back in his chair. "I'd like my objection to be on the record," he murmured. Looking at Tori, he said, "I'm sorry. A decision is based on majority."

"I understand." She uncurled her fingers and rubbed her moist palms against the outside of her thighs, before straightening her shoulders. "I'd like to be the one to tell Barry."

Deoul shrugged. "I have no objection." He glanced at his colleagues. "Caladh? Tobias?"

They both shook their heads.

The council president looked at Tori again. "He's in

one of the holding cells downstairs, which is where he'll stay for the next thirty days." His tone held warning, like he thought she'd try to break the guy out or something.

She might be tempted, but she wasn't stupid. She didn't want to ruin her life, or possibly put it in jeopardy because Barry was going to be shackled in silver for a crime he'd actually committed. As a liaison, part of her job in addition to investigating crimes was to uphold the law. She might not agree with it, but until someone changed it, she was duty bound.

Sometimes this job really sucked.

Tori gave a small bow and started to turn.

"Just a moment," Tobias said. "There's one more thing I'd like to bring up while Tori's here."

She frowned and turned back to face the council.

"It strikes me that having our liaisons make these face-to-face reports is a little...pretentious. Their findings can easily be sent through e-mail over a secure server."

Why the hell did he have to involve her in this? She didn't want to fight this particular battle.

"Pretentious?" Deoul's eyebrows climbed his forehead. "This is a time-honored tradition, Tobias. There is order in what we do."

"Yes, yes." Caladh waved one hand. "In this I must also agree." His glance toward Tobias held some humor. "This appears to be an off day for you."

"Apparently." Tobias crossed his legs and rested one elbow on the arm of his chair. "I just feel like it's more a matter of ego to make them come here in person and adhere to the old-fashioned greeting."

Deoul puffed up, his eyes glittering. "Ego! This is not about ego. It's about respect." He leaned toward Tobias.

"Do you not believe the council is worthy of respect?"

Tori watched the interaction with a horrified interest that was reminiscent of watching a train wreck. She wanted to look away but couldn't. Apprehension crept up on her, because she knew that soon enough one of them would turn to her for her opinion.

"Of course," Tobias responded to the most egotistical and pretentious pret among them. "But wasting our liaisons' time by making them come to the office is hardly respectful of *them*."

Then came the moment Tori had been dreading. Caladh looked at her and said, "You're a liaison. What do you think of Tobias's proposal? Do you believe we disrespect you?"

Hell, yeah. Tori searched her mind for a tactful way to agree. "There could be more efficient uses of our time," she finally murmured.

"I see." Deoul began drumming his fingers on the table. "Should we discontinue these face-to-face meetings then? These in-person reports where we can gather so much more information through body language and attitude that doesn't come across in an e-mail?"

You mean so you can try to figure out if your liaisons are trying to hide something from you. Sneaky, slippery elf. "I merely agreed with Tobias that e-mails would be more efficient as far as time goes." She made an effort to keep a melodious inflection in her voice. It had been known to calm the savage beast. She wasn't sure it would do the trick on three of them. "Though I will say that the greeting I could do without."

Deoul's eyebrows rose, as did Caladh's.

"It's just…" She huffed a sigh of frustration. Damn

Tobias for putting her in the middle of this. "We're not in the other dimension anymore. Many of us have been on Earth for centuries. Some of us for millennia." She looked at Deoul and Caladh. "Why are we holding onto a language from a place that cast us out?"

"Hear, hear," Tobias said quietly.

Tori tried to tamp down her irritation. He really was trying to make her job easier. She should cut him some slack. She just wasn't sure she would.

"Hmph." Deoul folded his arms across his chest and stared at Tori. Finally he said, "We'll take this under advisement. You may go."

She gave a slight incline of her head, shot Tobias a dirty look, and then turned and left the chamber. She knew Barry was on pins and needles, waiting for the verdict, so she headed down to the basement first.

Stopping at the check-in desk, she removed her weapon and signed it over to the guard on duty, who stowed it in a locker and handed her the key. She passed through a metal detector and went on to where Barry was.

The cell was really a large metal cage, maybe six by eight, with a bench against the back and three rings bolted into the cement floor. Barry was on the bench, one arm between his legs, a silver handcuff around his wrist. The other handcuff at the end of the foot-long chain was attached to one of the floor rings. He looked up as she stopped in front of him. "Well?" he asked.

"Thirty days of restraint in silver." There was no easy way to break it to him, and he was way past needing things sugarcoated.

He paled. "Even through the full moon?"

Tori nodded. "I tried for leniency, Barry. I really did."

"I know you did." He stared down at the floor. "I've never been unable to shift into the wolf at the full moon." He looked up at her again. "The urge is inescapable, Tori. I'll go crazy."

"No, you won't." Right then she made the decision to ride this one through with him. Werewolves were social animals. To be denied the opportunity to shift and run with the pack would be untenable. She couldn't let him go through it alone. "I'll be right here with you. We'll keep each other sane."

His eyes widened. "You'd do that?"

"Yes, I would." Tori knew Barry was a good guy. He was one of the prets who'd decided to look at his exile on Earth as a second chance—a way to atone for the lawlessness he'd practiced in the other dimension. He volunteered at a homeless shelter and worked as a nurse at one of the local hospitals. "Consider it a date."

His lopsided grin held self-depreciation. "Usually I can show a girl a better time than being chained up in a cell." He glanced at the handcuffs, waving his hand back and forth to give them a rattle. "Though something like this I could put to good use."

"I'll take your word on that."

His lips quirked again. Then he sighed. "Really, Tori, I appreciate the offer. But I can't let you do it. I got myself into this mess, and I'm the only one who should be punished."

She studied him and saw fear lurking deep in his eyes, though he did a good job at trying to hide it. "You're sure?"

"I'm sure." His gaze met hers. "You're a stand-up person, Tori. Thanks."

"No problem." She rested one hand against the wall of the cell. "You keep your chin up, okay?"

He gave a nod. "I will."

She lifted her hand in good-bye and headed back to the front where she retrieved her sidearm from the locker, dropped the key off with the guard, and went back upstairs.

Ash was still in the break room. When she pushed open the door he looked up from a scandal rag he was perusing. "Did you know that you can tell a pret from a human by the hair between our toes?"

Tori pursed her lips. "Really?" Last time she'd looked, she didn't have hair between her toes.

"According to this article." He held up the paper. "It amazes me the crap people will believe just because it's in print. Idiots," he muttered, as he let the paper drop to the sofa beside him. "So, what did you want to talk about?"

"The attacks going on in your quadrant."

"Not you, too." He scowled and shot to his feet. Dark blond hair lifted and then settled against his head. His eyes filled with the amber of the wolf. "I don't have to justify myself to you."

"Whoa there, Bartholomew." She lifted her hands in a gesture of surrender. "I'm not judging you here. I just want some information."

"Oh." He cleared his throat. "That's different, then." He plopped back down on the sofa and stretched long legs out in front of him. Slowly the wolf surrendered, the light going out of his eyes. "Don't call me Bartholomew."

She grinned. His full name was Bartholomew Maxwell Asher, but he preferred to go by the nickname Ash. She only called him Bartholomew when he was being a butthead.

"What do you want to know?" he asked.

Tori sat beside him, one leg bent so she could face him. *Let's just get this one out of the way.* "Do you think Barry's responsible?"

"Hell, no. Why? Do you?" His look was disbelieving.

She shook her head. "No, but until I can check out his alibis on the days of the attacks, I really just have my gut to go on."

Ash stretched one arm out along the back of the sofa. "Your do-gooder wouldn't stray far enough away from his little lost sheep to run around biting people in the north quadrant."

"I agree." Both with the statement that Barry was a do-gooder and that he wouldn't leave his homeless guys for very long. "What's your gut telling you?"

Ash heaved a sigh and raked his fingers through his hair, frustration written in every long, lean line of his body. "I think it's a clever SOB we're after, and he's not going to stop until we catch him. That's what my gut tells me." He stared at her. "If you're asking me if I have a list of suspects...No, I don't. And it's frustrating as hell."

"I hear the suspect uses bleach to break down his DNA."

He nodded. "And drops about fifty gallons of ammonia at the scene to override his scent." He gave a low growl. "Okay, I'm exaggerating. But the end result is I couldn't smell a thing for about twelve hours after I left one of those scenes." His scowl proclaimed his aggravation with that state of affairs. "Some damned werewolf I am when I can't smell a damned thing."

"Ammonia, too? Dante didn't mention that."

"Dante? MacMillan?" At her affirmation, Ash asked,

"What the hell is MacMillan doing getting involved with something in District Four? He's based out of District Two." His scowl deepened. "Like you."

"Don't get your panties in a wad," Tori muttered. "Some cop named Rivera called him this morning about Barry, wondering if it could be the same guy. I told Dante I'd talk to you."

"Uh-huh." A look crossed his face she couldn't quite decipher. "Rivera's getting desperate, too. His boss probably gave him the same ass-chewing I got from mine."

Tori hunched forward and rested her chin on her fists. "So, why hasn't a BOLO gone out on this?"

"A BOLO that says what? Be on the lookout for a werewolf who's biting people?" He rolled his eyes and then stared up at the ceiling, his head on the back of the sofa. "There's no fur, no hair, no fiber, no nothing. It's like he's wrapped in plastic, for God's sake."

That set Tori's brain whirling. How would a werewolf, or even a human for that matter, keep from leaving bits of himself at a crime scene? Little booties would mask shoe prints. Latex gloves would hide fingerprints. But what about hair and skin cells? People shed hair and skin at a fairly rapid rate. For a crime scene to have none of that... "Maybe he *was* wrapped in plastic," she mused out loud. "Or... he shaved?"

Ash seemed to consider that seriously. "Well, if he shaved all over, head to toes, he'd have no hair to lose. But humans and prets alike shed something like fifty thousand skin cells a day. Even if he was already in his wolf form, well, there'd be fur, wouldn't there?"

"You'd think so." Tori drew in a breath and held it a moment, rolling things over in her mind. Finally she shook her head in defeat. "I don't know what to tell you, Ash. It doesn't make any sense."

"Thank you! That's what I was trying to tell *them*," he said with a gesture in the general direction of the main chamber. "Not that they listened."

"Yes, well, they often don't, do they?" Tori pushed to her feet. "I'll let you know if I hear anything."

"Thanks." Ash stood as well and raised his arms above his head in a stretch. "Let's just hope someone else doesn't take a page out of this guy's book and decide to do the same thing in another quadrant." He shot her a dark look. "Maybe *yours*."

Tori walked out of the building, Ash's last words tumbling around in her mind. And she was struck by one thought: Why had the werewolf decided on District Four? Why not the other quads? What was so special about the north?

Chapter Five

The next morning Dante carried his travel mug of coffee out to the stables. Monsoon season was in full swing and while they wouldn't see any rain until later in the day, the humidity was already in the fifties and climbing. He was used to humidity in the teens, or lower, so this was nearly unbearable, especially when coupled with triple-digit heat. But he couldn't forgo his morning cup of coffee. Setting his mug on one of the flat-top rails, he pulled out his smartphone and re-read the e-mail Tori had sent him yesterday.

Ash said the suspect uses a lot of ammonia at the scene so determining his scent is impossible. The ammonia temporarily fries the olfactory sensors in the nose. I was able to check Barry's alibis for the dates in question, and he checks out. He's not the guy. Unknown suspect remains at large.

After he'd gotten the e-mail, Dante had called and left a message for Rivera, letting him know what Tori had reported. He could imagine the other detective's disappointment. And dread. Since Barry wasn't the suspect in the "werewolf incidents," as Captain Scott called them, that meant there was another attack coming.

His Appaloosa nickered, obviously impatient for his grooming to begin. Dante put his phone away and picked up the rubber curry. "All right, Benny. All right." He'd fed the horses about two hours ago, and this brushing was a weekend ritual he and Big Ben both looked forward to. On the other hand, his buckskin quarter horse, unlike the Appaloosa, merely tolerated being groomed, so he always got his grooming last. Even the little burro who acted as stable mascot enjoyed being brushed, but the quarter horse had his nose in his feed bucket, trying to get every last little nugget that might still be in there.

As Dante got started with slow circular motions of the curry on Ben's neck, he reflected on yesterday's incident. He was torn between feeling just a little aggrieved at being called out on a drunk and disorderly and feeling somewhat relieved that it hadn't been anything more serious.

The vampire slayings he'd investigated earlier in the year had been gruesome, so much so that the images still scrolled through his mind every now and again. And while he, Tobias, and Nix knew who had been behind the murders and why, they hadn't been able to make that particular report because of the uncertainty of the players' identities. He and his friends had been victorious in the end and had managed to get their hands on the device the bad guys were using to communicate through the rift. But having been informed that some of the council members were at the very least aware of those communications and had seemingly been doing nothing about it had added a level of danger that made this particular tightrope hazardous to traverse.

In the end, they'd all decided that for the moment no

one but the three of them—and later, Tori—needed to know they had the device, or that there even was a device. For now, the official report was that the slayings had been related to a group of rogue preternaturals but the motivation was unclear.

Tobias had held onto the apparatus and corresponding schematics, waiting for things to cool down. He'd given them to Tori within the last several days, asking her to look it over and see if she could figure out how it worked. But he hadn't told her where he'd gotten it or from whom.

Dante had been itching to look it over, too, but he had held his tongue. This was more of a pret issue than it was a human one. And he trusted Tobias to do the right thing. If the new council member felt Dante needed to be brought into things, he'd call.

So Dante told himself to be patient. He'd soon enough get a chance to see inside that thing. And a chance to work with Tori on something unrelated to being a city detective.

Not that he should be looking forward to spending more time with her. She was a temptation he just didn't have the luxury of giving in to right now. Because he knew as surely as he breathed that once he had a taste, it would be impossible to walk away.

Deciding he didn't want to think about that now, Dante forced himself to concentrate on grooming his horse. He let himself be calmed by the motions and soon was lost in the rhythm of the process.

He'd just picked up a towel to wipe down Big Ben in the final step of grooming when his sister, Liliana, walked into the stables.

"How are my boys doing today?" she asked.

The burro brayed and shoved his head over the gate of his stall. Lily stopped and scratched his forehead, grinning when he draped his chin across her shoulder. "Hello, Sugar," she greeted.

Dante noticed his sister looked a little pale this morning. He turned away before she could catch him staring, and he sighed, making sure the sound was vexed without any trace of the concern he really felt. "I don't know why you insisted on givin' him that sappy name."

"Don't you listen to him," she crooned to the burro. "Sugarplum is a perfectly acceptable name for a sweet boy like you." She glanced at Dante, mischief dancing in her dark eyes. "Besides, who's the softie who adopted him from a Bureau of Land Management roundup three years ago?"

"Only because you wouldn't stop pestering me about it."

"Uh-huh." She let Sugarplum nuzzle her palm. "Look at this face. How could anyone resist it?"

Dante finished up with Ben and draped the towel over the top railing of the stall. He patted the gelding on the side of the neck and closed the gate behind him. Handing his sister the curry comb, he said, "Why don't you groom this refugee from the glue factory while I take care of Stud over there?"

Sugarplum hee-hawed again.

"See? He wants it." Dante walked over to the equipment storage area and grabbed another curry. As he went into the quarter horse's stall, he asked, "How can you say no?"

She stuck her tongue out at him but went into the stall with the little burro. "Okay, sweetie. Let's get you clean."

Two hours later Dante put all the grooming equipment back in storage while Lily gave each of the horses a few slices of apple she'd had in a plastic baggie tucked away in one of her pockets. She gave Sugarplum a carrot and another scratch on his forehead. As she walked toward Dante, her shoe caught on a rough patch of cement and she stumbled.

Dante rushed forward, stopping at her glare. "What? I'm supposed to let you fall?"

She shot him a look. "Of course not. But even if I did fall, I'm not some fragile little thing you need to keep wrapped in cotton." As she walked toward him she muttered, "I can take care of myself."

"I know you can." He kept his voice gentle. He knew how hard she'd found it to have to rely on him while she went through chemo and then radiation treatments for her breast cancer. But the stress of a divorce right after her diagnosis had sent her into a tailspin. Dante understood that her ill-humor was not directed at him so much as at her circumstances. "But having family means you don't have to."

She crossed her arms and stared at him in silence for a few seconds, then muttered, "You know, it's really hard to be irritated at you when you act so sweet."

He grimaced. "Now you're just bein' mean."

Lily laughed and punched him on the shoulder. "Come on. Let's go fix some lunch." She looped her arm through his and they went back into the house.

She took a clean dish towel from the drawer and ran it under the cold water, then held it to the nape of her neck. Dante tried to hide his continuing concern, but as she took celery from the fridge and started chopping it for the salad she insisted he eat at least once a day, she kept glancing at him and shaking her head. Finally, she turned toward him and propped one hand on her hip. "Out with it."

He eyed the knife she held in her right hand. "What?"

"Just say it. Whatever it is you're thinkin', just get it out so we can talk about it."

He cleared his throat and went back to forming hamburger patties. "And what makes you think I have anything to say?"

She waved the knife. "Don't be cute, Dante. I can see it in your eyes."

He tried to deflect the conversation. "It's hard for me not to be cute." He gave her a wink.

Lily rolled her eyes. "Oh, get over yourself already." She turned back to the celery and started chopping again, her movements slow but steady.

Dante had to wonder if her knife strokes were controlled so he wouldn't see her hands shake with fatigue. He rubbed the back of his neck. God, he hated this. He was helpless against cancer—he couldn't intimidate it, he couldn't punch it in the nose. Unlike her worthless ex-husband.

He smiled at the memory of the last time he'd seen Tony Fabrizio. The other man had been lying on the floor of the living room in the house he and Lily had once shared. The home to which Lily's name had never been added to the deed. The plush cream carpet had been spattered with the blood from Tony's broken nose, and Dante had walked out of the house with a hand that had hurt like hell.

The pain had been worth it. Now, though, fear gnawed

at him constantly, and frustration that he couldn't do to the cancer what he'd done to her ex. He had to be crazy to think he was anywhere near being ready to get involved with a woman, especially Tori.

God, the need to punch something made his hands ball up into fists. Where was Tony Fabrizio when he needed the bastard?

"What's brought that smile to your face?" Lily asked with a sidelong glance at him. "It looks like trouble."

He shrugged. "Just thinkin' 'bout Tony."

"Uh-huh." She gathered up the chopped celery and put it in a bowl, then reached for a red bell pepper. The look on her face told him she knew exactly what he was replaying in his mind, and her next words confirmed it. "You're lucky he didn't file assault charges against you."

She was probably right, but he wouldn't change a thing. Tony had deserved much more than Dante had dished out. As far as he was concerned, the bastard was damned lucky all he'd ended up with was a broken schnoz. "We wouldn't have had that little chat if he'd been a man and taken care of you."

"I do *not* need a man to take care of me!" Lily slammed the knife down and turned toward the refrigerator. As she yanked open the door, she added, "The only thing the men in my life have done is cause me heartache."

"Well, some of us are just tryin' to help," Dante murmured. He carried the burgers over to the counter and placed them on the electric grill.

Lily sighed. She closed the refrigerator and walked over to him, rubbing her hand across his shoulder. "I know, Dante. And I appreciate it, I do. You've given me the chance to focus my attention on getting better without having to worry about paying bills or taking care of a home on my own. I just…" She pressed her lips together and walked to the other side of the kitchen island. She heaved a sigh. "I'm sorry. I realize I'm being defensive. But I hate this, having this enemy that's eatin' me from the inside out. The doctors say the cancer's eradicated, but they won't know if I'm in true remission for another couple of months." When she looked at him her eyes shone with tears. "There's just so much I want to do. I'm not ready to die."

"Hey, now, none of that." Dante put the lid on the pan and turned to face her. "You're not gonna die. You're gonna live long enough to be a little old lady who gripes about her eccentric, doddering older brother."

A slight smile tilted one side of her mouth. "I do that now."

He brandished the spatula. "I'm neither eccentric nor doddering. Not yet."

"That's a matter of opinion." She gestured toward the dining room table. "What about all that crap?"

Dante looked at the computer parts lying on the table. "What about it?"

"It's been on that table for over a month."

"I'm working on it."

She raised her eyebrows. "Really?" She looked at the table again. "Every piece is in the exact spot it was in on the Fourth of July and hasn't been moved in five weeks." She shot him a look. "Hasn't even been dusted."

"So now you're complaining about my housekeeping skills?"

"Not at all." Her smile became more of a smirk. "I

can handle a little dust. Besides, I'm sure you have other strengths, brother dear."

"Hmph." Dante was glad to see her smile, even if it was at his expense. He glanced at the table laden with a couple of hard drives, a motherboard, a quad-core processor, and a keyboard. "I've been busy." He felt the need to defend himself.

"I know." She tossed the chopped bell pepper into the salad bowl. Her tone was as placid as her expression. "Burgers are gonna burn." She tilted her head toward the grill.

Dante rescued the hamburgers before they carried their food out to the covered patio. In the shade and with the misters and overhead fans going, the heat was almost bearable. Over the next hour their banter continued, and he did his best to coax his sister to eat more every time she put her fork down.

Finally, she gave a sigh and pushed her plate away, half of the burger and part of the salad uneaten. Before Dante could say anything, she held up one finger. "Don't. I'm stuffed. At least I won't be throwing it up," she added on a sigh.

Her last chemo treatment had been six months ago and her dark hair had started growing back in a few months later. Right now it was about three inches long and as silken as baby hair. She missed having long hair, but he thought she looked adorable.

"Well, if you're sure," he said as he reached for her plate.

She rolled her eyes. "Oh, my God. You *are* a human garbage disposal, just like Mom always said."

He grinned and bit into her leftover burger.

"I still have salad, too."

Dante pushed his food to one cheek. "I'm good."

"Uh-huh. Your colon must love you."

"My relationship to my colon is personal and not something I want to discuss with my sister."

"Okay, okay." She stood and picked up her plate and glass. "As usual, your grilling skills are the best, bar none." She yawned. "I think I'm gonna go lie down for a few minutes."

Dante shot to his feet. "Lily..."

"Don't start." She gave him a warning look. Dante knew her insistence on independence was a defense against the uncertain turn her life had taken. His sister went on. "I'm just a little tired, that's all." When his phone rang she gave a small wave toward him. "I'll clean up the kitchen. You take your call."

"Lily, I can—"

When she raised one eyebrow she reminded him so much of their mother that he fell silent. Lily looked satisfied with his reaction and went into the house.

Dante pushed his plate out of the way and answered his phone. "MacMillan."

"It's Tobias."

Tobias Caine, the only vampire friend Dante had.

"What's up?" Dante stood and walked to the edge of the patio, making sure to stay in the shade.

"I've been talking to Tori, and she's hit a wall on that, ah, unresolved matter of a few months ago."

He could only be talking about the rift device. Dante knew Tobias had given it to Tori, who had experience with various types of radios. From what Tobias had told him, she'd been some sort of radio communications officer during World War II. He tried not to think too hard about that, because then he'd be focused on how long she'd been alive and his head would explode. "What's the problem?"

"It's apparently more computerized than she's comfortable with. I need you to give her a hand if you don't mind."

Mind? Dante had been itching to get his hands on that little gizmo. Plus, it would give him an excuse to see Tori outside of work.

He scowled. It had been only about five hours ago that he'd told himself to lay off those kinds of thoughts. Yet here he was... "Sure, no problem." He was satisfied with how nonchalant he managed to sound. "Does she know you're asking me to help?"

"I just got off the phone with her. She sounded pleased."

"Did she now?" Dante pondered that a moment. Tori had been overt in her interest in him, which could cause all kinds of problems in and of itself. He wasn't ready to commit, for one thing. For another, she could kill him in an unguarded moment, or bite him and turn him into a werewolf. He was happy being human and really didn't care to change. On the other hand... she was funny, sexy, and intelligent. Completely his kind of woman, and he was an idiot not to pursue her. Crap. He was damned if he did and damned if he didn't.

"I think she likes you." Tobias's deep voice held humor.

The last thing Dante wanted was to be teased by his bloodsucking friend. "What's not to like?" he responded, keeping his tone flippant.

Tobias's snort came across the line loud and clear. "One of these days that devil-may-care attitude of yours is going to be knocked for a loop."

Dante forced a laugh. "Maybe, chief. Maybe." He glanced at his watch. "How soon do you need me on this?"

"We're still keeping it off the radar, so there's no need for you to go racing over to her place, even though I know you want to," he added on a dry note. "But I'd like you two to hook up in the next couple of days."

So in spite of his trying to play it cool, Dante obviously hadn't fooled his friend. He cleared his throat. "No problem. I'll just wait for Tori to give me the word."

"That'll work. Oh, and I still haven't told her where I got the thing. I'd like to keep it that way."

"You don't trust her?"

"Eventually, just not right now." Tobias sighed. "He's so close. The fewer people who know Natchook is behind this rift thing, the better chance I have of finally catching him. Okay?"

"Yeah, fine."

Tobias started to ring off but Dante stopped him. "How's Nix?" Dante asked.

There was a slight hesitation, then the vampire said, "She's adjusting. Slowly." He paused. "I appreciate your giving her some space. It's been only a few months since her turning. She definitely needs to take it easy for a while, so she's not seeing any visitors. I know her—she'd feel like she had to put on a brave face, especially with a former colleague, even though you two are friends," he added. "It would make things worse."

"I understand." Dante blew out a breath. "Let me know if there's anything I can do, okay?"

"You got it." Tobias cleared his throat. "Listen, maybe give her a buzz in a week or two."

After Tobias ended the call, Dante slipped his phone back into its holder on his belt and returned to the table. He picked up his plate and cup and carried them into the house. In the kitchen, he rinsed the plate off and put it in the dishwasher.

"You are going to make some lucky woman a wonderful wife," Lily quipped from behind him.

He twisted to face her. "I thought you were gonna lie down for a while."

"I'm going. I'm going." She stifled a yawn. "Come get me if I'm not up in an hour."

"All right." Dante pasted an agreeable expression on his face. If she was still sleeping in an hour, there was no way he was going to wake her.

"I mean it." Lily wagged her finger at him. "If I nap the afternoon away I'll have trouble sleeping tonight."

"Okay. I got it," he said when she stood there looking at him. "If you're not up in an hour I'll come get you."

"You'd better." She sent him one last warning glare. Then her face softened and she walked over and gave him a tight hug. "I love you."

He put his arms around her and held her until she pulled away. He lightly flicked the tip of her nose, grinning at her exaggerated scowl, then watched as she walked back to her bedroom and closed the door behind her.

Dante went into the dining room and stared down at the computer parts on the table. He really should get this mess cleared up. The circuitry on the motherboard directed his thoughts toward the rift device again. And Tori.

Just the fact that she had the device put her in danger. Right now only four people on the planet knew she had it, but secrets had a way of getting out. The sooner they knew what it did and how it worked, the sooner they could get it back to Tobias and let him deal with disposing of it.

Tori was a werewolf and therefore probably more capable of protecting herself than Dante was, but that didn't stop him from worrying.

Tori dropped the last two bags of groceries on the kitchen counter. She'd had her five-mile run earlier this morning, while it was still relatively cool, then ran a multitude of errands, including shopping for food. The local neighborhood market had been a madhouse. Everyone who worked during the week tried to do all their shopping on Saturday, parking their carts in the middle of every freaking aisle. It made her crazy, how many times she'd had to say "Excuse me" while subduing the urge to run her cart into people when they'd had the chutzpah to look at her like she was the rude one because she'd politely asked them to move out of the way.

She'd also dropped by council headquarters to see how Barry was faring. He'd been calm but resigned, not looking forward to the upcoming full moon but knowing there was nothing he could do at this point except get through the ordeal as best he could.

She knew what he faced, because she'd been subjected to the punishment of silver binding during a full moon before, nearly a century ago, and it was something she'd reserve only for her very worst enemy. She could only hope that someone as sensitive as Barry would get through this without breaking. There'd be a part of him, the good, decent part, that might not survive the ordeal.

She put everything away and took a deep breath, the silence of the house thundering in her ears. Rand hadn't come home last night, and it worried her. Not that he couldn't look after himself, but as far as she knew he hadn't made friends yet. If he had, he hadn't told her about any of them, which worried her even more.

The kind of friends you didn't tell your big sister about were the kind of friends who got you into trouble.

Tori opened the fridge and leaned on the door, staring inside. She was hungry—she'd bought a lot more than she should have and everything had looked so good at the store. Now nothing seemed appetizing. But in just a little bit she'd need to get dinner started. She just wished she knew if she should fix dinner for one or two.

With a sigh she pulled out a small can of veggie juice, downing it in three long gulps. After tossing the can into the recycling bin, she scooped her wallet and keys off the counter and headed toward her bedroom. She opened the door and stopped dead in her tracks. "Rand!"

Her brother gave a start and looked up from the small black device he held in one hand. "Uh, hey, Tori."

With deliberate movements and never taking her eyes off her brother, she put her wallet and keys on the dresser. He'd been so quiet she'd had no idea he was home. "What are you doing in here?"

He shrugged but didn't do a very good job of hiding his nervousness. "Just wanted to see why you're always holed up in your room." He glanced at the small device in his hand. "So, what is this?" His voice was matter-of-fact and filled with just enough nonchalance to make her even more suspicious. For him to have found that device where she'd hidden it in the toe of her hiking shoe meant one of two things. Either he'd been spying on her and had seen her hide it, or he'd searched her room, which meant he was sneakier than she remembered. It also meant she needed to find another hiding spot.

She held out her hand and waited until he placed the device on her palm before she said, "It's just a little something I'm trying to fix for a friend." It was her turn to give a nonchalant shrug. "Nothing earth-shattering."

"Maybe I could help?"

Tori stared at him. "I don't think so." She forced a smile. "But thanks, though." She curled her fingers around the cell phone–sized contraption and, as he got up from her bed, asked, "What do you want for dinner?"

Another shrug. "I can just grab a couple of steaks from the fridge."

"I'm talking about a *cooked* dinner, Rand. One where we sit down and eat together. As a family." She'd missed gathering around the table, eating and talking with her loved ones. She tended to make friends easily, but it wasn't the same as having people who were your flesh and blood. And while technically Rand's "flesh and blood" was that of a stranger, his soul was as familiar to her as her own.

Her brother rolled his eyes. "What is it with you and family meals?" Disdain colored his tones. "It's not like our family meals were all that special before."

They obviously had different memories of those days. "I've missed you," she murmured, wondering what her brother had experienced here on Earth that had made him so aloof. "Tell you what," she said as she slid her hands into her front pockets. "I'll grill up a couple of steaks and we can catch up. What do you say?"

His sigh was less than enthusiastic. "Fine. Just don't expect me to eat salad or anything like that."

She rolled her eyes. "How about a couple of rare steaks and a baked potato?"

"All right." He walked out of her room.

Tori waited until his footsteps faded before she pulled the rift device out of her pocket. Now, to find a better hiding place for this thing, then on to tackle dinner with a brother who didn't seem to want to be anywhere near her.

When she was sure Rand was sulking in his bedroom, the door closed, she went into the kitchen and carefully wrapped the gadget in cellophane, then put it in a baggie and shoved it down into the canister of flour. Rand didn't cook; she had no fear that he'd find it hidden there.

Half an hour later they sat down at the dining room table, both with a rare steak, baked potato, and green peas on their plates. Rand ate his eight-ounce steak in about six bites and reached to fork over another steak from the serving platter.

Tori set down her fork and took a drink of water. "So," she said, trying not to sound like she was desperate to fill the silence that felt as awkward as walking in heels for the first time. "I hope you've decided to stay in town, at least for a little bit. It's nice having you around."

Rand played with his peas before scraping several onto his fork. "I don't know. Maybe." He shoveled the peas into his mouth and cut into his steak. "No offense, but I don't think I want to live with you." He met her gaze. "I want to be on my own."

She fought back the hurt shredding her gut like sharp

blades. The one person in this town who was family, and he didn't want to be with her. She understood the desire to be independent, but this felt like something more than that. Deciding to get it all out in the open, she clasped trembling hands in her lap and leaned forward slightly. "What have I done to you, Rand?"

Her brother raised his eyebrows. "What do you mean?"

"We haven't seen each other since right before we were put into the holding cells, and we stayed in there for years before getting sucked through the rift. I've missed you, yet you don't seem to feel the same way," she said, her voice husky.

He bit his lip and glanced down at his plate. "I did miss you, Tori. I did." He looked up again. "Let's just take this one day at a time, okay?"

"Okay." Tori picked up her fork again and watched Rand do the same. He separated some peas from the rest and then with his knife pushed them onto his fork. She watched him do this a few times before she realized he gathered six peas onto his fork before shoving them into his mouth. Six. No more, no less. Maybe this was the only way he knew how to deal with the chaos going on inside him.

She just hoped he'd let her help. If they had each other, they could face anything.

Chapter Six

A couple of hours later Tori went into the living room and stopped by the sofa where Rand lounged, watching some inane reality TV show. She needed to get out of the house, and it was clear she needed to get *him* out of the house as well. "I'm feeling the need for some action," she said. "What d'ya say we go out?"

Her brother never looked away from the television. "Nah, I don't want to. You go ahead."

This apathetic attitude of his wore her nerves thin. She bit back a sigh and forced gaiety into her tone. "Come on, Rand. You didn't come to Scottsdale just to stay cooped up in my house all the time." Maybe Byron Maldonado's mega-popular nightclub would tempt him. "We can go to the Devil's Domain."

His eyes flickered but then he shrugged. "I don't want to miss the end of this episode."

Seriously? Tori glanced at the digital clock on the DVD player. "So we'll go in forty-five minutes."

"Would you give it a rest already?" Rand finally looked up at her, his face dark. "I said I don't want to go out tonight. God, you nag worse than a wife."

"But wouldn't you like to—" She broke off when his

lips tightened. Her own temper flared. "Fine. Sit here and numb your brain with this stupid crap." She flung an arm out toward the TV. "I'm going out." She stomped back to her bedroom to change clothes.

Thirty minutes later her hair was in an up-do style and she had slipped into a slinky red dress and four-inch red heels. She grabbed a small matching sequined shoulder bag and slid the thin strap over her shoulder. In the little handbag were her essentials—council credentials, hairbrush, credit card, lipstick, and her cell phone.

As she walked through the living room toward the front door, she told him, "Don't wait up." Without stopping to see if he was going to respond, she went through the front door, letting it slam behind her.

She was still fuming when she arrived at the club. The air conditioning was a welcome change from the heat of the outdoors. In just the few minutes it had taken her to walk from her car to the front door, light perspiration dotted her upper lip. Temps in the upper eighties with humidity in the sixties was stifling.

Tori paused just inside the doorway, letting her senses get used to the change. Between the voices of the crowd and the techno rock music, the din was nearly overwhelming. Various scents wafted her way, including one she recognized. She cast her gaze around, stopping when she saw the muscular man sitting at the bar. Finn Evnissyen, a bad-boy demon she had a tenuous friendship with. She had never felt like she could completely trust him, because she couldn't tell what agenda he had. She was pretty sure he always had one.

The rumor was that Finn worked directly for Lucifer Demonicus as an enforcer, keeping other demons in line or exacting the demon leader's retribution when one strayed over the very broad line demons followed. It was said he could be outnumbered six to one and still come out victorious. But since demons didn't discuss their business and Finn was as close-mouthed as they came, it wasn't easy getting a definitive answer from him.

It was also whispered that Finn was more than Lucifer's sword. He was one of Lucifer's sons, which would add a whole new dynamic to that relationship. Tori had never been able to get the real skinny on that one either, which made Finn all the more attractive back when she'd first met him. There was nothing quite like walking on the dark side to make a girl feel alive, which was what she liked most about Dante, only he was someone she could trust. She couldn't say the same about Finn.

As she walked up to him he leaned back against the bar and let out a long, low whistle, his gaze traveling the length of her body and back up to meet her eyes. "Victoria, sweetheart, you're liable to send every man in here tonight into heart failure, looking like that."

She grinned. In the mood she was in, his appraisal was just the thing she needed to boost her ego. She did a slow pirouette. "Glad you approve."

He shook his head. "Not sure approve is the right word, but…" He gave her another once-over. "I guess it'll do." He raked his dark blond hair off his forehead and motioned toward the seat next to him. "Have a drink with me?"

"Sure." She eased onto the stool and set her clutch on top of the mahogany bar. To the vampire waiting to take her order she said, "I'll have an Almond Joy."

The bartender gave a nod and turned away to fix her drink.

"What is it about women and mixed drinks?" Finn's raspy voice held a musing tone. "You couldn't just order a scotch?"

"Scotch is boring." She smiled her thanks at the bartender when he put a frosted glass of perfection in front of her. "This…" She took a sip. "Mmm. *This* has chocolate in it."

She held up her glass and Finn did the same. They toasted each other, she with her froufrou drink and he with his scotch.

"So," he said after he took a sip, swirling the drink around in his glass. "I'm still a little rankled by your defection the last time we were here."

"That's what you call it? A defection?" She raised her eyebrows. "As I recall, you were being your usual arrogant, annoying self, provoking Tobias and Nix. And let's not forget, you wouldn't cooperate during the investigation into Amarinda Novellus's death. Which you still haven't said much about, by the way. That's still an open case, so you're not off the hook by a long shot." She shook her head and took another sip of her Almond Joy. "You're lucky Tobias didn't haul you off to the council." She pursed her lips and sent him a mock scowl. "I have to admit, you did a good job giving me the slip afterward."

He laughed, blue eyes sparkling with good humor. "I figured Tobias would send you after me. I'm like a Boy Scout, always prepared."

Though hardly honorable, she thought. Finn was the kind of guy who would lie, cheat, or steal to accomplish his goals, which he always kept hidden from everyone but himself. And sometimes she wondered if he knew why he did what he did.

He shot her a sidelong glance. "I really didn't expect the cop to tag along. You two got something going on there?"

Tori smiled at the memory. After Finn had left the club, Tobias had given Tori the signal to follow him, and Dante had muttered, "I think I'll hang with Tori for a bit," and hurried after her. Within ten minutes Finn had lost them, leaving them both embarrassed.

They'd recovered their equilibrium, stopping at a small diner for coffee. They'd talked, flirted, and Tori had had some hope that something might develop between them. But in the intervening months Dante seemed to have cooled toward her. Well...in between the moments when he wasn't looking like he wanted to devour her.

She understood that he had a lot on his plate right now, but she didn't take up that much room, and she wasn't too demanding, either.

But to think they might have something going on? Her smile faded. "No, I really don't think there is," she said in answer to Finn's question. She stared at him. "And Amarinda Novellus?"

He sobered as well. "I had nothing to do with Rinda's death, Tori. You can trust me on that."

She studied him a moment. He wasn't giving off any outward signs that he was lying—his pulse was steady, no discernable changes in the blood flow to his face. She gave a nod and glanced around the club, noting the usual assortment of prets—vampires, shapeshifters of just about every variety, pixies, and in one corner a glum-looking troll hunched over his beer. Above the cacophony of voices and dance music she heard the front door squeak open and in reflex looked in its direction.

Dante entered the club and paused, looking around. His gaze landed on her, and even from here she could see heat flare in his eyes.

"Well, speak of the devil," she heard Finn mutter.

She looked at him, torn between good manners and going over to Dante to see what she could stir up.

"Go," Finn said. "You don't owe me anything. It's not like we're on a date."

"I'll see you later," she murmured and picked up her clutch. "Thanks for the drink." Grabbing her glass, she slid off the barstool and headed toward Dante.

Finn watched her go, appreciating the feminine sway of her hips. Tori was a strong woman, yet feminine and sexy. She was just his type. He still hadn't been able to figure out why things never clicked between them, but they hadn't. It wasn't for lack of trying on his part. He had a reputation to maintain, after all.

He swiveled around and pushed his empty glass toward the bartender. "Give me another." As the vamp poured more scotch, Finn rested his folded arms on the counter and stared at his reflection in the mirrored shelves behind the bartender. He scrubbed his hand across his jaw, realizing he needed a shave, a haircut, and some sleep.

But sleep only brought dreams, dreams that he could make no sense of. He grabbed the glass the bartender placed in front of him and downed his drink in one throat-burning gulp. "Another," he demanded.

From a couple of stools down he heard a husky feminine voice murmur, "I'll have a Glenlivet, straight. Make it a double." The rolling hills of Ireland tinted her honey-eyed tone.

Finn turned to see a slender woman in a black barely there dress. Her auburn hair fell in thick curls to the small of her back. Hell, there was more hair than there was dress.

Which sent his thoughts off in a whole other direction.

"See somethin' interestin', boyo?" Her sultry voice broke through the fantasies playing through his mind.

He looked into her blue eyes and felt like the world fell away all around him. The only stable thing was the barstool beneath him. What the hell? He cleared his throat and did his best not to show just how poleaxed he felt. "I see a lot of something that interests me," he drawled, making sure to put a bit of a flirtatious smirk on his lips. Picking up his glass, he moved down to the stool next to her. "I'm Finn." He held out his hand.

She put her soft fingers in his. "Keira." Her grip was firm yet tender. She smelled light and sweet, like a spring day. She was one of the fey. Elf, most likely. Or maybe a sprite. Didn't really matter. She was lovely.

"Keira." It suited her. Strong, yet feminine, like the hand he still held. He brought it to his lips and pressed a kiss on her knuckles.

"Well, now, aren't you the fine gentleman. For a demon." She withdrew her hand and picked up her glass.

"You have something against demons?" he asked, lifting the scotch to his lips. It wouldn't surprise him. The fey were the snootiest of all preternaturals, most of them looking down on all other prets as if they were subpar.

"Not generally, no. I like to get to know someone before I make a judgment." She took a dainty sip of her drink. "So, Finn. What do you do?"

"Oh, a bit of this and a bit of that," he hedged. Part

of his...charm was the aura of mystery surrounding him. He nurtured that, encouraged people to think there was more of a dangerous edge to him than there might necessarily be. Not that he wasn't plenty dangerous, though right now he needed people to be acutely aware of that if he were to succeed in his current...endeavor.

"Oh, a mystery man," Keira murmured. "I like that."

"I haven't seen you around here before," he said, leaning one elbow on the bar, angling his upper body toward her.

She shook her head and took another sip of her twelve-year-old scotch. "No, this is my first time." She glanced around the club. "I'm new to the city," she said, her gaze focused on the dance floor.

"I'd be happy to show you around."

She looked at him, one eyebrow quirked. "I bet you would." A slow burn entered her eyes. "What's a girl got to do around here to get a man to dance with her?"

He grinned and held out his hand. "Your wish is my command, m'lady."

Her answering smile was full of mischief and flirt. "I thought you'd never ask." As they walked to the dance floor, Finn noticed how light on her feet she was and how delicate she seemed next to him, though she stood just shy of six feet tall. That still put her six inches shorter than him, even if her high heels had put them almost eye to eye. She was the perfect height for dancing, both the vertical and horizontal kind.

The song they danced to was fast, upbeat, and he found himself wishing for a slow dance. He knew all about the ugly side of life, had been through all sorts of things that could make an hour feel like a year, had done things he could never be cleansed of. She was beauty to his ugliness, soft to his hard, light to his dark. If he put his big, rough hands on her he might break her, yet here he was, wanting to do just that.

As Tori made her way through the crowd toward Dante, a familiar scent wafted her way, one she hadn't smelled in centuries. She stopped and searched the club before she saw him.

Her cousin Stefan was standing in the back, near the door to the special rooms that vampires used to dine in private. She held up a finger, signaling to Dante that she'd be right there, and walked toward her cousin, placing her drink on the tray of a passing waiter. As she reached him, Stefan leaned his shoulder against the wall, his face in deep shadow. His host body was shorter in stature than the one he had in the other dimension. He was swarthy skinned, dark haired, and dark eyed.

"Stefan!" She leaned over and kissed his cheek, then gave him a quick hug. Underneath that thinness was wiry strength. Stepping back, she asked, "When did you get here?"

"Here at the club? I've been in the back getting a bite to eat," he said.

She rolled her eyes at what she could tell was his deliberate obtuseness. "No, here in Scottsdale."

His quick smile lightened his features. "I've been looking for you and your brother. I found out what names you were going by a few years ago and just recently heard you were in Arizona. So... here *I* am." He sobered. "It's been lonely, living all these years without family. I'm so glad I found you." He reached up and cupped her cheek.

She wanted to believe him, she did. But Stefan was the king of con. "Family didn't matter so much to you before," she said, her voice hard. "Rand and I wouldn't even be here on Earth if it weren't for you." The memory of being arrested and summarily tried for crimes they'd had nothing to do with was as fresh as if it had happened five minutes ago. Some things were impossible to forget and maybe forgive, but she had tried. "They took us from everything we knew, everyone we loved, and sent us through the rift. Because of you." She still hadn't gotten over the shame of it. As much as she loved him, she'd told no one on Earth of her relationship to him.

"I know, and I'm sorry." Stefan dropped his hand to his side. "Though, on the flip side, you and your brother have had almost a hundred and fifty years to get acclimated here." He smiled. "It's not so bad, is it?"

"Yes, well, being a werewolf isn't always all it's cracked up to be." Tori kept her voice low as she glanced around to make sure no one was eavesdropping. "You *murdered* someone, Stefan. A very important someone."

His lips thinned. "I was...misguided. Perhaps even a little out of control, but—"

"A little?" She leaned in closer. "You call what you did a 'little' out of control?"

"But I have a second chance, Tori. A real chance to live my life right. I've been doing charitable works, feeding the poor...I know it doesn't return the life I took, but it has to count for something, right?" He took her hands in his. "I need your help. Your understanding."

God, she wanted to believe he was sincere. She *needed* to believe he was sincere. Stefan hadn't always been so driven. So inflexible. "You realize there are prets out here who plan to kill you? And they mean to carry it out."

Stefan squeezed her fingers. "Look, let me worry about that, all right? When the time is right, I'll turn myself in to the council, but I can't do it just yet. I have...things to do first."

Her investigative senses flared to life. "What kind of things?"

"*Things*." His eyes hardened though his face didn't lose its pleasant almost placating expression. "I'm not going to do anything to mess up the life you have here, I swear." He touched a knuckle to the tip of her chin. "You have nothing to fear from me."

For the moment she would accept him at his word. And for the time being she'd go against her training, against her *duty* and keep his presence in town a secret from the council until he was ready to turn himself in. He was family. She owed him that much. However, she'd do her best to keep tabs on him, starting this minute. "Come over to the house tomorrow," she invited. "Or let's go right now. I know Rand will be thrilled to see you again."

Stefan opened his mouth but then his attention was caught by something behind her. "I'd love to, but not tonight. I'll stop in soon." He turned toward the door to the private rooms.

"Wait!" Tori grabbed his arm and yanked him to a stop. "You can't say hi and then leave."

"I'm not leaving town, honey. Just the main floor of the club." He chucked her under the chin. "We have plenty of time to get reacquainted. I'll be in touch." Before she could stop him, he went through the door.

"At least give me your cell number." Tori tried to follow but was stopped by a beefy security guard who bared his fangs at her.

"Off limits unless you're a vamp or a donor," he said. His gaze tracked over her neck and then downward.

She was tempted to say she was a donor, if only for a second, but she really had no desire to be a snack for a hungry, randy vamp. Most of them preferred to dine on humans, but every once in a while there was one who had a taste for pret.

With a low growl, she turned away and decided she'd had enough for the night. Except…there was Dante. The tall sex-on-a-stick detective headed her way, his face set in pleasant but determined lines. It would be an outright slight were she to leave now, and she didn't want to do that to him. She had the fleeting thought that Dante was why Stefan had ducked out so early, but then she dismissed it. There'd be no reason the two men had ever crossed paths.

"Hey," she greeted Dante when he stopped in front of her.

"Hey yourself."

He seemed more than pleased to see her. His gaze slid down her body with the same intense focus that Finn's had earlier, but the demon bad boy hadn't sent the slow shiver through her that this good-guy cop did. This close, she saw the shadow of stubble over his strong jaw. Her gaze tracked over each of his long, silky lashes and every strand of his thick, dark hair. Before the night was over, she'd get her fingers tangled in that hair even if she had to knock him down to do it.

Dante stared at the back door. "Who was that you were just talkin' to? He seemed familiar but I couldn't get a clear look at his face."

Tori's heart stuttered. She couldn't tell Dante who Stefan really was. Not yet. He'd feel obligated to tell someone or inform the council, and she'd be ordered to turn in her cousin. She couldn't do that. Everyone deserved a second chance, and she believed Stefan when he'd said he wanted to turn his life around. She had to give him that opportunity. "Just a guy," she said. "A vamp I know." When Dante didn't look convinced, she waved a hand in negligent dismissal. "He's nobody, believe me."

Dante stared at Tori. She was being cagey, and his first thought was that the other guy was an old lover of hers. Jealousy surged, irrational and unwelcome, but undeniable. He didn't like the thought of someone else touching her, some other man seeing her face flushed with passion, her eyes glazed with desire. It made absolutely no sense at all. Tori had lived for almost a hundred and fifty years, so he knew she'd had lovers before. Hell, it wasn't as if he himself had lived like a monk. But damned if he wasn't green-eyed over every single faceless man who'd ever touched her.

This was not the mind-set to have in order to keep his thoughts off having a relationship with her.

"He's nobody, huh?" he said, his voice gruff with aggravation directed at himself. If he were honest, the gruffness was because of hard-fought control. That red dress she had on was smoking hot. The front dipped down nearly to her navel, and when he'd first seen her she'd turned and headed in the opposite direction, almost giving him a heart attack when he saw the way the back was cut all the way down to the dip at the base of her spine. It was a dress that just begged for a man to put his hands on the revealed expanse of silky, tanned skin. He shoved his hands into his pockets to try to disguise the growing interest his cock was showing, and he cleared his throat. "I didn't expect to see you here tonight."

She frowned, obviously taken aback by his abrupt tone. "I hang out here sometimes." She started to turn away. "Yeah, well, anyway, I thought I'd say hi. Have a good night."

Dante could almost hear the muttered "jerk" he was sure she wanted to add. He couldn't let her leave like that. "Wait." He put a hand on her shoulder and resisted the urge to stroke his fingers across her soft skin. "Tori...Look, I'm sorry." He could barely hear himself over the loud rock music blaring from the speakers. "Can we get a booth and sit down?" Just as he added, "I'd like to talk to you," the music stopped and his last words came out loud and clear, turning heads toward them and eliciting a few snickers from those around them.

Tori smiled. Slow, sensuous music started up. "Forget about talking. You can dance with me," she said and held out her hand.

Even as his rational brain told him to walk away, his pulse picked up speed. Here was a chance to hold her, to feel her softness against him. He couldn't shake the feeling that getting her in his arms would be a very bad idea, but to leave her standing there would be beyond rude, and he didn't want to embarrass her.

At least, that's what he told himself as he drew her onto the dance floor. He put his hands on her waist, then slid them lower to curvaceous hips. Tori was a pret. A werewolf. Her body transformed whenever she wanted it to. She was built for speed and meant to take down prey larger than herself. He knew she had a lot of strength, but it was packaged in silky softness.

She clasped her hands behind his neck, and he felt her fingers sift through his hair. Her eyes fluttered closed, face wearing a mask of contentment. For a few moments they danced in silence. She swayed to the music, her pelvis bumping against his every few seconds, her fingers stroking the hair at the nape of his neck. She sighed and opened her eyes. "So, you wanted to talk?" That voice was the definition of sultry.

There were too many people on the crowded dance floor to talk about what he wanted to. The rift device. Plus, he wasn't sure he could keep his mind focused on the conversation while she was plastered against him like she was. "Not here," he murmured close to her ear.

Dante felt the shiver that went through her. She turned her face so that their lips were less than an inch apart. Amber flickered in her eyes and her breath tickled across his cheek. The slight curve of her belly brushed against his groin again, eliciting a resulting hardness to his lower body.

Before he could talk himself out of it, he dropped his mouth onto hers. His entire focus centered on the woman in his arms. Everything else—all the noise, the smells of the club—faded away. His heart thundered in his ears, pulsed in his cock. Her tongue, tasting slightly of chocolate and amaretto and wholly of hot, sensual woman, twined with his.

She moaned into his mouth and pressed closer, breasts flattening against his chest. Dante moved his hands from her waist to the small of her back, pulling her lower body firmly against his. Her fingers tightened on his shoulders.

He reluctantly became aware that the music had stopped. Stepping away from Tori, he kept his hands on her waist and stared down into her eyes, feeling like someone had cut him off at the knees. He was stunned by the primal urge to claim this woman right then and there, in the middle of the crowd.

He'd had no idea he could be as primitive as a Neanderthal. Or a preternatural.

With a smile full of feminine promise, Tori took one of his hands and led him off the dance floor. He trailed behind her, willingly following her lead, feeling just a little off his game.

She slid into a booth at the back of the club and Dante took a seat across from her. She flagged down a passing waiter and in a husky voice said, "I'll have a Screaming Orgasm, please."

"I'd like one of those, too," Dante rasped. He cleared his throat. "But give me a beer, whatever you have on tap."

"You got it." The waiter walked off, a grin on his face.

"Chicken." Tori leaned forward and traced a finger across the table. Back and forth, back and forth. It was mesmerizing, the rhythm.

Made him think of another kind of back and forth he'd like to do.

The waiter dropped off their drinks and Dante took a long draw of his beer. "So, tell me, how'd you end up as a council liaison?" Time to get things back on neutral territory.

While he and Tori had worked together for the past several months, they hadn't really taken the time to talk about personal things. Keeping the "personal" focused on the job somehow managed to keep it less intimate.

She sat back in the booth. One of her feet bumped his beneath the table and he quickly moved his foot to one side. She sighed and sipped her drink. Her tongue swept out, leaving her lips shiny and inviting. She gave a little shrug. "I needed something to do with my time."

"And so you applied to be a liaison?" Dante stretched one arm out along the back of the booth. "Seems to me you could've found less dangerous work." He'd decided a long time ago not to get involved with another cop, because if he ever had kids, well, they deserved to have at least one parent who wasn't in a hazardous occupation. The fact that Tori was a preternatural made her whole life, not just her job, dangerous.

"Like you did?" One slender eyebrow rose. She leaned forward and cupped her glass. "Why'd you become a cop?"

He shifted on his seat. "I come from a long line of con artists. I thought it was time to leave a new legacy."

Her lips pursed. "I bet you've gotten a lot of ragging from your fellow cops."

"At first. Especially after my granddad got indicted for selling counterfeit goods my rookie year."

Tori's mouth formed a perfect little O. Then she pressed her lips together, he figured, against a grin. "That couldn't have been easy."

"It wasn't. But it was SOP for Granddad. He was in jail the day I was born. And the last time he got sent up *was* the last time. The old man died in prison."

"Oh, wow." She reached out and touched his hand where it rested on the tabletop. "And your parents?"

"My dad had his fair share of run-ins with the law. He

was killed in a car accident when I was fifteen. My sister was ten." Dante rubbed his hand along the back of his neck, trying not to let the memories get to him. "My mom died several years later after a lingering illness. Lily, though she was only eighteen, had been married by that time. I figured she was taken care of, so I joined the army and got as far away from family as I could."

"But Lily didn't stay married," Tori murmured.

"No, she didn't. I got out of the rangers and came home to find her in an unhappy marriage."

"Dante, there's not a whole lot you could have done about that." Tori shifted on her seat, her foot bumping against his under the table. "She's responsible for her own happiness."

"I know I couldn't have prevented her marriage going down the toilet, but I could've at least been there for her, not halfway around the world fighting someone else's war."

"So you joined the police department to fight a war closer to home?"

He shrugged. "The job uses skills I already had. And this time, when Lily really needed me, I was around."

"I'm sure she appreciates it." Tori circled the rim of her glass with one finger. "You've been with the police department how long now?"

"Almost ten years." He wet his lips, then took a swig of beer. "I feel like I still have a lot to prove, to my colleagues, to my sister." He blew out a breath. "To myself. Hell, when it comes right down to it, I'm just this side of being a wet-behind-the-ears newbie when it comes to being on the Special Case squad."

He didn't usually open up like this with people, not

even his sister. Feelings weren't something he was comfortable discussing and usually he deflected the subject with humor. He was surprised how natural it felt to confide in Tori.

"Anyway," he went on, "it's just me and Lily now, so..." He gave a one-shouldered shrug.

"Lily's doing okay?"

Dante nodded. "Now she is." At Tori's questioning look, he said, "Right about the time that her ex filed for divorce she was diagnosed with breast cancer. She's been living with me while she tries to find her footing again."

"That's nice, isn't it?" Her smile seemed sad. "You're not alone."

"No. She's there to nag me about leaving my socks on the floor and she gets me to eat better. Well," he added on a laugh, "she tries, anyway. I don't know what I'd do if..." He swallowed the emotion threatening to clog his throat. Redirecting the conversation now was a good idea. "What about you? You just hooked back up with your brother, right? That has to feel good."

"It does," she responded quietly. A look passed through her eyes before her lips curved upward. "But that's enough serious talk for one night." She dipped into her drink and brought her hand to her mouth, slipping her finger between her lips. A foot slid up his calf, scrunching beneath his jeans so that bare toes touched his skin.

Dante felt the shock of that flirtatious touch like a punch to the gut, and it weakened his resolve. Would it be such a bad thing to relax a little and see where things went with her? He could always find the time. He knew she could take care of herself; otherwise she'd have been killed a long time ago. But if he went down this road, if he allowed himself to feel anything more than friendship for her, would his heart survive if she were taken from him?

Probably. But her loss would scar him. And right now, still fearing he might lose his sister, he wasn't prepared to face losing Tori.

As she rubbed the pad of her foot up his calf again, he stared at her. He knew she was doing her best to change the subject of family, which made him wonder why. Were things not as good on the home front as she'd made out? He moved his leg and leaned back in the booth, keeping his fingers wrapped around his beer. His investigative instincts kicked in. Why didn't she want to talk about her brother? "No, no, sweetheart, I want to know more. Tell me about this brother of yours. Randall's his name, isn't it?"

What could she say about her brother? Tori shifted her weight on the seat and took another sip of her drink. "Uh, well, he's younger than me by five years. He's smart, really smart." And rebellious and bratty and acting like a five-year-old at the moment. But she didn't say all that. She gave a shrug. "That's really all there is."

"Uh-uh." Dante wagged his finger at her. "What's he do? Where's he been all this time?"

"He's in between jobs right now," she said. "As you can imagine, over the last hundred years or so he's done a lot of things." She signaled a passing waiter and asked for another drink, then said to Dante, "He's been on the East Coast for the last twenty-five years. He was finally able to track me down and . . . here he is."

"It took him that long?"

"What?" She frowned.

Dante lifted one shoulder. "It just seems to me if I lost contact with Lily, I'd do all I could to find her."

"It wasn't that easy back in the day," she muttered.

"I understand why he had trouble a hundred years ago, but these days? With the Internet—"

"Which is how he finally found me. It took him time to find out who I'd gone into, and I'm not the only Victoria Joseph in the world, you know. It took him a while to sort through everyone." She wasn't certain of that last bit, because Rand had never said so, but it made sense. It was the only thing that *did* make sense. But she wasn't ready to look too closely at Rand's apparent lack of interest in finding his only sister, and she didn't want to talk about it. She took a breath. "So, that's enough about me. What do you say we get out of here?" she asked, rubbing her foot up his muscled calf again.

His gaze sharpened. *Crap*. She'd awakened his investigative instincts, which she hadn't meant to do.

He leaned forward, clasping his hands around his glass. "You'd tell me if something was going on between you and your brother, right?"

She frowned. "What do you mean, 'going on'?"

"I just mean . . . you seem uncomfortable talking about it. I'm just wondering why . . . if he threatened you—"

"No." She smiled nervously. "It's nothing like that."

She pressed her lips together. She couldn't— wouldn't—admit that she was jealous of the relationship he had with his sister. As much as he tried to make it out like Lily was a nag, it was evident from the tone of his voice, from the emotion he couldn't hide, that he loved her and would move heaven and earth to find her if she disappeared from his life. And Tori, now that she'd found Rand again, would do as much for her brother.

She just wasn't sure he'd do the same for her.

"Rand and I haven't seen each other in over a hundred years, Dante." She looked at him. "It's like we're two strangers getting to know each other. It's...hard."

"I can understand that. It'll take some time." He glanced around the club. "Which is why I'm kinda surprised to see you here tonight. Figured you'd be at home with him." Dante looked out at the dance floor. "Or that he'd be here with you."

"He was busy." Watching mind-numbing reality TV, instead of spending time with his sister. And it made Tori mad all over again.

"I can't see how anyone would be too busy to spend time with you, particularly your brother..."

Tori couldn't understand it either, especially when she hadn't seen Rand in over ten decades.

She tried to hide the sadness that overcame her.

She couldn't deal with this tonight. Didn't *want* to deal with it. "Yes. Look, I've gotta go." Tori slid out of the booth. "I'll see you later."

She caught the look of surprise on Dante's face but didn't wait around for him to respond. She was here to have a good time, not talk about things that made her upset. Didn't Dante know men weren't supposed to be so talkative?

Chapter Seven

Tori didn't need this emotional crap right now. She'd come to the Devil's Domain for a good time, and she was going to have one, damn it. She headed toward the bar. She'd find Finn and get him to dance with her so at least the night wouldn't be a total loss.

As she walked she glanced around the club, searching for the demon. She saw him near the front door, hand flat against the wall, bracing his weight as he leaned toward the woman he was talking to. She was turned away from Tori, so all Tori could see was flowing auburn hair that ended at the small of the woman's back.

Well, hell, it looked like Finn had already hooked up with someone. She wasn't going to horn in and ruin whatever action he might be about to get. She looked around the club but didn't see anyone else who could keep her company and help get her out of her funk.

Leaving the noise of the Devil's Domain behind, she had just made it to her car when she heard footsteps behind her.

"Hey. We're not finished." Dante sounded concerned, but she also caught the tangy scent of his confusion.

Turning toward him, Tori tried to ignore the heat that

blanketed the night. It had rained, leaving behind wet pavement and a muggy feel to the air. She could smell the nearby mesquite trees, and in the illumination of the parking lot lights she saw the determination on Dante's face as he came to a halt in front of her.

"If all you want to do is talk about my brother, then I don't think we have anything left to say."

His brows drew down over eyes dark with frustration. "Hey, I'm just tryin' to get to know you a little better, that's all. I didn't know it would upset you. I'm sorry."

He was sorry. So was she. She knew she'd overreacted and now was starting to feel like an idiot. "Don't worry about it. Rand and me...it's complicated."

"Probably doesn't help that you're prets, right?" He moved a little closer, so close she could feel the heat radiating from his big body.

"You're right. Rand hasn't..." She blew out a sigh. "I don't think he's accepted what he is. He's...restless."

Dante raised his chin in acknowledgment. "I get that." His hand lifted as if he were going to touch her, then dropped back to his side. "So, I guess I'll see you around," he said turning away from her.

"Dante, wait." She stared at him, trying to figure out the puzzle of this man. Here he was caring and compassionate, his eyes broadcasting his attraction to her. Yet he seemed hesitant to follow through on it. "Can you just tell me one thing? Are you interested in me or not?"

"You're a beautiful woman, Tori. I'd have to be dead not to be interested," Dante said in that slow, sexy drawl of his. "But I just don't think I have the time to commit to a relationship right now."

She frowned. That was his thing? He didn't want to get

involved because he didn't have time? Genuinely confused, she asked, "Who said anything about commitment? I'm not necessarily interested in getting serious with anyone, either." She spread her hands. "We're both adults. Why can't we just enjoy each other and see where it takes us?"

"You're not the kind of woman a man can just enjoy." Almost as if he couldn't help himself, he reached out and caressed the bare space at the nape of her neck. The weight and warmth of his broad hands made her sway with desire. The sweep of his callused thumbs along her skin made her want to moan. His deep voice husked across her eardrums, sending tiny shivers through her core. "A man gets one taste of you and it only makes him want more." His voice dropped lower. He moved one hand to cup her jaw. "Makes him want it all."

At that husky admission, Tori's heart picked up speed. She moved closer until she rested lightly against him, her belly nestled in the V of his slightly spread thighs. The evidence of his interest rose behind the zipper of his jeans. "Then take it all, Dante. I don't mind." She raised her arms and looped them around his neck. "And I promise I won't bite. Unless you want me to."

His bark of laughter was abrupt, though sensual humor lingered in his eyes. She slid her hands up to cradle his skull, gently urging his mouth down to hers. He resisted, but for only a second, before she felt the shock of his lips on hers all the way to her toes. With a moan she went up onto the balls of her feet, holding his head, pulling him closer. The hard ridge of his erection pressed against the softness of her stomach. His big hands slid down to her hips, tilting her pelvis. She lifted one leg, wrapping it around his thigh.

His low, deep groan rumbled against her breasts. He brought his hands up to her face and took control of the kiss, tilting her head to the angle he wanted, thrusting his tongue between her lips to lay siege to her mouth.

She willingly allowed him to conquer her as she ran her hands over his back, feeling the softness of his shirt and the hardness of flexing muscles beneath. He was hot under her fingertips. Strong.

And he smelled so good, like the fresh outdoors and a healthy male in his prime. The combination called to everything within her, both feminine and feral. With an impatient growl, she pulled his shirt free from his jeans and spread her fingers over the warm flesh of his back.

When she started toward the buttons, he wrapped his hands around hers and rested his cheek against the top of her head. "Wait," he rasped, his breath coming fast and hard.

"Why?" She pressed a kiss to the dip in his throat bared by his open collar. "Consenting adults here." She dropped another kiss onto his Adam's apple. "Though I suppose we should move this to someplace more private."

He cupped her face and gently moved her back. "It would...complicate things, Tori. I'm not saying it won't happen. I'm just saying I'd like us to be friends first." His hands dropped to his sides.

Her brow dipped, just a little. Usually when a handsome man told a woman he just wanted to be friends, it meant one of two things: he was gay or he just wasn't that into her. She didn't think Dante could kiss her like that and not be straight, and she also didn't think he could kiss her like that and not be interested. "I'm confused."

"You're a beautiful woman. Sexy as hell. But I have

obligations that take up most of my time right now, and it wouldn't be fair to you to always be last on my list." His gaze was steady on her and his sincerity seemed real. "I want to get to know you better, I do."

"But..." she prompted.

He shook his head. "I've already told you the 'but.' Let's keep things simple for right now, okay?"

"Things don't get much simpler than I want you and you want me, but all right." Battling back her hurt ego, Tori glanced toward the club and decided she didn't want to go back inside. There were too many people in there for her current frame of mind.

Plus, Stefan might still be around, and she didn't want to take the chance that Dante would somehow recognize him. She needed to figure out what her cousin was up to before anyone official got involved. And since Dante seemed willing to proceed as friends, she didn't want to miss an opportunity to spend time with him. "Why don't you come to my place for coffee? Just as friends," she stressed. When he didn't say anything right away, she added, "I have pie," hoping to further entice him.

He seemed torn. "What kind of pie?"

"The best kind. Homemade." She had a bit of a sweet tooth, and sometimes the craving for dessert was impossible to ignore, so she just about always had something on hand. Or the ingredients ready to whip up a treat. "Dutch apple and peach. And triple-bean vanilla ice cream."

He grinned. "You've just talked me into it."

"Excellent." Tori adjusted the strap of her evening bag. "Just follow me home."

Dante pulled out his smartphone. "Give me your address."

She rattled it off and he input it into the device. "Got it." He looked up at her, his dark eyes still holding banked lust, though mostly he seemed intrigued by her pies.

If she had to start with his stomach, so be it.

"Where're you parked?" he asked.

She motioned to her right. "I'm a few rows that way."

"I'll walk you to your car." He cupped her elbow.

It was nice, being treated like a lady. She didn't have the heart to remind him that, as a werewolf, she could protect herself better than he could. She drew her keys out of her purse and remotely unlocked her Mini Cooper.

As she opened the door, he shook his head with a muttered, "This is like driving around in a tin can." He looked at her. "It's not safe. Someone in a bigger vehicle could roll right over you."

"You mean like someone driving a big heavy-duty pickup?" she asked with a glance over his shoulder at his truck.

"Yeah. Or a Hummer. Lots of Hummers in this town."

She shrugged. "I'm a good defensive driver. And I get great gas mileage." She ran a hand over the roof of her car. "Besides, it's such a cute thing. If it makes you feel better, for its size, it's gotten great safety ratings."

He grimaced. "I can see this is one argument I'm not going to win. Just be careful."

"Yes, sir, officer." She grinned at his scowl. "I'll see you in a few minutes."

She got in the car and started it up, waving at him to get him to go back to his own vehicle. She waited until he had climbed behind the wheel and started the big truck, the diesel engine rumbling like some great behemoth, and then she pulled out of the parking lot and headed home. Time for some pie and maybe a little cop on the side.

Dante made a right and followed Tori's tin can of a car into a residential neighborhood. He kept replaying that kiss in his head, remembering how good, how right, she'd felt in his hands. How hot, how sweet she'd been on his tongue.

He hadn't been wrong—one taste of her had only made him want more. God, what had he been thinking? He should never have followed her home. Just walking into her house would change their relationship. Seeing where someone lived, how they lived, lent an intimacy he wasn't sure he could handle.

He should just turn his damn truck around and go home. Stop this before it got out of his control. He lifted his foot off the accelerator and watched Tori's little Cooper move farther ahead of him. His gut tightened as the distance increased. With an oath, he picked up speed. He wasn't going to be an ass about this. He said he'd have pie with her, so he had to see this through. As long as he kept things work-related for the time being, he should be fine.

Time to think about something else. He put his attention on the neighborhood he was driving through. As he passed house after house he wondered how many prets lived there. Were humans outnumbered here? Were they soon to be?

Was that the purpose behind the rift communications? To send more prets through the rift? Their primal need for survival would compel them to take over human hosts, and the human souls already housed in the bodies would be suppressed.

Dante just hoped he wasn't ever randomly—or otherwise—chosen to become a host. He didn't want to lose who he was. It would be better to become a pret by the bite of another one, though that did limit him to being either a vampire or a shapeshifter of some sort. They were the only ones who could create others of their own kind. Other than in the time-honored way of making babies, everyone else had to wait for another rift in order to grow their population.

Hmm. Maybe that was it. Maybe the person behind these communications was neither vampire nor shapeshifter. Maybe Natchook was acting on behalf of someone else.

Dante followed Tori into a driveway and pulled his truck to a stop behind the car she parked beneath a carport. As he shoved the gearshift into park and cut the engine, he studied her home. It was a typical brick ranch house from what he could tell. The light from the portico shone onto the front yard, which he could see was desert landscaped with prickly pear and a saguaro standing like lonely sentinels to one side.

He got out of the truck, tucking in his shirt as he went and hoping like hell he hadn't made a mistake by coming here. As Tori unlocked the front door and invited him in, he gave himself a little pep talk. *No sex, MacMillan. Just pie and coffee.*

And maybe a look at that rift device.

But no sex. Sex would complicate an already complicated situation, and he had a feeling that once he got her underneath him he'd never want to let her go. That wouldn't be a bad thing, except he wasn't a love 'em and leave 'em kind of guy. If he took Tori to bed, it would mean he had feelings for her. Feelings he wasn't ready to accept.

"The kitchen's through here," she said.

He followed her down a short hallway and into a larger-than-expected kitchen. "This is nice," he murmured. Stainless-steel appliances and marbled green counter tops complemented the dark stained cabinets. "Are you a closet gourmet chef?"

A smile lit her face. "Not gourmet by any stretch of the imagination, but I do like to cook." She placed her small evening bag on the counter near a set of ceramic canisters decorated with bright red, orange, and yellow chilies. As a matter of fact, the entire kitchen was bright with smatterings of chili pepper decorations, even down to a couple of magnets on the fridge. He grinned at seeing a Snoopy magnet, too. It didn't surprise him to see that slight hint of playfulness. "I like to eat more than I like to cook," she went on. "So cooking's rather a necessity."

Dante laughed. The admission was unexpected, yet not. Most women he knew were always on one diet or another, but he supposed that Tori, with her increased werewolf metabolism, didn't have to worry as much about gaining weight.

She bent and took off her sandals, giving him a great view of her shapely ass. As she straightened, holding the straps of the sandals between her fingers, she said, "I don't think Rand is home, but let me check. I'd like you to meet him."

"Sure." Appreciating her grace and beauty, Dante watched her walk down another hallway and stop in front of a closed door.

She knocked with one knuckle. "Rand?" There was no

response. With a slight frown she put her hand on the knob, her expression deepening as she twisted it. He saw her lips press together and then she turned and came back into the kitchen. "His door's locked, but he's not in there."

"How can you tell? Maybe he's asleep."

"His scent is too muted. If he were here, I'd be able to smell him more." She glanced back toward his room. "He didn't want to go out earlier. I guess he changed his mind." She sounded a little peeved.

Dante wasn't sure he'd ever get used to the olfactory abilities many prets had. Especially those of shapeshifters. To be able to smell not just scents but also emotions... He gave a slight shake of his head. He could understand why some prets looked upon humans as being inferior. He didn't agree, but he understood it.

Tori opened the refrigerator and pulled out two pies. "Which kind would you like?"

Dante walked over to stand beside her and looked down at the desserts. The Dutch apple had that crumbly topping with what looked to be a drizzle of caramel over the top, and the peach pie had a crust that was flaky and golden.

Tori laughed. "Maybe a slice of both?"

"Works for me." Dante met her gaze. "Can I help?"

She shook her head. "Nope. Just have a seat." She motioned toward the adjacent dining area. "I'll bring it over."

"At least let me start the coffee," he said.

Pleasure softened her face. "Of course. Coffee's in the cabinet above the coffeemaker."

Dante quickly got the dark brew going and leaned one hip against the counter, watching Tori cut large slices of pie and dish them onto two plates.

"I'm assuming you didn't want small pieces," she said without looking at him. He could hear suppressed humor in her voice.

"You assumed right," he responded. "Where are the forks?"

"Drawer to your left. By the sink."

He put his hand on the knob of a drawer only to stop when she said, "Not that one. Next one."

With two forks in hand, he turned back to the coffee-maker. "Mugs?"

"Cabinet by the fridge."

As he turned toward the refrigerator, she did, too, and they both stopped, eyes melded. Her hair was beginning to come out of her elaborate upswept style, and he wondered how much of that was because he hadn't been able to keep from touching her. He didn't have the pleasure of tangling his hands in her thick mass of chestnut brown hair, and that was probably a good thing. The feel of it cascading over the back of his hands would have started fantasies about how other parts of his anatomy would feel with her tresses dragging over them. His belly, thighs. His cock.

It had a mind of its own and perked up, taking notice of the directions Dante's thoughts had gone. With a soft oath, he sidestepped Tori and yanked open the cupboard door, staring blindly at a neat row of coffee mugs until Tori said, "Just grab any."

She took a gallon of ice cream out of the freezer and carried it back over to the counter. "How many scoops?"

"Two's fine," he managed to say through a throat gone tight.

Tori finished with the ice cream and replaced it in the

freezer, then picked up both plates. "I take mine black," she said with a jerk of her chin toward the coffeemaker.

Dante usually took a couple of sugars in his, but tonight he thought he could use the extra jolt the bitterness of the brew would give him. He poured coffee into both mugs and carried them over to the dining room table, hoping Tori wouldn't notice, or at the very least wouldn't comment on, his renewed erection.

She sat in the chair at one end of the table, and he took the chair to her right. He forked a piece of apple pie into his mouth. As the taste of fruit, cinnamon, nutmeg, and caramel hit his taste buds, he gave a little hum and closed his eyes. "This is really good," he said and took another bite.

"Thanks. It's nice to see my cooking appreciated for once. Before Rand came, I often ate alone, and appreciating my own cooking isn't quite the same thing." Her tone was dryly self-deprecating.

He looked at her with a slight grin. "My sister always goes on about what a grill-master I am. Between you and me, I think she does it so she can get out of doin' the cooking."

"She's all right now?"

Dante nodded. "She still gets tired easily, but her energy levels are leaps and bounds over what they were when she was going through chemo."

Tori stared at him. "You haven't said a whole lot about her. She had cancer, right?"

"Breast cancer." He cupped his hands around his mug and stared down into the dark coffee. "She got her diagnosis two days before her loser of a husband told her he was filin' for a divorce."

"Oh, my God. Like she needed that kind of additional stress on top of everything else."

"Exactly." He took a long chug of coffee. "My now ex-brother-in-law understood me clearly when I made that same point to him."

"I imagine he did." She leaned one elbow on the table. "I take it you made it with your fists?"

Dante started into the peach pie but paused at her comment. "Now, what makes you say that?"

"Oh, I dunno. Maybe because I know you, and I know you wouldn't let your sister get hurt and upset like that without doing something about it. Since you can't fight her cancer for her, I have a clear picture of your brother-in-law—"

"Former brother-in-law," he made sure to correct.

"I have a clear picture of your *former* brother-in-law," she repeated with a grin, "on the ground with a bloody nose and a black eye."

"Close enough." The bastard had had both eyes blackened to go along with the broken nose and split lip. Dante finished his dessert and pushed the plate away, replete. "Damn, woman. You could put a man in a coma with food like that."

"I'll take that as a compliment."

"You should." He stood, coffee mug in hand. "Get you a refill?"

She shook her head.

Dante filled his mug almost to the brim and went back into the dining room.

As he sat down, Tori said, "I think it's wonderful that you opened up your home to Lily." Melancholy touched her dark eyes. "You have no idea how lucky you are.

How lucky you've been to have your sister with you."

"But you have your brother."

She nodded, her smile so sad it broke his heart. "For now, yes." She seemed to come to a decision and opened up to him in a way she'd refused to in the club. "But I can tell he's pulling away from me. I feel as if I'm losing him and I don't know why."

Chapter Eight

Dante leaned back in the oak chair, his dark eyes fixed on her. "Tell me about him."

"Rand?" At his nod, Tori blew out a breath and wrapped suddenly chilled fingers around her coffee mug. There wasn't much heat left, but it gave her something to do with her hands. "He's five years younger than me. He's smart. A little…indecisive, I guess. But he has a good heart."

"Where's he been all these years?"

"After our Influx he ended up in Leeds. England," she clarified. "I was in London. Just a few hundred miles apart, and we didn't know. I wouldn't have had any idea whom he'd jumped into so finding him was virtually impossible. Of course, I could have traveled the countryside sniffing people," she added dryly.

Frankly, she'd been too busy trying to survive. Being a woman in the East End of London in the latter half of the Victorian era had not been an easy introduction to life on planet Earth. She'd done things that, once she'd gotten out of London, she'd vowed to never do again.

Humans talked about how violent prets could be, but human beings could be just as vicious. And a woman on her own on the backside of poverty in the late 1800s, even if she was a werewolf, was a woman at risk every damn day.

"So how did you find him?"

"I didn't. He found me." Tori scrunched her face at his expression of surprise. "I know, right? He just showed up on my doorstep a week ago . . . well, not quite a week yet, but there he was. Said he'd been looking for me for a while and had finally gotten lucky."

"Really?" Dante looked skeptical. "How did he do it?"

"He said he kept doing online searches for me, and eventually my name popped up in conjunction with the regional council of preternaturals."

"Wow, I'm surprised it took him that long." He took a sip of coffee. "You've been doing this job for how long now? About three years? He must really suck at using the Internet."

She frowned. He had a point, and she'd wondered the same thing. If she'd been able to locate Rand, nothing on Earth would have stopped her from getting to him. But he'd shared enough about himself that she knew he was close to being, if not actually, destitute. "He doesn't have a lot of money, Dante. Some people can't just pick up and go whenever or wherever they want to. They have to plan for a trip. Financially."

He gave a small shrug. "Regardless, I imagine you were shocked."

"Shocked doesn't begin to describe how I felt. Stunned. Gobsmacked." She grinned, remembering the moment she opened the door to see that familiar stranger on her modest front porch. "I knew right away who he was."

"How?" He leaned forward, his entire demeanor one of keen interest.

She shrugged. "It's kind of hard to explain. It's a...sense that I had. Plus, he...smelled like I remember."

"But his name wasn't Randall in the other dimension, right? Just like yours wasn't Victoria."

"Right." Tori crossed her legs and swung one foot. "But that's who we are now. Randall Langston and Victoria Joseph, formerly of Great Britain."

Dante twisted in his seat to hook one arm over the back of his chair. "Funny, you don't sound British." His square-tipped fingers played with the handle of the mug.

She shot him a dry look. "I've been in America since just after the Civil War. Plenty of time to lose an accent." She gave a slight shake of her head. "Or pick up a new one. Whatever." She was tired of talking about her brother and their relationship. Or lack of one. The closeness that Dante and his sister had put a bright spotlight on what she didn't have with her brother. She didn't want to be so mean-spirited as to feel envious, but she did. She was jealous of the bond Dante and Lily shared.

Tori sure as hell wasn't about to volunteer that her cousin had recently wandered into her life as well. Any thoughts of physical intimacy with Dante tonight fled as sadness and regret came over her. All she'd ever wanted was to have her family close by, and now that she did, it wasn't like she'd thought it would be.

Dante seemed to sense her discomfort, because he leaned forward and said, "So, since we're talking about the rift..."

She raised her brows. "Were we?"

"Yeah. We were."

Smart man, to know when to change the subject.

He pushed his mug to one side. "Can I see the device?"

"I'm surprised it took you this long." She grinned and got up from the table. Going into the kitchen she took the lid off the flour canister and rooted around, carefully pulling out the baggie. She held it over the sink and swiped clinging flour away, then grabbed a dishtowel and took both into the dining room. "In case Rand comes home," she said, holding up the towel before she dropped it onto the table. "If he comes in, put that over the gizmo." She opened the plastic baggie and wrapped her fingers around the small black contraption, holding it out to him.

Dante took it from her, the tips of his fingers grazing her palm, sending a frisson of sensual awareness through her nerve endings.

"Finally I get to see this damned thing up close," he muttered, turning the cell phone-sized device over in his hands. "Doesn't look like much, does it?"

"Uh-uh." Tori pointed toward one of the tiny silver knobs on one end. "This one turns it on."

He looked at her, dark eyes holding a mixture of concern and curiosity. "Have you? Turned it on, I mean."

"Oh, yeah. A couple of times." She grimaced. "But then someone always asks me for a password and I have to shut it off. We need to figure out how to turn it on without anyone on the other end knowing about it." She took the seat next to him. The warmth from his big body was intoxicating, and she had to fight against leaning closer.

"Turn it on." Dante held the device out to her.

Tori took it from him, her fingers brushing his once again. Thoughts of physical intimacy immediately flooded back into her mind. She wanted those strong hands on her skin, caressing her breasts, stroking her sex. Before she could do anything to act on those thoughts, Dante jerked his hand away as if he'd been zapped. With a sigh, she twisted the knob and turned on the rift device.

For a few seconds nothing happened, then static emitted from the speaker. Several moments later, a male voice spoke in the standard language from the other dimension. Tori quickly twisted the knob and switched off the device.

"What'd he say?" Dante asked.

"He asked for the password." Tori shook her head. "The other couple of times I've turned it on he's done the same thing."

"Same guy?"

"Don't know. Don't care." At his lopsided grin, she said, "Does it matter?"

"Probably not." He picked up the device and looked at where the two sides were attached. "Do you have a small Phillips-head screwdriver?"

"Sure." She got up and grabbed the toolbox from the laundry room. She handed him the screwdriver and watched as he worked the small screws loose. With slow care, he slid the battery off the back and then separated the two sides of the device's casing. "I opened it up a couple of days ago and realized it looks much more like a computer than a radio, so I called Tobias and asked him for help." She stared down at the inner workings of the device. "This all looks like a bunch of wires and bits of...bits."

Dante gave a low whistle upon seeing the inside of the gadget. "Would you look at that." It did in fact look like a computer, but it was by far the smallest one he'd ever seen. He pointed to a tiny square that was no bigger than a quarter of an inch wide. "That's probably the microprocessor, and these"—he put his finger above thin copper wires—"lead to that." He looked at what appeared to be an external connector. Studying the sides of the casing, he mused, "Looks like a USB port."

"To hook up to what?" Tori leaned closer, a long tendril of hair escaping her upswept style. It curled against her cheek.

Without thinking, he reached out and brushed it behind her ear, his fingers lingering on her soft skin. When her eyes closed as she leaned forward, he remembered his resolve not to get romantically involved with her and dropped his hand to the table. He cleared his throat and her eyes flew open. "Sorry," he muttered.

She heaved a sigh. Her look was one of exaggerated disappointment, though he saw the hurt she couldn't hide. The gaiety in her eyes seemed forced. "You are such a tease, MacMillan. A fisherman...woman...gets tired of baiting the hook only to have the fish get away time after time. So be forewarned: One of these days I may not let you get away so easily."

He met her gaze. "Hopefully one of these days I won't want to slip your hook."

She clapped a hand over her heart. "I can only live in hope."

"Smartass."

Her grin chased the lingering hurt from her eyes and made the humor genuine.

Glad he could restore her normal upbeat mood, Dante gave her a wink and turned his attention back to the device. "Is there anything on the schematics about what this port is for?" he asked, pointing at the connector.

"No. I don't think so, anyway." Tori pushed back her chair. "I'll get it so you can take a look, just in case I missed something." She returned in under a minute and placed the document on the table. Once unfolded, the paper was roughly three feet by three feet wide.

Dante leaned over. "Okay, so this is a microcontroller, not a microprocessor. That would explain why I'm not seeing any other chips." His finger followed the lines drawn on the schematics.

"English, please."

He glanced at her. "I thought you were up on this."

"I know radios. Communications. Not computers." She shot him a dry look. "Why do you think Tobias asked you to help me?"

"Right." He pointed toward the chip. "This little guy has the core processor and memory, possibly some RAM. That's one of the ways they could make this device so small, to have it all on one chip." He studied the schematics. "It doesn't look like there's anything like a GPS, so that should mean the device's location can't be electronically tracked by anyone. Okay. So this little doohickey is a transceiver, right? It can transmit and receive messages."

"Right."

"So maybe this port"—Dante tapped his finger on the corresponding spot on the diagram—"is to hook up to some kind of external memory? Or a power source of some kind? Or maybe it's for a transponder. Something to amplify or retransmit the signal on a different frequency." He looked at Tori. "What do you think?"

"I think we're missing some schematics is what I think." Frustration colored her tone. "If all this does is send and receive radio waves, why would they need external memory? And so far it hasn't seemed to need charging."

"Have you had it on much?"

She shook her head. "Just a few times. And I shut it off almost right away because that guy always asks me for the damned password." She picked it up. "If this port does go to a transponder, why would they need one? The reception on this thing is just fine."

Dante sighed and leaned back in his chair. Lifting one hand, he rubbed the nape of his neck and then glanced at his watch. "Aw, hell. I didn't realize it was so late."

Tori grabbed his wrist to see the time. "It's only just after one A.M."

"Lily and I are taking the horses out early, before it gets too hot. Once I go back to work Monday—well, tomorrow, I guess, since it's so late—I won't have much of a chance to ride until next weekend." He started reassembling the device and fought back the urge to haul her into his arms. Just the feel of those delicate fingers on his wrist had made him want them wrapped around another, needier part of his anatomy. *Keep things light.* "I need my beauty sleep." He dropped one lid in a wink.

Her bark of laughter ended with a snort. "You get any prettier there, and we might just have to slap a dress on you."

"I've got the legs for it." He grinned at her eye roll.

"Since you're playing so hard to get," she said with a sidelong glance, "I guess I'll have to take your word for that."

He flashed her another grin and handed her the device, taking care to let it drop into her palm so he wouldn't touch her. He watched while she wrapped it up in plastic and then returned it to the canister, shoving it deep and moving stuff around before she replaced the lid.

"Flour," she said as she turned around, her fingers coated with white powder. She rinsed off her hand and dried it on a dish towel lying on the counter. She swiped the towel over the surface, wiping up flour that had spilled. "Rand doesn't cook, so there's no reason for him to look there."

"Does he know you have it?"

She didn't answer him right away. Instead, she fiddled, straightening canisters that didn't need straightening. Finally she murmured, "He may have seen it." She muttered something else he didn't catch.

"Hey, one of us doesn't have preternatural hearing. What'd you just say?"

She sent him a little glower. "I said he found it in my bedroom." She went into the dining room and scooped up the schematics, folding them into a square that was roughly the size of his palm.

Dante stood. "What, you just happened to leave it lyin' around on your bed?"

Tori frowned. "No." She looked away and went back into the kitchen. "I had it in the toe of one of my hiking boots. Be right back," she said over her shoulder as she walked down the hallway.

Dante waited until she returned, empty-handed, before he said, "So he was snoopin'." He leaned one hip against the table and folded his arms over his chest. "Maybe your house isn't the safest place to hide this thing."

She sighed. "It's safer here where I can keep an eye on it. Besides, he doesn't know what it is."

"You sure about that?" Dante walked into the kitchen. "What if he does? What if he tells someone you have it?" He put his hands on her shoulders. "You're not safe with that thing here. Let me take it."

"And do what with it? Keep it at your house? With your sister? If it's not safe here, it wouldn't be safe there, either." She shook her head. "It's okay. Rand won't find it again."

"I have a gun safe in my bedroom. I could at least lock it up."

"And that'd probably be the first place someone would look. Besides, your sister is there by herself during the day." She shook her head again. "I don't want to put her in danger."

He bit back a sigh. She was right. He couldn't take the device home and put Lily in harm's way. He dropped his hands and took a few steps away. "We're assuming someone would know I have it." He blew out a breath. "Do you trust him?"

"Rand?" Her brow furrowed. "He's my brother," she said as if that explained everything.

"That doesn't answer my question." He braced himself with one hand on the counter. "Do you trust him?"

Her lips thinned. Something flickered in her eyes before she responded with a soft, "Yes. I trust him."

"All right. That's good enough for me." It would have to be. He'd trust her judgment until it was proven faulty. With a flick of his wrist he checked his watch again. "I really gotta go."

They started toward the front of the house. "Thanks for the pie," Dante said. "You're a good cook."

"Well, I don't know about my cooking," she rejoined with a smile, "but my baking skills are pretty good."

"Damned good." He paused by the front door. Now that it was time to go, he wasn't sure what to say. Before he'd gotten on the Special Case squad, and before Lily's life had fallen apart, he'd give the woman he was with a good-night kiss. Hell, he'd probably be giving her a good-morning kiss after a hotter than hell night. But he had to keep his hands off Tori for now. Get the job done and maybe in another year or two he could make some time for a relationship. He hoped she'd wait. Maybe he could shave that down to six months. "Uh, thanks for the pie," he said again, then felt like an idiot for repeating himself.

Her smile widened. "You're welcome."

"I guess I'll see you around."

"Most likely." Humor sparkled in her eyes, making him realize she was laughing at him.

Dante let it go. After his vacillations tonight he deserved to be laughed at. He probably deserved a slap, but what he got was humor and pie. She was a hell of a woman. As he reached the door, he heard her say, "Oh, wait a minute." He pulled his hand back just as the door swung open and a startled young man stood in the opening.

"I heard him at the door," she said to Dante. "This is my brother Randall." Tori put a hand on the guy's shoulder. "Rand, this is my colleague Dante MacMillan."

At the word "colleague" Dante felt something—hurt? disappointment?—slash through him. But he had only himself to blame. Sure, they were just starting to really get to know each other, but he'd at least thought they could call themselves friends.

Dante eyeballed the guy. He looked like the type who would snoop through someone else's things. Taller than Dante had expected, he had shifty eyes and a nervous quality that piqued Dante's interest. Randall's skin was baby smooth with a light dusting of hair on his arms. The hair on his head was as dark as Tori's, cut in a marine style with buzzed-cut sides, and slightly longer hair on top.

"You're human." Randall's voice came out flat, his British accent full of disdain.

Tori's brother was apparently a bigoted jerk. Dante was always surprised when people showed their prejudice, whether it was over the color of someone's skin, their religion, or species. "Yep. Sure am." He hooked his thumbs over his belt and rocked back on his heels. "And you're a werewolf, like your sister."

"Sure am." The younger man tried and failed to mimic Dante's drawl. He crossed his arms, then uncrossed them, repeating the process a few times before he left them folded over his chest. "So you work with my sister?"

"I'm on the Special Case squad assigned to her district." Dante could tell by his demeanor that Randall really wasn't interested, but if he wanted to put on a good face for his sister, Dante was willing to oblige. "We work cases together when there's a werewolf involved."

"How nice for you." Randall dropped his arms against his sides and drummed the fingers of one hand against his leg. "Are you a wannabe?"

"Sorry?" What the hell was the kid talking about now?

"Do you want to be a preternatural when you grow up?" A pronounced sneer lifted Randall's upper lip.

"Rand." Tori's voice was hard.

Dante frowned. "Not particularly," he said in answer to her brother's question.

The sneer turned to a scowl and Randall's brows drew down over darkening eyes. "So you think you're too good to be one of us?"

"That's not what I said." The guy was apparently itching for a fight, and under other circumstances Dante might be willing to get into it with him. But not with Tori looking like she wanted the floor to swallow her whole. Dante glanced at his watch again and said to her, "Listen, I really have to be going." To Randall, he said, "It was nice to meet you."

"Yeah, nice to meet you, too," Randall muttered, his tone suggesting he felt the exact opposite of his words. He pushed past his sister. "I'm going to bed."

"I was surprised you weren't here when I got home," Tori said. Her brother stopped and turned toward her. She added, "You weren't interested in going out earlier."

His blue eyes narrowed slightly. "I didn't want to go out with *you*. There's a difference."

Dante saw the hurt flare in Tori's eyes while embarrassment colored her cheeks. He wasn't going to stand by and let Randall talk to her like that, even if the little pip-squeak was her brother. "What's your problem, buddy?"

Randall scrubbed his hand over the top of his head. With the rebellious streak the young wolf had, Dante was surprised at the military cut of his hair. He would have expected a longer style and a cigarette hanging out of one side of his mouth, especially since shapeshifters' bodies healed too fast for them to be bothered with pesky diseases like those from which humans suffered. Lung cancer would be of no concern to him.

"My problem, *buddy*, is that you think you're too good to be one of us, but it's apparently all right for you to screw my sister." Her brother's eyes went from blue to wolf-amber in the span of a heartbeat.

"Rand!" Tori put a hand on his chest when he started toward Dante. "That's enough. He's not...we haven't..." Anger was beginning to flare in her voice and on her face, but he could tell she was more embarrassed than anything. "And, anyway, it's none of your business if we were."

Randall's lips curled back, revealing canines that looked remarkably long. And sharp.

Dante broadened his stance, preparing for a fight. He'd never duked it out with a werewolf so he wasn't so sure how he'd fare, but he wasn't going to back down just because the guy was a pret.

"Rand, stop it, right now." Tori put herself between the two of them, her hands on their chests. When she glanced toward Dante, he saw her eyes held the same amber glow as her brother's. "You, too, Dante."

He raised his brows. "I'm only defendin' myself."

"I know what you're doing. Stupid, macho..." Her mutters trailed off as she glared at her brother. "And *you*...you should know better."

"I'm just trying to look out for you."

The look on Tori's face told Dante she knew that wasn't exactly true. It was clear he had a thing about humans. When her brother didn't budge, she let out a low growl that raised the hair on the back of Dante's neck.

Randall threw up his hands. "Fine. Whatever. You do whatever the hell you want to. You always do. I can see where your loyalties lie." With one final glower at Dante, her brother turned and went to his room, slamming the door behind him.

"What is he, fourteen?" Dante glanced at Tori, glad to see her eyes slowly return to normal. That growl she'd given had been like something out of a movie. Deep, gravelly, and a clear warning of danger. He was damned happy it hadn't been directed at him.

She sighed and lifted her shoulders. "I'm so sorry about that. I guess it's his way of protecting me." Her expression lightened for a moment and she seemed pleased by her assessment. "He's always been a little...high-strung. He'll get over it."

Dante could almost hear her unspoken "I hope." He worried that he might have made things worse between the two siblings. That was the last thing he wanted to do, to make Tori choose between her brother and him.

He had a hard time believing the guy was a werewolf, as juvenile as he seemed. He came across as hostile but harmless. Plus, with all the fidgeting, Dante sensed that Randall was nervous and not at all confident like his sister. "What he said..." Dante held her gaze. "It's not true. I don't think I'm better than you."

"Oh, I know that. And despite what Rand may have led you to believe, being a pret is not a be-all-to-end-all. We have issues, too."

No kidding. Dante ran into plenty of issue-laden preternaturals on his job. All the time. But right now specifically...

"Like brothers who are ungrateful little bastards,

right?" Dante looked down the hallway toward the bedrooms.

He wanted to teach the little runt a lesson. Something he'd probably never get the chance to do. Besides, Tori was a grown woman. It was her decision on the direction she wanted her relationship with her brother to go. If she wanted Randall to stay with her badly enough, which Dante suspected was the case, she'd probably end up taking more crap from him than she'd ever take from anyone else on the planet.

Including Dante.

That was a sobering thought, and yet another reason why the timing wasn't right. For either of them.

He drew in a breath and exhaled. "So, for the third time, I'll see you later."

She nodded. "Drive safe." Her green eyes were big and dark, serious.

He bent closer and whispered as low as he could, "Find a better hiding place," and then pressed a kiss against her satiny cheek, hesitating, wanting more than anything to move his mouth just an inch or so to those luscious lips. But he restrained himself and instead drew in a breath, holding her scent in his lungs for a brief moment. "Good night," he murmured and turned away.

As he walked to his truck he thought about her brother and that hot temper he had. Little shit. Tori was a saint to put up with all of that snark. The guy needed an attitude adjustment and Dante wished he was able to give it to him, but he knew once Randall brought out the fangs and claws, Dante's chances of adjusting anything would be slim to none. Even having a gun loaded with silver bullets.

Not that he wanted to shoot Tori's brother. Doing that would ruin the friendship they had built and do a hell of a job putting the brakes on anything romantic between them.

Damn it. Things got complicated way too fast around here.

Chapter Nine

Tori felt like she'd just gotten to sleep when her cell phone rang. She grabbed it from the nightstand and peered at the screen, her vision blurry. The time display read five thirty. "Hello," she answered.

"It's Ash." The gravelly voice of the werewolf liaison from District Four came over the line. "Sorry to wake you, I thought you'd be up already."

"It's okay. What's going on?" She rubbed her eyes, trying to wipe away the remnants of slumber.

"There's been another attack up here. I thought you'd want to know."

She struggled to a sitting position. "When?"

"The ME estimates TOD around midnight. The crime scene techs just opened the scene, so I'm doing my initial walk-through."

"He killed this one instead of turning him?" That didn't make sense. "Maybe it's a different attacker."

"How likely is it that we have two rogue werewolves attacking people?" His voice went dry. "Besides, there were two victims. The man was killed; the woman survived and most likely was turned. We'll know for sure in another couple of hours."

"Any clues at the scene?"

He sighed. She could picture the frustrated look on his face. "No, damn it. He's a clever bastard. Same MO, bleach used on the bodies so there's no DNA. There were a couple tufts of fur left at the scene, but they're soaked in bleach and ammonia, too, so no help there. It's like he's a fucking ghost. Pardon my language."

"That's okay," she responded absently. She'd heard worse every day on the job. Hell, she'd *used* worse. "Are you any closer to figuring out why he's doing this?"

"Uh-uh. It could be that he's just a crazy son of a bitch."

"Could be, but most people, including the crazy ones, have a reason for what they're doing ... even if that reason doesn't make sense to the rest of us." Tori plumped the pillow behind her back. "Tell me what I can do to help."

"That's what I like about you, kid. Always willing to jump in and lend a hand." He sighed. "There's nothing, really, other than keeping your ear to the ground. Let me know if you hear anything that seems pertinent."

"Will do." She ended the call and pondered for a second whether she should call Dante, but decided against it. There wasn't anything he could do and, besides, the man himself had said he needed his beauty sleep. She'd call him later and let him know there'd been another attack. He might want to consult with his counterpart in District Four.

Dante. She shook her head and put the phone back on the nightstand. Sliding down into bed with a yawn, she couldn't keep her thoughts off him. He'd been so ready to come to her defense with Rand. It had made something inside of her melt. She'd never really had someone, a man, stand up for her like that before. It made him all the more attractive to Tori.

Her mind bounced back to the kisses they'd shared. God, that man was a good kisser. A great kisser. She got stirred up just thinking about it.

He was smart *and* funny. A lethal combination. She could kind of understand his reluctance for a relationship, to a point. She got that he put in a lot of hours on the job—so did she. She got that he had obligations to his family—so did she. Or, at least, she was trying to. And she got that he had a hobby, his horses, that also demanded time from him.

There they differed. She could never focus her attention on something long enough for it to become a hobby, unless you considered working off the clock to be one. And she didn't do pets, because she was all the animal she cared to look after.

For the next hour she tossed and turned, trying to get her mind to shut down long enough to fall asleep. It didn't happen.

Finally, she got up and put together a big breakfast of pancakes, hash browns, and lots of sausage. She got Rand out of bed, smiling when his grousing stopped as soon as he found out what she'd fixed. As they sat down at the dining room table she tried to get him to talk to her about the night before, but he remained reticent and noncommittal about his impressions of Dante, except for a snarly "The cop's human."

When had he become such a bigot? He hadn't acted this way in the other dimension. It seemed as if this planet had changed him, and not for the better. "Since when do you care if someone's human or pret?"

Rand sent her a look over his coffee mug. "You don't know me, Tori. Not really. I'm not the same person I was back on our home planet. Neither are you."

He was right about that. The personality and life experiences of her human host had changed her. For the better, she'd like to think. She wasn't so sure about Rand. "So tell me about yourself. Let me get to know you."

He forked pancake and a bit of sausage into his mouth. "Nothing to tell," he said as he chewed.

Apparently he wasn't ready. Tori could give him time. She hoped so, anyway. She never knew when she might wake up to find he'd left without saying good-bye. Thinking she could get a topic going that he would want to talk about, she said, "So, I ran into Stefan last night at the club."

Rand's face brightened. "You did? Why didn't he come over?" He squirmed like an eager puppy that had just heard its master's voice.

"I asked him to," she replied. "I guess he had other things to do. But he said he'd see us soon," she added at Rand's look of distress. "I'm sure he'll make sure he sees you while he's in town."

Using his knife and fork, her brother pushed bits of sausage around on his plate, grouping them together in neat little rows. "Well, I'd like to see him." Rand chuckled before saying, "He's so clever."

"He is." Tori drew in a breath and held it a moment. "Don't you feel even the slightest resentment toward him?"

Rand lifted startled eyes to hers. "Why should I?"

She leaned forward, resting her elbows on the table. "He killed someone. He's the reason we got sent through the rift, Rand. We lost everything." She pressed her lips together. "I should have called the council right away and let them know he was here."

"No! You can't!" Rand shoved to his feet, his chair skittering across the tile floor, banging against the wall. "Everyone agrees that being here on Earth is our second chance. Stefan deserves the same."

Tori fiddled with her fork. "I know, Rand. That's why I haven't turned him in yet." She sighed and searched his eyes. "But what if he hasn't changed? What if he's still a criminal?"

"He's not. I won't believe..." Her brother grabbed his chair and sat back down. "He's just passionate about what he believes, that's all."

Passionate. That was one way to look at it. Insane would be another. Only time would tell which way he went with his second chance.

Rand speared several small pieces of sausage and forked them into his mouth. "What do you know about the werewolf attacks up north?" He stared down at his plate as he cut into his pile of pancakes. "I think the investigators are clueless. I mean, they aren't any closer to catching the guy now than they were after the first attack, right?" He lifted his gaze to hers.

At the admiration she saw shining in his eyes, Tori's appetite fled. She put her fork down. "He's attacking innocent people." She took a sip of orange juice. "Anyway, it could be a woman, you know."

"Well, whoever it is, he or she is making more of *us*. That's not a bad thing, in my opinion." Rand finished his meal and pushed his plate forward. "Don't you ever feel outnumbered? Outgunned? Or are you so fond of humans that you don't care that they might enact laws to put us in communes or, worse, behind bars?"

She frowned. "No one's even talking about doing that, Rand." Where was he coming up with all this crap?

"Really? What about the senator who's trying to microchip us? He says it's so they can have an accurate count, but the chips could have a GPS function and track us."

She shook her head. "People wouldn't let that happen."

"Are you sure? How would we know if it did?"

"We'd know. They couldn't keep something like that a secret."

"Right." He shot her a glower. "You are so naïve sometimes."

Tori clasped her hands. "Rand, think about it. The government's too disconnected and there'd be way too many people involved for something like that to be kept under wraps. We'd know. The council would know," she stressed.

"And if they knew, would they tell?" His expression turned sly.

Now there was the million-dollar question. Some of them knew about the rift device and hadn't shared that knowledge, so it was possible, even probable, that they had other secrets they were keeping. Hell, prets were all about secrets. Up until about four years ago their very existence was a secret.

"Well, I don't think there's any kind of conspiracy going on, and you shouldn't either," she finally said. What else could she say?

"Don't tell me what to think." Rand leaned back in his chair and folded his arms over his chest, then repeated the action several times. "I'm allowed to have my own thoughts. Just because you're older than me doesn't mean you can tell me what to think."

"I never said that." She reached out a hand as if to touch him even knowing she was too far away. "I just don't want you worried about something that probably isn't happening."

He shrugged. "But it's my worry, right?"

She lifted her hands in surrender and sat back. He was right. It was his worry. He'd also been right when he'd said he wasn't the same man. He *had* changed, and she was afraid it wasn't for the better.

Rand got up and carried his plate to the sink. "So, tell me about your new lover. The human cop."

"He's not my—"

"Maybe not physically, yet, but I saw how you looked at him. How he looked at you."

She couldn't see his face, and the tone of his voice was neutral, like they were discussing the weather.

However, that last piece of information sparked her curiosity. "How did he look at me?"

"Like he wanted to lay you out and feast on you." He rinsed off his plate and put it in the dishwasher, then dropped his fork and knife in the utensil container.

Tori took her plate into the kitchen and scraped the leftovers into the wastebasket. When Rand held out his hand, she gave him the plate and watched while he rinsed it off. "It feels so strange talking to my brother about this," she muttered. She was heartened that he seemed interested, but she couldn't shake the uneasy feeling she had that he seemed also to be aligning himself with radicals in the preternatural community.

"But you like him."

"I like him. We're just friends, though." If she didn't think about those kisses maybe she could make herself believe they were co-workers and nothing more. It had really been that almost-kiss there right before he'd left that had her most bothered. To have him so close, to feel the rasp of his stubbled cheek against hers, his warm breath on her skin, the heat of his body radiating to hers... She fought back a shiver. "He's my co-worker."

"You've never had any of your other co-workers over for pie at one o'clock in the morning." A teasing note entered Rand's voice.

"We ran into each other at Devil's Domain." She leaned one hip on the counter. "You could have met him there if you'd gone with me. Where'd you end up going, anyway?"

He shrugged. "Just... out. Went for a run. Stopped off at a gym to shower, then came on home."

She'd thought last night that his hair looked a little wet. It was hard to tell; he kept it cut so short. "That doesn't make sense. Why didn't you wait and shower here?"

"I just didn't. Jeez, I'm not one of your suspects for you to interrogate." He leaned down and rearranged the silverware in the dishwasher basket and then pushed the rack into the machine and closed the door.

Tori noticed he started tapping his foot. One-two-three-four-five-six. Pause. One-two-three-four-five-six. Pause. Repeat.

"Honey, are you okay?" She walked forward and took his hands in hers. She stared into his eyes. "You seem..." While she searched for the right word he jerked away from her.

"I seem what? Sick and tired of you always being a council liaison? Never my sister?"

She frowned. This wasn't the first time she'd caught this attitude from him. How could he be tired of her doing her job when he hadn't even been here a week yet? "I'm worried about you. I noticed you've been acting a little…" She sighed. "I think your OCD is getting worse. Maybe you should see someone."

"See someone? Like a shrink, you mean?" He shrugged off the placating hand she tried to put on his shoulder. "There's nothing wrong with me."

"I didn't say there was, but sometimes talking about a problem can help. Maybe there's a medication that could alleviate some of the symptoms." She hated to see him like this.

"I'm fine," he insisted, his eyes amber with anger.

"Okay." She'd let it go for now. "You know I'm here for you."

"Right. Yay me." He scowled and turned on his heel to head toward the front of the house. "I'll see you later."

"Where are you going?"

"Out." The door slammed behind him.

Tori sighed and leaned over the counter, letting her head hang. The muscles in her neck and shoulders ached in protest as they lengthened, loosening from the stress that had tightened them. When had things gotten so strained between her and her brother? Had they always been, in the other dimension, and she hadn't recognized it? Or had she chosen not to see it?

Dante gave Lily a boost onto her horse and then rechecked the cinch, making sure it was properly fastened.

"Stop motherin' me," his sister said. "You've already checked it three times."

"And now I've checked it a fourth. You can never be too safe when it comes to riding horses."

She pressed her lips together, but not before a dimple flashed, telling him she was fighting a smile. "Okay there, Ranger Rob." She gave him a two-fingered salute.

"Lily."

"What?" She shot an innocent look his way. "Oh, just stop it, Dante. Muffin's such a sweet boy. He would never do anything to make me fall off, would you?" She leaned forward and patted his neck.

The quarter horse turned his head and shook it a couple of times, nickering low in his throat.

"See?" Lily sat straight with a grin. "He's a good boy."

"All right, all right." Dante hoisted himself into the saddle and clicked his tongue. Big Ben set off at a slow walk, Muffin catching up to walk by the Appaloosa's side.

"So," his sister said in that sly, teasing way of hers, "tell me about her."

"Who?"

"Don't be coy with me, mister. You've met someone, I can tell. Spill."

Dante concentrated on guiding Ben around a flat-paddled prickly pear cactus. "I don't know what you mean." He barely had a handle on his feelings about Tori. There was no way he was ready to talk about it, least of all with his sister.

"Ha!" Lily moved Muffin closer so she could reach over and smack Dante on the shoulder. "You do so know what I mean. Who is it? Is it someone you hooked up with at the club last night?"

"I don't 'hook up' with women." He shot her a frown. "And if I did, I wouldn't be talking to my little sister about it."

"Okay." She held up one hand in surrender. "You don't want to talk about her, I get it."

He knew his sister. She wouldn't let go of it for very long. She should've been a cop. "There's nothing to talk about," he insisted. "I...was working."

"Uh-huh." She eyed him. "You went out to that night-club and didn't come home until almost two. You don't usually stay out that late when you know we're getting up early for a ride."

"Talk about mothering," he muttered.

"Fine." She gave a scowl but couldn't hold it and broke into a grin, shaking her head. "Let's talk about something else, then."

"Yes, let's." He tipped his cowboy hat farther forward, giving more shade to his eyes.

"Any interesting cases you're working on?" Lily clicked to her horse, urging him up a slight incline and then back down. She was a natural horsewoman, riding Muffin with ease. She looked...happy for the first time in a long while.

Dante was glad he could give her some peace of mind. He knew for himself there wasn't anything quite as relaxing as riding a horse, out in the desert where there was only the sound of nature—a few caws from the ravens circling overhead, the rustle of leaves as a slight breeze blew through the nearby mesquite trees.

"Had a werewolf and vampire get into it a couple nights ago," he said. "Well, the werewolf tried to get into it with the vamp, but I don't think he quite managed it."

"What do you mean?"

Dante glanced at her. "He bit a human on his way to the vamp."

"Really?" Lily's eyes went round. "Wow. Is the human okay? Will he…will he turn?"

"No. The werewolf didn't let loose any of his preternatural stuff."

"Stuff? Is that the technical term for it?" Her lips tilted in a smile.

"As a matter of fact, it is." Dante shared a grin with her.

"So how does that work?" she asked. "I've never been sure."

Dante pulled Ben to a stop in the shade of a mesquite and waited until Lily maneuvered her horse next to him. He grabbed the canteen off his saddle and handed it to his sister, then took a swig of water after she passed the canteen back to him. "It's just like in the legends. Werewolves can make another werewolf with just their bites. Vampires have to seal the deal with blood because they're the weakest of all the prets."

"The weakest?" She frowned. "Just a few days ago there was a news report about a vampire who picked up a minivan full of tourists and set it down on top of another car just for shits and giggles."

"Yeah, that's the weird thing…*one* of the weird things about vamps," he clarified. "They're the weakest of all prets when they first come through the rift. They can only take over bodies that are close to death or have just died. Once they've acclimated to their host, though, physically they're the strongest." Big Ben shifted his weight and Dante leaned over and stroked the horse's neck.

"Can you imagine? Living forever." Lily turned Muffin

and started back toward the trailhead where they'd left the truck and horse trailer.

Dante pressed his heel to Ben's side and followed his sister.

"Seeing history as it unfolds and being a part of it... You'd have all the time in the world to do what you want to do, not having to worry about getting sick or dying." She turned her face away from him, and he knew she was fighting back tears.

"Well, they can die," he informed her. "It just takes some doing."

She met his gaze, her eyes sad and full of the worry that he knew was her constant companion these days. "But they're not going to get some kind of illness that eats 'em from the inside out."

"No, probably not." Dante urged Ben closer to her. "Honey, you've got this thing beat."

She looked down and then back at him. "I know." She pressed her lips together. "What if it comes back, Dante?"

"Then you'll fight it again." He tugged off one of his gloves and reached over to brush a tear from her cheek. "And I'll be right there with you."

Lily gave a tremulous smile. "I know you will be. I'm a lucky woman, to have a brother like you. I love you, you know."

He lightly chucked her on the chin and then pulled his glove back on. "And I love you too, squirt."

She laughed. "You haven't called me that in years."

"Yeah, well, I outgrew callin' you names to make you mad." He dropped one eye in a wink. "I have other ways."

"Oh, boy, don't you!" She shook her head and sent him

a sidelong glance. "You sure you don't want to talk about your woman?"

"I don't have..." He rolled his eyes and tipped his hat back. "You just don't give up, do you?"

"Nope." She pulled her horse to a stop beside the trailer. "I'll get it out of you, sooner or later."

She probably would, too. Not that he minded. He wasn't trying to keep Tori a secret. But talking about her made things more... solid. Real.

For once, Dante couldn't control where his heart was heading, and he wasn't sure he was ready for what that meant.

Chapter Ten

After a refreshingly uneventful Monday at work, Dante was bent over the computer parts on the dining room table at home when his cell rang. He pulled the phone from his belt and put it on speaker. "MacMillan." He set the phone on the table.

One of the police dispatchers said, "We've got a real situation at Hades' Hideaway over on Stetson."

"So call Grover," Dante murmured, holding the motherboard in one hand so he could look it over more closely. "I'm off duty."

"Uh-uh. Grover's off with some kind of bug. Breckinridge can come on early in the morning, but you're it for tonight."

Dante sighed and put down the motherboard. He twisted his wrist to check his watch. Seven P.M. "Damn it." He pinched the bridge of his nose. "All right. Hades' Hideaway, huh? That's one of Maldonado's clubs, isn't it?"

"Yep. It's owned by a vampire so it's not surprising something happened there, right? One of the 911 calls said a vamp got staked. Wonder if it's the big bad himself?"

Dante raised an eyebrow. "Was it fatal?"

"Dunno. The person didn't say."

Dante ended the call and went into his bedroom to re-trieve his gun from the gun safe. He stared at the small safe in the deep drawer of his dresser and thought back to his conversation with Tori the night before. Even though he didn't want to put Lily in jeopardy, he really thought the device would be more secure with him. But if some-thing happened...He hadn't helped her get back on her feet only to let her be killed by a rogue preternatural.

He shoved his feet into his work shoes and tied the laces, then slipped his belt through the loops of his pants, pausing to attach his holster. He shoved his Glock 22 home and grabbed an extra clip of silver bullets. After he attached his badge next to the gun, he headed toward the front door, scooping up his cell phone as he went through the dining room. Stopping at the doorway into the family room, he told his sister, "I got a call. Be back later."

She twisted around on the sofa to stare at him. "I thought you were off duty."

"Not anymore." He gave a shrug. "I'll see you later."

"Just when you were making progress on that mess in the dining room," she mumbled as he walked away.

"I heard that," he called over his shoulder. Her laugh echoed down the hallway.

Pulling into the parking lot of the club ten minutes later, he stayed in the truck surveying the scene for a few moments. It had rained earlier so the pavement was still wet. There were police cars with flashing lights, and a few other vehicles, including Tori's Mini Cooper. Her pres-ence surprised him because she should have been done for the day, like he had been. He wondered why she got stuck on this call.

People were gathered in groups in front of the club,

a few of them with dirty, tattered clothing, looking like they'd rolled around on the ground a bit. He noted two vampires, a handful of guys clutching blankets around themselves, and several humans. Piper was already there, taking notes as she talked to the group of humans. She had a typical cop stance, making sure her firearm was facing away from the men, and was dressed in her usual pant suit and flat-soled shoes. Her pink-trimmed Sig Sauer was secured in a belt holster that also had two additional clips.

A couple of women stood off to one side with a tall, slender man who had his back to Dante. The man turned and Dante realized it was one of the quadrant's fey liaisons. Dante figured the women must be fey of some sort, but hell if he could tell what. He always had a hard time discerning the difference between nymphs, elves, pixies, and the like.

He climbed out of his truck and headed toward the scene. "I see the gang's all here," he said as he reached the crowd.

Piper told the humans to stay put and walked over to Dante, combing her fingers through her dark blonde hair as she came. "It looks like it was the vamps who started things. These guys"—she gestured toward the group of human men—"were just too drunk to back off."

"Anyone hurt?" Dante cast a glance over the various groups, looking for wounds. He stopped when he saw the wooden stake sticking out of the shoulder of one of the vampires.

"Just him," Piper said. "Everyone else has some scrapes and bruises, but nothing serious."

"What the hell happened?" Dante started toward the group of humans, Piper at his side.

"They happened." She pointed toward the two women talking to the fey liaison. "Couple of pixies rattled some cages and got them fighting each other."

"Got who fighting who?"

Piper made a circular gesture to encompass the entire gathering. "All of them. Humans. Vamps. Werewolves."

Ah. That would explain the blankets. The werewolves had shifted in order to fight, and then turned back to their human forms, a process that left them naked.

He glanced at the women. They were very attractive, he admitted that. However, in his opinion, they were not worth going up against vamps and werewolves for. "I take it these bozos are drunk out of their skulls," he said with a nod toward the human men.

"They were. They've sobered up a bit now."

Dante took a moment to review Piper's notes and asked a few questions of his own. The men were tired and anxious, and he couldn't blame them. The vampires were sending glares that promised dire consequences for the night's activities.

The door to the club swung open, catching Dante's attention. Tori walked through the doorway, heading toward them. Now there...*there* was a woman he'd risk his life for. She waved toward the werewolves. "You can go," she said, her voice hard. "But you'd better not leave town."

Dante raised his eyebrows. Usually she sounded so melodious, sultry. But not now.

"What?" she said as she stopped in front of him. "They screwed up my evening." Her scowl was accompanied by a snarl.

He held up his hands. "I didn't say anything." He stared down into her gorgeous face, fighting the desire to pull her into his arms. He was the one who kept pushing her away, telling her he needed to focus on his career, yet he continually wanted to touch her, kiss her.

He wanted her. More than that, he liked her. A lot.

Dante cleared his throat. "What're you doin' here, anyway? Where's your other liaison?"

"There was a thing between two different clans of werewolves over on Camelback Mountain. He got dispatched to help out over there, so I got stuck with this bunch of yahoos." She shot the departing werewolves a glare. When she looked at Dante again, her gaze softened. "I still have pie left, by the way."

There was the sultry note he'd been listening for. His body tightened and the memory of the heated moment they shared flooded his mind. He could see by her eyes she was remembering, too. Scrubbing a hand over his jaw, he looked at Piper. "So what's the verdict? Do I really need to be here?" *Please, God, tell me no so I can get out of here before I do something I'll regret.*

She glanced from him to Tori and back again. "I don't think so," she finally said. "The pixies started it, the werewolves continued it, and the vamps finished it. The humans were just kinda caught up in it because they were drunken idiots."

When Tori snagged his gaze by running her tongue across her lips, Piper propped her hands on her hips. "Hey, what's going on with you two?"

"Nothin'," he said at the same time Tori muttered, "I don't know what you mean."

"Right," Piper drawled. "Listen, whatever this is"— she gestured between the two of them—"I don't care as long as it doesn't hinder any investigations we do. I mean, you're both consenting adults and whatever it is you consent to is really none of my business."

"We haven't consented to anything," Tori said with a frown.

"Okay. Whatever you say." Piper clearly didn't believe her. She looked at Dante. "You probably don't need to stay. I'll file dual reports at the council and at your precinct."

"Is that your conclusion, too? That the humans were only peripherally involved?" he asked Tori.

She shoved her fingers into the back pockets of her jeans. Dante tried not to notice how the motion thrust out her breasts. She nodded and said, "They admitted as much. The pixies flirted, got the vampires' blood lust up, then the werewolves horned in and the girls turned their attention to them. The vamps got mad."

"And those guys?" he asked with a nod toward the humans.

"Just another bunch of yahoos," Piper said dryly with a glance at Tori. "Those numb nuts got in the way and then were too drunk or too macho, or maybe a little of both, to back down. A couple of them carry stakes with them, and that's how the vamp ended up with one in his shoulder. He was lucky it didn't end up somewhere else."

"Tori, do you think any of the werewolves are viable suspects for the attacks going on in the north?" Dante asked.

She pursed her lips. "I don't think so, but I'd already thought of that. I got their alibis for the nights in question, and I'll follow up on those as soon as I'm done here."

He noticed she was looking at the crowd gathered on the far side of the parking lot. "What's up?" he asked her.

"I see someone I want to talk to." She glanced at him. "Be right back."

As he watched her walk away, those full hips swaying with each step, he was aware of Piper staring at him with her arms folded over her breasts. He looked her way. "What?"

"Nothing." She watched Tori for a minute and then said, "Listen, I want to ask you something."

When she didn't go on right away, Dante said, "You wanna ask me now or later?" He really hoped she didn't want to talk to him about Tori.

She grimaced. "Now. Give me a second." She motioned for the humans to come over to where she and Dante stood. When they got there, she said, "Is there anything else any of you want to add?"

There came a mumbling in the negative. A couple of the guys kept glancing toward the vampires, whose gazes still threatened retribution. The other humans studiously ignored the vamps, as if hoping the bloodsuckers would disappear.

Dante could see this thing escalating out of control once the police presence was gone. He needed to get these guys away from the vamps. He motioned to a couple of uniformed officers. When they came over, he said, "Take these guys to the station. We'll finish questioning them there."

"Thanks, man," one of the men said, relief and genuine gratitude in his voice.

"You might not thank me once this is all over." Dante gave him his best stern-cop look. "Carrying stakes is like carrying a gun. You have to have a concealed weapon permit. Do you?"

The guy held up his hands. "Wasn't me who staked him, man."

Dante glanced over the group. "Who did?" he asked.

They shifted their feet, didn't meet his eyes, and otherwise seemed disinclined to confess.

"Fine." To the uniforms Dante said, "Take them to the night commander. Fill him in, and once he gets a copy of Piper's report he can finish up with these...gentlemen."

"You got it," one of the officers said. "Come on," he told the group of men.

Dante kept his gaze on them as they trudged away, then asked Piper, "What was it you wanted to talk to me about?"

"How do you deal with all this?"

"All what?" He looked at her. "Preternaturals?"

She shook her head. "I know how to deal with prets. My great-grandfather was taken by an entity when he was in his sixties, well after his kids had started their own families, so we've known about the rift and prets for a long time." In a drier tone she added, "The Petersons are experts at keeping secrets."

"Good to know."

"How do you deal with the violence? I mean, I've been around prets all my life, but it's been in familial surroundings, not...not this." She gestured toward the wounded vamp who was being taken back into the club, the wooden stake still in his shoulder. Most likely they'd remove the stake and have a willing donor or two standing by so he could regain his strength and heal.

"But you've been a liaison for a few years, yeah?" Dante hooked his thumbs over his belt. He glanced toward Tori and saw her talking to Finn Evnissyen. He ground his jaw at the familiar way the demon leaned toward her. With effort, Dante put his attention back on Piper. "You've seen stuff like this before."

"Stuff like this, yeah. In my other post I usually ended up dealing with minor skirmishes and meaningless squabbles." She sighed. "I'm just not sure I can deal with the tougher cases." Meeting his gaze, she said, "Like that one you had late last year, with the vamp slayings. I don't think I could've handled all that blood and gore." Her eyes darkened. "How do you do it?"

Dante thought about his answer a moment. "Some of it just comes with experience, Piper. I hate to say it, but once you've seen some of this stuff, you become inured to it. You have to in order to be effective. What helps most is keeping your attention on the victim." He drew in a breath and let it out slowly. "We're the voices for those who can no longer speak for themselves."

"I suppose."

"It's really not that different than working any other type of crime." He put a hand on her shoulder and gave a light squeeze. "You focus on finding who did it so the dead can have justice. You can do that." He gave her shoulder another squeeze and then dropped his hand to his side.

Piper nodded. "Yes, thanks." She looked around the scene and sighed. "I guess I'll go file those reports. See ya later."

"See ya." Dante walked back to his truck and sat on the front bumper, waiting for Tori. She was still talking to Evnissyen and some red-haired woman. Even from here Dante could tell she was gorgeous, but he only had eyes for his wolf.

* * *

"Finn, stop jerking me around." Tori crossed her arms and glared at the grinning demon. "I know you. It wouldn't surprise me a bit if somehow or another you're mixed up in this mess."

"You know, I don't think I've ever seen you this worked up." Finn leaned closer, his smile as wicked as they came. His voice was a raspy whisper as he said, "I seem to bring out the wildness in you."

"What you bring out is my total lack of tolerance for BS." She heaved a sigh and looked at the auburn-haired woman at his side. She'd introduced herself to Tori, giving her name as Keira O'Brien, and from her scent Tori knew she was an elf. From the faint traces of an accent, she could tell the woman had originally been from Ireland. Tori glanced her way. "I'd rethink my decision to hang out with this guy if I were you."

"Thanks, but I can handle myself." Keira smiled. She seemed nice enough, Tori supposed. Not at all uppity like a lot of fey she ran across.

"Would you please just tell me what you saw tonight?" Tori fixed her gaze on Finn.

He shrugged broad shoulders. "I'm sure it's nothing you don't already know. The pixies started it, really, flirting with the vamps and then backing off and taking up with werewolves." His eyes crinkled at the corners. "I guess the vamps didn't like that too much."

"And the humans?"

"Just a gaggle of drunken idiots."

"Who staked the vamp?" She'd already been told one of the humans had done it, but she wanted to see what these two would say. Knowing Finn, he'd tell her a werewolf had, just to play with her.

"A human did it," Keira chimed in. "But in all fairness, it was in self-defense." When Tori looked her way, the elf added, "But that was all I saw."

"You're sure?" Tori studied her closely.

"Positive."

"All right." Tori looked at Finn again. "Anything else you'd like to share?"

His eyebrows lifted. "Not that I can think of."

Tori narrowed her eyes. He kept an innocent look plastered on his face. She huffed a sigh. "Fine. Thanks." She lifted a hand in farewell and turned back toward the club.

Almost everyone had gone. There were a couple of patrol officers wrapping up witness interviews and several bystanders milled around. The combatants either had been allowed to leave or had been taken into custody. She was glad to see Dante was still there. She walked over and sat beside him on the bumper of his truck. "So, I got a call from Ash early this morning," she said. "There was another attack up in quadrant four."

He looked at her. "A turning?"

"Probably. I haven't heard yet." She heard a rumble of thunder and hopped up. "Why don't we get in your truck where we can actually sit down?" When he hesitated, she added, "Or we can go sit in my car."

He stared at her Mini. "Uh, no, thanks." He fished out his keys and unlocked the doors.

Once they were inside, she told him, "One person was killed in the attack and the other, a woman, was bitten. I thought you'd like to know in case you talk to your counterpart in quadrant four."

"Yeah, thanks." Dante switched on the ignition and fired up the AC. Cool air circulated through the truck from the vents in the dash. He reached out and adjusted the one by the driver's door so that it blew on his face. The hair at the back of his neck curled over his collar, damp with sweat from the heat and humidity.

Staring at the curls, Tori imagined running her fingers through them. She squeezed her hands closed to keep from giving in to her desires. She swallowed hard, trying to control her thoughts.

"When can we get together again to look over that device?" He twisted in his seat to face her, one long arm resting along the upper curve of the steering wheel. He turned away to look through the windshield.

She loved his strong profile. He really was a handsome, masculine man, though his eyelashes were beautiful and long. "Just about any time is good for me. As long as Rand isn't home." A thought struck her, and she said, "Monday night would be good. Rand's planning on being out, and after I take care of a . . . thing, I'll be available."

His brows dipped and he glanced at her again. "What thing?"

"You remember Barry? From the grocery store?"

"Yeah, I remember. It was just a couple of days ago." His lips twisted in a wry grin. "Senility hasn't quite set in yet."

Tori grimaced good-naturedly. "No need for sarcasm." She brought her left leg up onto the seat, her knee bumping against his thigh. When she met his gaze, she saw his eyes had darkened. She had no doubt that he wanted her and sooner or later he'd realize that love hardly waited for convenience. She hoped it was sooner. "His punishment for biting the human was to be bound in silver for thirty days. He can't shift," she added in explanation when Dante seemed a little bewildered.

"Ah." He gave a nod.

"I promised I'd be with him the night of the full moon." She watched him closely for his reaction.

His eyes narrowed slightly. "You mean you'll be sitting outside his cell, right? You'll still be able to shift."

"Well, that would be downright cruel, wouldn't it? Shapeshifters can control when and how often they shift, but during a full moon it's agonizing if you don't change into your animal form. And I mean agonizing." She closed her eyes briefly, remembering all those years ago when she'd been clapped in silver chains, rendered impotent of her shifting abilities. She'd deserved the punishment. Barry didn't. "It's...difficult to get through. Anyway, he turned me down, but I want to check on him before sunset." She couldn't explain to herself why it was so important to make sure this one werewolf was as emotionally prepared as possible to get through this punishment, except that she'd been there. She knew how excruciating an experience it was, and if she could help, she had to.

"Why would you do that?" Dante's eyes narrowed even further. "He's not your responsibility. He's there because of choices he made."

She sighed. "I just...Wolves are pack animals, Dante. We're not loners. We want our own kind around us, especially when we're sick or injured." She leaned toward him, trying to make him understand. "Barry's not exactly an alpha male. He'll have a hard time of it. The effect is not only physical but emotional, too."

"And that's your responsibility how?" When she shot him a glare, he held up one hand. "Look, I don't mean any disrespect. I think what you offered to do says a lot about the kind of woman you are." His tone suggested he wasn't sure if he should admire her or call the men in the white coats. "But I..." He leaned forward and took her hands in his. "I for one am glad he declined your offer. I don't want you to be in pain."

He was the sweetest man ever. She'd known a lot of good men, but none had even come close to making her feel the way Dante did. Tori got mutant-sized butterflies in her stomach when he was near, and everything seemed brighter and full of hope when she was with him. With him, she felt like she was living, not just surviving like she'd done just about all of her life. She squeezed his fingers. "That means a lot to me, that you feel that way."

"I appreciate your compassion, honey, I do."

Her heart jumped at the endearment he didn't seem to know he'd used. He also didn't seem to realize his thumbs were sweeping over the pulse points of her wrists.

But *she* had noticed the action. With every sweep, her pulse skittered, her breath came faster, and everything feminine deep inside her softened with desire. With a soft moan, she leaned into him and pressed her mouth to his.

His lips opened beneath hers, his low groan lost in her kiss. He stroked his tongue along hers, tasting dark and all male. His arms wrapped around her, pulling her closer.

He trailed a path to her ear, giving her lobe a light nip, not hurtful but enough to send a shock of arousal jolting through her.

"Dante," she moaned. She shifted her position, draping herself over him, flattening her breasts against his broad chest. She ignored the steering wheel digging into her rib cage. The small amount of pain was worth getting close to this man again.

With an oath, he wrapped his hands around her upper arms and lifted her off him. He set her gently on the passenger seat. His breathing came hard and fast, chest rising and falling. "Wait."

"Wait for what, Dante?" She stroked her fingers down his cheek, but he stopped her. She whispered, "What if you're about to pass up something beautiful, something right, because the timing doesn't fit your schedule?"

Regret, stark and sharp, passed over his face. "I really like you, Tori. But I have so much on my plate right now, with a job that isn't exactly a forty-hour-a-week thing, and my sister..." He blew out a breath and pressed her palm to his face, holding it there. "That's not entirely it. I...I'm afraid of losing you. If I fall in love with you and then you get killed by some other pret..."

Her breath hitched. "You're not alone in this, you know. You also do dangerous work and could get killed on the job."

"Yeah, you're right." He held her gaze. "One thing I know for sure, the first time I make love to you is not going to be in the cab of my pickup."

She smiled, a slow build up to a full-fledged grin. "You are such a gentleman. What if I want it to be right here, right now? What if I'm ready to see what you look like naked?"

He shook his head even as his eyes darkened with desire. "You say the most romantic things." When she didn't laugh, he said, "Not here, because..."

"Yes?"

"When I have you stretched out under me, I'm gonna take my time."

A shiver wracked through her. She had to admit that

Dante was right about their bad timing. However, she couldn't stop her mind from thinking of the possibilities when they did find someplace private. She swiped her thumb across his sexy lower lip. "I can't wait," she murmured. She withdrew her hand from his and opened her door.

"Why don't you come over Monday night after you check on Barry? Lily's going out with friends. I'll fix dinner and you can bring the, uh, thing."

Her mind went blank for a moment, then she started sorting through all kinds of items he might be meaning by "the thing" before she finally landed on the rift device. "Oh. Right. The thing." She smiled again. "I actually have a council meeting, a sort of meet and greet for new prets in town, at seven. Is five o'clock too early to come over?"

He shook his head.

In a throaty voice she murmured, "I'll see you then." She climbed down from the cab of his truck, grinning at his mingled look of desire and dismay. It wasn't often Dante MacMillan could be knocked off his stride. She couldn't wait to do it again.

Finn leaned against the corner of the building and watched Tori get out of the human cop's truck. Things had been getting interesting, and for a minute he'd thought they were going to make out right there in the parking lot. Not only would it have been entertaining, it would have given him something to throw into Tori's face whenever she got too big for her britches. But to his disappointment they hadn't.

"So you're also a voyeur," a lilting voice said from behind him. "Good to know."

He turned his head and looked at Keira as she walked up to stand beside him. "I spy on people only when it might lead to something useful."

She cast him a sidelong glance. "Do you play Peepin' Tom much, then?"

Finn shrugged. "I lurk. That's what I do." He shifted his position, leaning his back against the wall. "And just what do you mean by 'also a voyeur'?"

Her smile was a slow dance of pure wickedness. "Oh, you've quite the reputation." She drew one finger down his shoulder, leaving a trail of sparks he could feel even through his clothing. "Playboy. Ladykiller." Her expression sobered. "Ne'er-do-well."

"Oh, a ne'er-do-well, really?" He crossed his ankles, bearing his weight on his heels. Shoving his hands into the front pockets of his jeans, he said, "Now you're just flattering me."

"Do you think so?" Keira reached into her purse and pulled out some sort of plastic hair clip. Holding it between her lips, she lifted her arms and gathered her long hair up off her neck, then fastened it. Stray strands fell around her face, curling in the humidity of the approaching dusk. Without thinking he reached out and scooped several strands behind her ear.

She drew in a startled breath but her expression didn't change. "You have an odd opinion of yourself then."

He made note of her reaction and determined some day, and someday soon, he was going to get that reaction from her again. "I'm a demon," he said, figuring that was explanation enough. He glanced around the nearly empty lot. "What're you doing here?"

"Oh, meeting new people." She gave a dainty shrug.

"Gettin' the lay of the land. You know." She moved a little closer, tilting back her head to look up into his face. "I'm findin' that Scottsdale's an interesting place."

She didn't know the half of it. He heard a car start up and peered around the edge of the building to see Tori's tiny piece of tin she called a car pulling out of the parking lot. For God's sake, who ever heard of a werewolf driving a Mini Cooper?

Not him. As much as he hated to leave Keira's side, he had to keep an eye on Tori and her family. He'd been hearing things, things that surprised him and piqued his interest. He turned back to Keira. He hated to bail on this gorgeous woman, but he needed to see what Tori was up to. He had reports to file, and the lord of demons didn't like to be kept waiting. "I've gotta go, sweetheart. Catch up with you later?"

"Sure." She adjusted her purse strap on her shoulder. "You know she has her eyes on that detective, don't you?"

"Who?" He frowned. "What're you talking about?"

"Tori."

"I'm not…" He stopped. "It's complicated. And not what you think."

The lifting of her eyebrows was both regal and skeptical.

"Seriously." Finn pulled his keys out of his pocket. "I'll see you."

"Sure."

He felt her gaze on him as he walked around the back of the club to his motorcycle. As he pulled on his gloves, he watched her walk toward a neon-green Beetle. He scowled. What was it with the women around here? His frown lightened when she went past the Volkswagen and unlocked a black BMW M3. He admired her choice of vehicle—it was small enough for good maneuverability yet had a big enough engine for excellent acceleration.

He made sure she got under way before he left the parking lot and headed after Tori. Something was going on in this town, something not good, and he had a feeling she knew what it was.

Chapter Eleven

Things were quiet for the next couple of days. Dante and Tori handled a few minor skirmishes here and there, both of them glad that things seemed to be calming down. Even the attacks in quadrant four had stopped. Tori hoped the rogue was finished but her instincts said otherwise.

Rand seemed unusually quiet. He hadn't asked about the rift device since that day in her bedroom. She didn't know for certain if he'd looked for it again, though she thought he might have searched her closet. A couple of her shoes were askew on the shoe rack, shoes she hadn't worn in several weeks and didn't remember touching. She kept the incident to herself because she didn't want to draw attention to the device at all. She started thinking again that maybe Dante was right—she needed to get it out of the house. She just wasn't sure where to put it, and she hated to admit she couldn't keep it out of Rand's grasp. It hurt her to think that she was unable to trust her own brother. As soon as she got the chance, she'd talk to Dante about it. It seemed like his gun safe might be the best place for it after all, but she couldn't help but think about Lily. She would be in danger just by virtue of the fact that the device was in Dante's home.

At least as werewolves, Tori and Rand had a fighting chance against anyone who might come for the device. Lily would be helpless.

Unsure of a good hiding place, she took it out of the flour canister and put it in her fanny pack. She always wore it to work, anyway, so no one would think anything of it. Despite the new location, she still carried the damn thing everywhere she went, even into the bathroom, where she stashed it in her box of tampons while she showered.

As she took off her clothes, she thought about the meeting at headquarters, which she really wasn't looking forward to. The new prets didn't like being put on display under the auspices of introductions to the council and its liaisons. Tori supposed it was a necessary evil. This way, when the newcomers got themselves into trouble—which most of them invariably did to one degree or another—Tori and her colleagues knew with whom they were dealing.

After her shower, she dressed in a flowing sky-blue skirt, a two-toned silk tank top, and a bright pink short-sleeved jacket with high-heeled sandals to match. She fitted the fanny pack in place, grimacing at how it ruined the look of her outfit, and made sure the jacket wasn't caught under the straps. She left a note for Rand, letting him know she'd see him at the meeting, and drove to Dante's.

As she drove up the winding driveway, she admired the natural landscaping of prickly pear and saguaro cacti, mesquite, and palo verde trees. When she pulled up in front of the house, she put the car in park and turned off the ignition, sitting for a few minutes to look the place over. It was a one-story adobe ranch house with a long front porch and roofed with Spanish tiles. Potted flowering plants lined the walkway leading to the front door. She couldn't see Dante taking the time to plant flowers, so no doubt they were Lily's handiwork.

A separate barn sat about twenty-five yards away from the house on the south side, complete with a corral that, at the moment, was empty. His horses must be in the barn.

She got out of her car and slammed the door, hitting the button on the remote to lock it. She drew in a breath and smelled various scents—the flowering bougainvillea and oleanders, horses, hay, and the pungent odor of manure. The sound of hooves stomping, low nickers, and the aroma of fear wafted to her from the horses. They smelled her, and they were afraid. She pressed her lips together. Sometimes she regretted what she was, and this was one of those times. She'd love to be able to get close enough to the horses to really appreciate their beauty, but she'd probably never be able to.

She headed toward the house. As she reached the front door it swung open and Dante stood there, a wide smile on his face. "You made it. Any trouble finding the place?"

"Nope, none." She entered the house. "Nice," she commented, seeing how it reflected his masculinity from the oversized leather recliner and matching sofa in the living room to the décor in various shades of browns and greens. There were a couple of pillows on the sofa that had splashes of red in them and a few decorative pots on the hearth of the beehive fireplace in the corner that suggested a woman's touch. Again probably due to Lily.

"Thanks," he said. "I can give you the tour a little later, if you'd like."

She followed him through to a large country-style eat-in kitchen, complete with a distressed pine table that seated six. There was also a formal dining room off to the left of the kitchen with another large table, this one a darker wood.

"I know I said I'd fix dinner," Dante said. "But since you can't stay long, I figured we should spend most of the time working on the device instead of eating. So..." The doorbell rang and he held up one finger. "I ordered pizza. Have a seat," he said, motioning toward the kitchen table. "I'll be right back."

Tori went over to it and pulled out a chair, admiring the Southwest pattern on the padded seat. Dante came back in with a couple of boxes in his hands. The smell of pepperoni and pizza sauce wafted her way, as well as the spicy aroma of barbecue.

"Got some wings, too." Dante flipped open the boxes and grabbed a couple of plates from a cabinet. He placed one in front of her and handed her a paper towel. "You want beer? Soda?"

"Soda's fine," she said. "Since I have to drive."

"Okay. Soda it is." He grabbed two cans from the fridge and handed one to her. Taking his place in the chair across from her, he said, "Dig in."

She took two slices and put them on her plate.

"Get some wings, too," he urged.

"In a minute," she said around a mouthful of food.

Once she'd scarfed down her pizza, she started on some wings. After a few minutes, Dante reached over and swiped his thumb across the corner of her mouth, letting it linger on her lip. "You had some barbecue sauce there," he said, his voice husky.

In reflex, she swept out her tongue, the tip sliding over the pad of his thumb. His indrawn breath flared his nostrils. He rubbed across her bottom lip and leaned closer. "God, you've got the most beautiful mouth." He bent his head, his lips closing over hers.

He tasted like pizza sauce and pepperoni with an underlying tang of heated desire. He ate at her mouth like a starving man and she was just as voracious. When they pulled away for air, they both breathed heavily. Dante's eyes were heavy-lidded, the brown of his irises almost black with passion.

As much as she wanted to say to hell with the rift device, she had limited time to work on the thing, and they needed to get results. She stroked her fingers down his cheek, thrilling to the catch of his breath, the flare of his eyes. He must have read the intent on her face, because he husked, "Why don't I clear the table and we can take a look at that device?"

She cleared her throat. "All right." As he put the leftover pizza and wings in the fridge, she gathered up the plates and used napkins and set them on the counter. Then she unsnapped her fanny pack and took it off, pulling out the rift device and placing it on the table.

"We have to figure out how to check this thing out without alerting that guy who keeps asking for a password." Tori blew out a sigh.

"Did you bring the schematics with you?" Dante asked, standing next to her to look down at the small device.

"Yeah." She pulled the paper out of her fanny pack and handed it to him.

"Ah, excellent." Dante unfolded the document and

spread it out on the desk. He bent over it, studying it in silence.

Tori got closer to him to look it over as well. She was able to pick out the various parts that made up the radio component, but anything more than that left her confused. She drew in a breath, struck by how good he smelled— like soap and hot, virile male. Holding it in a moment, she trapped his scent in her lungs. After a few seconds she exhaled. If only they had more time...for now she'd keep things directed toward the job at hand. "We make a good team," she murmured. "You know computers and I know radio communications."

"Mmm."

His focus was so intent on the schematics she doubted he'd really heard what she'd said. Pursing her lips, she decided to put it to the test. "My brains to your brawn. Your ability to bullshit with my unwavering search for the truth." Only it wasn't so unwavering these days, was it? There was still that small matter of finding out if her brother was involved with the werewolf attacks. She pushed that aside for the moment. "You look good in pink while I tend to stick to more muted colors."

"Right."

A slight smile curved her lips and she shook her head. Typical male. Able to focus on only one thing at a time. While in bed, that wasn't necessarily a bad thing; outside of it could be damned frustrating. For now, though, she was having too good a time to be irritated with his one-track mind.

"All right, so we determined last time that this doohickey is the processor running the works. And if I'm reading these schematics right..." He picked up the device and turned one of the small dials on the top. Another dial, the one that Tori had been using to turn the device on, he twisted to the right.

Slight static came across the speaker. Dante fiddled with one of the antennae and the static faded.

Tori carefully sat down, trying not to make any noise, and waited for the guy on the other side to ask for a password. After a minute or so of silence, she glanced up at Dante. "Well, this is new," she whispered.

The speaker crackled. She tensed and bit her lip, shooting a chagrined look at him. He shook his head, finger to lips, but humor danced at the corners of his eyes.

A man's voice came from the device, speaking in the standard language of the other dimension. He seemed to be filing a report of some kind. Tori motioned for Dante to get her something to write with, and as soon as he fetched a long, thin pad and pen from next to the phone in the kitchen, she began transcribing the message. The man spoke for a few moments, and then the speaker went silent again.

Dante twisted the dials and turned off the device. "Okay, what'd he say?" He pulled out his chair and sat down.

"He's reporting that they're at twenty-four percent of goal and hope to be at or above fifty percent within the next two months. They should achieve maximum capacity by the target date." She turned to look at him. "He suggests that we keep turning people into werewolves in order to further supplement our numbers."

"Further supplement your numbers?" His face grim, he stared at her. "So now we know it's not really a rogue, right? Whoever's behind these attacks is following orders."

"Looks like it." Tori glanced into the kitchen and caught sight of the clock on the stove. "Oh, crap!" She stood. Grabbing the schematics, she started folding them up. If she didn't leave now, she was going to be late for her council meet and greet.

"What?" Dante stood, too, alarm on his face. "What is it?"

"I've gotta go. I'm gonna be late."

"Oh. Right." He picked up the device. "Can I hold onto this? I can keep fiddling with it while you're at your meeting."

She hesitated. It wasn't that she didn't trust Dante—she did. She'd trust him with her life. But Tobias had entrusted the device to her, and she was loath to let it out of her sight. She stared at the schematics in her hand and then looked into Dante's face. "Here," she said, and handed him the paper. "Hang onto them. We still need to know exactly what that thing is capable of," she said, nodding toward the device he still held. She zipped her pack closed. "Thanks for dinner."

He grinned. "Such as it was. Listen, why don't you come over tomorrow night, and we'll do a real dinner. Lily will be here," he said almost apologetically.

"Sure. I'd love to meet her." Tori walked through the kitchen toward the front door. She stopped in the living room and asked, "Can I bring anything?"

"Just your gorgeous self." He opened the front door and followed her to her car. After she got in, he stood there, his arm along the top of her door. "Do me a favor, will you?"

"If I can."

"I got a call earlier from a buddy of mine in Vegas

He said the number of prets moving into the city has more than doubled from last year. And he said a couple of his friends pretty much told him that the same thing is happening in Denver and Albuquerque." His serious gaze held hers. "And that's just the number of prets who register with the regional council. You know as well as I do that the real number could be a hell of a lot higher."

"Yeah?" She wasn't sure where he was going with this.

"Have you heard any numbers for the greater Phoenix area?" At her nod, he gave a sigh. "It might not mean anything, but I think an increase like this in our region needs to be looked into. Can you ask around, find out at the council meeting tonight?"

"I'll see what I can turn up, but the councilors tend to keep things very close to the vest."

"Just see if they'll tell you anything."

"I will."

Dante bent down and gave her a kiss, his mouth lingering, promising at things to come. Then he straightened. "See you tomorrow," he husked.

"Bye," she said, her pulse fluttering in her throat. It took just one touch of his mouth on hers and she was rendered speechless. She kinda liked it.

As she drove away from him, her mind went back to what he'd said about the increase in pret numbers. She couldn't help but wonder if that growth had something to do with the rift device. What if someone was positioning preternaturals in key areas in order to . . . what? Take over the world?

She dismissed that idea as soon as she thought it. That couldn't happen. Prets were only ten percent of the overall population on the planet. Even if the number was double what was reported, humans still outnumbered preternaturals seven to one.

Of course, that would change with the next rift due to happen in just a few months. And in the meantime, there was a pret running around turning people into werewolves, adding to the fold.

Within twenty minutes, she pulled into the parking lot behind the council building. As she went through the back door and walked down the hallway she saw that one of the guards, dressed in his red-on-black security uniform, was posted in front of the main chamber and another was at the security desk near the front door. She knew at any given time there were at least two other guards patrolling the building or running errands for council members. Others were down in the basement, either protecting prisoners or taking it easy until they were called.

Wall sconces placed roughly four feet apart provided ample lighting, and a polished concrete floor that almost looked like wood inlay lent an aristocratic ambiance to the entry.

Most of the city's liaisons were already there, gathered in small groups throughout the hallway. The various scents of each pret assailed her. It was like a meeting of the United Nations, only this time instead of a gathering of representatives from various countries it was a gathering of a variety of species, werewolves and other shapeshifters, vampires, numerous types of fey, and humans.

The low murmur of voices made conversations difficult, but not impossible, to listen in on. The human liaisons in their midst wouldn't have been able to distin guish separate voices, but her werewolf hearing allowed her to do just that. After a few seconds, she decided no one was talking about anything interesting enough for her to intrude on the conversation. The vamps spoke of some new blood bar that their leader, Byron Maldonado, had just opened. A couple of the fey liaisons argued over who was funnier, the Three Stooges or Abbott and Costello. The group of werecat liaisons complained about the price of milk, which struck Tori as hilarious. She snickered as she walked by, earning her a glare from one of the cats.

She stopped at the group of werewolf liaisons and said her hellos. She glanced at Ash, standing slightly to the side of the group, his back to the wall. He lifted his chin in greeting. *Talk to you later*, he mouthed.

Tori nodded. She saw Piper standing at the window at the end of the hallway. Excusing herself, she walked toward her and bumped shoulders with the other woman. "Hey," she said.

Piper smiled. "Hey yourself." She stared out the window again. "I really hate these meetings. Everyone's on display like they're a bunch of meat."

"That's not the way I see it at all." Tori crossed her arms and leaned against the wall, looking at Piper's profile. "This is our chance to get an early introduction to the newbies, and they get a chance to see who's going to come down on them if they screw up." She glanced back at the liaisons. "We all had to go through this when we first hit town."

"All of you except the human liaisons."

"Right. That's what I meant," she said dryly.

That drew a laugh from Piper, but then she sighed and shook her head. "I don't know. It just seems like they could send us a file with their pictures and particulars. What good does it do for us to come here in person? It's a gigantic waste of time."

Tori rolled her eyes. "That's the point I've been trying to make for years. So far I've only got Tobias on my side and maybe Caladh. I don't know about the rest of the council."

She understood the need to uphold traditions, but when tradition stood in the way of progress, when it impeded her ability to efficiently do her job, then something needed to give. However, until the council as a whole decided it wanted quicker results more than it wanted to lord its authority over its employees, nothing would change. And if the current council president had any say in the matter—and in reality, what he had to say carried a lot of weight—things would stay the same until the end of time.

Tori gestured toward all of the liaisons. "Doing it this way, I have to say, allows us to attach scents to the names and faces."

"Well, that only helps those of you who have an enhanced sense of smell. It doesn't matter though. You know Deoul will fight to keep things the way they are. Traditions and all," Piper said as if she'd read Tori's mind. "God forbid that his liaisons wouldn't have to kowtow to him in person." She paused, lips pursed, and sent Tori a sidelong glance. "Any idea how to kowtow through e-mail?" Piper's brows rose in hope.

"I haven't figured that out yet. When I do, you'll be the first to know," Tori said and grinned.

At that moment the doors to the main chamber opened and a guard stepped out. "The council is ready," he announced. "Please come in."

"Here we go," Piper said on a sigh as she turned around.

They joined the others and filed into the room. Tori stood next to Piper at the front of the room, about five feet or so from the mahogany table behind which all thirteen councilors sat. About a dozen preternaturals were lined up on one side of the cavernous room that was brightly lit with overhead lights and wall sconces.

Tori gazed at the group of newbies, searching for both her brother and her cousin. They were new enough to town that they should be here, but they weren't. Her heart skipped a beat. *Oh, God. Please don't let Rand and Stefan be behind these attacks.* She loved them both, but she couldn't turn a blind eye to the signs pointing toward their guilt. But what was she supposed to do? She couldn't betray the only family she had.

Looking back at the council, she lifted a hand in greeting to Tobias, who smiled in return. "I'd like to talk to you later," he said. "Can you stay after the meeting?"

Remembering that Ash wanted to talk to her, she glanced at him and he nodded a couple of times. She looked back at Tobias. "Sure, I can stay."

"Good."

As the guard closed the doors behind the last person to enter the room, the council president stood. "We'll begin the proceeding by introducing the council members, then the liaisons." Deoul looked at the sideliners, who all seemed as enthusiastic at being there as they would if they were facing a firing squad. "Finally, each of you will tell us your name, where you lived prior to coming to Scottsdale, why you came to our city, and what you plan on doing to become a contributing member of society. Hopefully, none of you will ever have to deal with the liaisons in anything other than a social situation." He gave a smile, apparently trying to be humorous.

Tori didn't think it was funny, and it looked like none of the newbies did, either, because no one's mouth so much as twitched as far as she could tell. Some of the liaisons put on their game faces and gave a few forced chortles. She caught Tobias's eye and had to press her lips together against a grin. He was doing his best to look non-committal, but she knew him well enough to know that at least in his head he was rolling his eyes in disbelief at Deoul's attempt at humor.

The council president cleared his throat and sat down as they began their introductions, starting with Deoul, of course. With his chest out and his voice booming like that of a radio announcer, he told the gathered throng that he was a high elf who came through the rift in 3463 BC, blah blah blah. The three vampire councilors introduced themselves next, then the witches and the lone specter member of the council. Next came the shapeshifters—a wereleopard, a werewolf, and the selkie member of the council, Caladh.

Tori kept her eye on the last three to introduce themselves, wondering the entire time which of the thirteen councilors besides Tobias were aware of the rift device. And of those who did know, just how involved were they? Did the members support the activity or were they trying to stop it?

The other fey shapeshifter on the council, Lorcan O'Shea, stood up. With his fingertips on the table, he stated his name and then added, "I'm of the pooka clan of feys and came through the rift in 251 BC." He started to sit but paused and said, "If anyone wants to go for a ride, let me know." Mischief sparkled in his hazel eyes.

Tori grinned. Lorcan was always willing to shift into his horse form and take on riders, the prettier the better.

The only djinn on the council rose from his chair. "I am Kaleb ibn Kalil. I entered this dimension in the year 908 BC." He glanced around the group. "I do not reside in a bottle nor do I grant wishes, so do not ask." He gave a slight bow and retook his seat.

Tori bit the inside of her cheek to hold back a smile. Kaleb was sensitive about the legends surrounding his people, and dismissive of magic carpets and jeweled bottles.

The final council member, Galen Kholkikos, got to his feet. "Welcome to Scottsdale. I'm a dragon and, yes, I can breathe fire. You may or may not be familiar with a little incident that occurred in the skies above Phoenix about fifteen years ago. Some of my friends and I were flying around and were mistaken for a UFO." He ran a hand over his dark hair. "We didn't do it on purpose. Honest." He sat back down amid light laughter.

The liaison introductions began. Tori was first since she was at the front of the room. She was happy to get hers over with, though there were still about twenty people who had to give their names, group affiliation, and quadrant. Thankfully, only half of the liaisons were in attendance that night.

Finally, they got to move on to the newcomers to the city. A troll named Trudie from Tazewell, Tennessee, stuttered through her intro, and a werewolf named Wanda from Walla Walla, Washington, was next. They both claimed to have moved to the area because of the drier climate.

Piper leaned over and whispered, "Seriously? Did they stand next to each other on purpose? You can't make this stuff up."

Tori grinned. "Like you have a lot of room to talk, Ms. Piper Peterson from Peoria." She snorted back a laugh at Piper's low growl. Coming from a human, it didn't carry much of a threat, but Tori got the point. "Sorry," she whispered.

"No, you're not," Piper muttered. A small smile tilted her mouth. "But that's okay."

Tori couldn't help but think that Dante would be fascinated by all this. He was like a kid when it came to prets—he was so curious. It really was too bad that the council kept these meetings closed to humans, except for their own human liaisons, of course. Tori held the opinion that the human cops assigned to the various Special Case squads would benefit from this just as much, if not more than, the liaisons did.

Several more introductions were made, with council members asking questions as they went along, sometimes delving deep into the newcomer's past.

Finally, they'd reached the auburn-haired elf whom Tori had met at the club. The slender woman took a step forward. "My name is Keira O'Brien. I'm originally from County Donegal, Ireland, and came through the rift in the Influx of 1419 BC."

Murmurs of disbelief went through the room. Tori was just as surprised. Coming through the rift when she did made Keira over thirty-four hundred years old. Except for Deoul and one of the vampire councilors, Keira was the oldest preternatural in the room. And that was saying something.

"What brings you to Scottsdale?" Deoul leaned forward and formed a steeple with his fingers. Tori couldn't determine if the note in his voice was his attempt at flirting or if he was just plain irritated. It was hard to tell with him most of the time, he was so bad at showing emotion other than anger or aggravation.

"I've wanted to visit the desert southwest for many years now," Keira replied, seemingly unfazed by his attitude, whatever it was. "There are many natural wonders that make your city beautiful."

"But it's very different from Ireland," he said. He leaned back in his chair and crossed one leg over the other.

"Yes." Her green eyes remained steady on him.

When she didn't continue, he frowned. "How long have you been in the States?" he finally asked.

Tori felt like she was at a tennis match, her gaze going back and forth between the two players.

"Since 1850," Keira answered. "From New York I went to Virginia, and in the early 1900s I made my way to Ohio." She gave a dainty shrug. "After living for such a long time through cold and snowy winters, I decided to follow through on my desire to live in a warmer climate." Her lilting tones were oddly soothing, almost mesmerizing. Tori could understand how the fey folk had gotten a reputation for enticement.

"Do you have family here?" Deoul asked.

Keira shook her head. "I have no family anywhere." Her voice was matter-of-fact.

Tori wasn't sure which was sadder, not having family or having family who wanted nothing to do with you. Actually, she knew quite well who was worse off. Her heart sank at the thought. Keira was the lucky one.

"What exactly did you do to get sent through the rift?" This came from Lorcan, the pooka.

Keira's slender throat moved with her swallow. For the first time, Tori saw the other woman's composure falter. Others had been asked this question and had also been reluctant to speak their misdeeds aloud in public, but when the council asked, they expected an answer. For a brief moment, Keira met Tori's gaze, and then she looked back to the front of the room and said, "My husband and I were grifters. We conned several prominent people out of a lot of money."

"And where is your husband?" Lorcan asked.

Keira's lips pressed together a moment before she responded. "He was murdered before..." She paused and cleared her throat. "We were released, under strict monitoring, to say our good-byes and get rid of any material items we had. He was killed before sentencing could be carried out."

"And now?" Caladh's voice was low and steely. "Have you come to us to defraud the citizens of Scottsdale?"

"No." She shook her head. "I have lived an honest and quiet life for many years now. I plan to continue doing so."

"For many years, eh?" The selkie councilor stared at her. "Upon your arrival to this dimension, you kept up your con-artist ways, did you not?"

Her generous mouth tightened. Her irritation wafted Tori's way on a wave of burnt cinnamon. When she spoke again, though, her voice was as serene as ever. "When I first came through the rift I was able to be an innocent. My human host was a wife. A mother. But when I outlived my family, when I was forced out on my own..." She drew in a slow breath. "There are things one must do to survive. I could grift or I could whore. I chose the former."

Tori wasn't sure, but she figured it would have been a very difficult thing to be a con artist back in Ireland before the Industrial Revolution. She gave Keira kudos for that.

"I see. I for one do not fault you for that decision." Caladh leaned forward and looked down the table at the other council members. "Does anyone else have any questions?"

No one did, and so the rest of the introductions were completed. Once the meeting was dismissed, Tori walked over to Keira and said, "You know, if you plan on living a quiet life here, hooking up with Evnissyen isn't likely to help."

The elf's smile was serene. "I can handle a demon. He won't throw anything my way that I haven't seen before." A crafty look flickered in her eyes. "He may prove useful. In my effort to assimilate, I mean." Her smile widened, and Tori was sure it was an effort to keep her from probing too closely. "Anyway," Keira went on, "I'm old and rich enough that no one will make me do anything I don't want to, believe me."

Of that, Tori had no doubt. There was something about Keira in this moment, with her hair pulled back in a long braid, wispy tendrils falling around her face, that put Tori in mind of the fierce Briton warrior queen Boadicea. She had no trouble imagining Keira as a similar warlike leader in Ireland back in the day. At any rate, Tori had a feeling she'd be seeing more of Keira. She only hoped it wasn't because the elf wasn't living honestly.

Keira murmured a good-bye and walked away.

Tori went over to Tobias. "How's Nix?" she asked upon reaching him.

His gray eyes lightened. "She's doing well, thanks. I'll let her know you asked about her." He folded his arms over his chest. "How are things going with you?"

"Good." She made sure to keep her voice low. Preternaturals had incredible senses and could hear the smallest of sounds. "Dante and I are working on a little project," she said as if Tobias didn't already know. "There's some interesting stuff going on. We're getting together again tomorrow night." That was as much of an update as she could give him at the moment.

He lifted his chin in acknowledgment. "You've been working closely with him on the past few cases, haven't you?" When she nodded, he asked, "What do you think of the detective?"

How was she supposed to say that she thought Dante was handsome, witty, and charming? That she lusted after him? That the more she learned about him, the more she liked him?

That she was afraid she was falling in love with a man who didn't want to love her?

In the end, all she said was, "I like him."

Tobias gave a quirky grin. "What's not to like, right? He's a good man." He put one hand on her shoulder. "I hear you offered to stay with Barry tonight."

She nodded.

"You've got grit. I'll give you that."

"That's what people keep telling me." She shrugged. "I thought it was the right thing to do."

"That's what I mean. The right thing to do is sometimes the hardest thing to do. That you were willing to go through that says a lot about your character." He gave her shoulder a squeeze and then dropped his hand to his side. "Keep me posted."

"Will do." When he started to turn away she called his name. "Have you heard anything about the stats for our area? I mean, do we know how many prets have moved into the greater Phoenix area in the last twelve months?"

He frowned. "We should be getting those figures together within the next week. We wanted to have this meet and greet first. Why?"

She moved closer to him. "According to Dante, three big cities in our region have had double the normal amount of prets moving into the area. I'm just wondering if Phoenix is the same."

"If it is," he said, his voice low, "the...situation we've been concerned about just got worse."

"My thoughts exactly."

"And with these rogue attacks happening..." Tobias leaned in. "They might not be as random as we'd believed. You keep your nose to the ground on this one, Tori."

"I will."

He gave a nod and left the room.

She watched him walk away, his formal robes swirling. He should have looked silly, but instead there was something regal about him. Being a council member suited Tobias well.

When she turned around she saw Ash waiting for her in the lobby. She walked out of the chamber and went with him to the employee break room. They sat down on the sofa, slightly facing each other. "So," she said. "What's up?"

"You know we've had a lull in the attacks." Ash frowned. "I should be grateful, but my gut tells me this is the calm eye of an ugly storm." His blue eyes took on a hint of amber as his disquiet grew. "There's something that's been bugging me."

"What?" Tori stretched her arm along the back of the sofa.

"Each crime scene has an area of pebbles or debris set up in some sort of pattern. Whoever it is has lined everything up in a neat, tidy row of six." He shook his head. "I think it's the rogue's signature, something he's compelled to do. I don't know." He huffed a frustrated sigh. "I'm going to talk to the department shrink about it. I think maybe the suspect's OCD or something."

Tori's heart stopped. OCD. Series of six, just like Rand's green peas. Oh God, this couldn't be happening.

Chapter Twelve

While Tori sat in shock, Ash went on. "It could be some sort of message, I guess. Maybe that he plans on a total of six turnings?"

She swallowed, hard, and tried to mask her emotions. It wouldn't help if Ash sensed her rising panic. "It could be a woman, you know." She wasn't trying to derail his investigation, not really. She just needed to buy some time to figure out what was going on.

Oh, hell. Who was she trying to kid? She *was* trying to point him in another direction, *any* direction that didn't lead back to her brother. She didn't believe, couldn't believe, that Rand was involved. It was a huge leap to go from having OCD to being a rogue killer, but she had to be sure.

Until she knew for certain, she wasn't going to say anything to anyone. If she could prove he was involved, in whatever way, then she'd know what she had to do. She only hoped that no other innocent people were turned or, worse, killed while she protected her brother.

If this went wrong, at the very least she could lose her job. At the worst, she could lose her job *and* be the one sitting in a cell in the basement waiting to suffer through thirty days of torment.

She wondered if anyone would volunteer to go through the torture with her.

Ash's brows dipped slightly. "I'm using 'he' in the generic sense." He scrubbed the back of his neck with one hand. "My gut is talking up a storm on this one, and it coincides with the statistics I researched. Most prets who go rogue are male. Something like ninety-two percent." He blew out a breath. "Ah, hell. I don't know. What do *you* think?"

Tori's heart had started beating again and now drummed in stunned, dull thuds against her ribs. *I think maybe it's my brother.* But she couldn't say that. Not without proof. "It might just be coincidence."

"At all three scenes?" His voice was tinted with light tones of disbelief. He shook his head. "I could buy it if it was one scene. It could be possible that maybe someone else had been there and did the thing with the rocks, but not at all three scenes."

She had to concede. "You're right." God. What should she do? If she did her job, she'd tell Ash that she knew someone who might fit the bill, except she was talking about her *brother*. Tori couldn't turn him in. Not yet. All werewolves could be killers. She knew Rand was capable of this. What she didn't know was why. Until she knew for sure, she had to keep this secret. She stood to lose so much, including the man she was falling in love with. Dante had definite ideas of right and wrong, and she didn't know if he'd understand why she'd kept this from him. What she did know was that when family was involved, there was no black or white. There were just endless shades of gray.

All she could manage to say now to Ash was, "I'll let you know if I hear anything."

"Thanks." Ash stood and looked down at her. "Where you headed to?"

Tori got to her feet. "I thought I'd check on Barry before heading out."

"I'll go with you," he said.

As they walked down the stairs and approached the holding area, Barry stood and walked to the front of his cell. He was dressed in denim shorts and a loud Hawaiian-style shirt. His feet were bare, though Tori saw a pair of sandals beneath the lone bunk that was bolted to the back wall. The smell of sweat and fear was heavy in the air.

A silver manacle was clamped around one of his ankles, and another one around his right wrist. With his fingers wrapped around the bars, he looked at her. "Hey," he said, his voice subdued. "I didn't expect to see you."

"I just wanted to see how you're doing." She covered one of his hands with hers. "You don't have to go through this alone," she said. "My offer still stands."

Barry drew in a deep breath and, for a moment, she thought maybe he'd change his mind. Finally he shook his head. "No. It was my mistake and I have to pay for it." He glanced over her shoulder at Ash. His expression hardened a little. "Did you want something?"

"Just making sure Tori doesn't give in to her soft heart, that's all." He lifted his chin. Icy blue eyes stayed fixed on Barry. "You better appreciate what she offered to do for you. Not many people would have done so." He gave the other werewolf a once-over and scowled. "I sure as hell wouldn't have."

"I know. And I do appreciate it, believe me." Barry began to pace. "I'm so sorry, Tori. I never meant to hurt anyone." He paused with a grimace. "Well, anyone other than the vampire."

"Whom you managed *not* to hurt," Ash muttered, his scowl deepening. "Good going there."

"Yeah, I screwed up, thanks for not rubbing it in." Barry looked at Tori. "I'm glad you're my liaison and not this jerk."

"You wanna see a jerk? I'll show you a jerk, you little pissant." Ash took a step forward, the dark amber of disgust darkening his eyes.

"Ash," Tori warned.

He paused, fists clenched.

Barry sighed and plopped onto the lone metal bunk bolted to the wall. His glower was directed solely at Ash. "It's not like I woke up one morning in 1939 and said, 'Hey! I think I'll turn into a werewolf today.'"

None of them had asked for this life. All of them did the best they could, some better than others. Barry wasn't one of them.

"Just what did you do to get sent through the rift?" Ash rested his hands on his hips and stared at Barry, curiosity shining through the lingering distaste in his eyes.

"You remember how the government passed what amounted to a three-strikes-and-you're-out law?"

Tori vaguely remembered that law being enacted a few years before her own trip through the rift. "They still had that one on the books?"

"Yeah." Barry shrugged. "I was in the wrong place with the wrong people at the wrong time. And now I'm here." He gestured to the cell.

"And still making bad choices," Ash said.

Barry popped off the bunk and headed toward the bars.

Testosterone-laden anger filled Tori's nostrils with a heavy odor of cloves. She threw out an arm and shoved him back. "Stop it, both of you." She frowned at Ash. "We've all done things we're not proud of, things we'd take back if we could. But there is no easy button in life, and pointing out Barry's shortcomings isn't helping at all." She sighed. "Just...keep me posted on your current case, okay?"

"Sure." Ash sent a lingering stare Barry's way, then looked at Tori again. "You coming?"

Dante leaned over the schematics and fought the urge to open up the device. That was something that should be done with Tori around. But these schematics were fascinating. Just as he started to trace a couple of lines with his finger to see where they ended, his cell phone rang. Manny Ramirez was on the line.

"Manny," Dante said in greeting. "You still at the conference in Vegas?"

"Yeah." Manny's heavy sigh came across the speaker. "I was going to stay another day, get a break from the job and the family...You know, have a 'me' day. Then my wife called. Her mother's health is failing and Rosa needs to go take care of her. I need to get home to be with the kids. Don't get me wrong, I love my kids, but with five of them, there's never any time to be alone."

"Then why'd you have five kids?"

" 'Cause we didn't want more than that," Manny said completely deadpan.

Dante chuckled at his friend's droll humor. "I'm sorry

to hear about your mother-in-law. Where does she live?"

"El Paso." He paused for a second and then muttered, "God, I hate to fly."

"The conference was worth it though, right?" Slouching down, Dante stretched his legs out under the table.

"Yeah." The other man cleared his throat. "Listen, I wanna run something by you, get your opinion."

Dante straightened. "Shoot."

"Ash and I think that the suspect is leaving either a clue or a signature." He lowered his voice. "Six stones, pieces of trash, or other debris are left at the scene in a perfect line."

"At each scene?"

"Yep. I didn't notice it at the first one, but after I saw it at the second and again at the third, I went over the crime scene photos and, sure enough, there it was. Always in a grouping of six."

"And you think the suspect has done this?" Dante figured it was a logical conclusion and one he would come to if it were his case.

"Sure. I mean, having it at all three scenes can't be a coincidence, right?" Manny heaved a sigh. "Ash called to tell me there haven't been any attacks since I've been out of town."

Dante raised his brows. "Is there something you wanna tell me, buddy?"

"What?" Manny muttered something in Spanish under his breath. "I am not a werewolf."

Dante's Spanish wasn't the best, but it sounded like Manny had questioned his parentage. He grinned, then sobered as he thought about the case. "Even if the suspect is lining all these things up in a row, he's not leaving any usable evidence, so it's really not going to help us much."

"Other than establishing a profile."

Dante thought about what Manny had said. He cast his mind back to a profiling class he'd gone through a few years back. "A signature would be something he's compelled to do, something that may or may not have anything to do with the actual crime. Maybe he's OCD." He sat up and leaned his elbows on the table. "What does Ash think?"

"He pretty much came up with the same thing. Said he talked to the werewolf liaison in your quadrant and she agrees. So does my captain." Manny cleared his throat again. "I just wanted your opinion."

Dante gave a little shrug. "It works for me." He heaved a sigh. "Guess that means you just need to be on the lookout for a rogue werewolf with OCD. Shouldn't be too hard," he said with a bit of sarcasm.

"Yeah, right. At least it's something."

Something was better than nothing, though not by much.

Chapter Thirteen

Around ten o'clock that night, Dante couldn't get Tori on the phone, so he decided to head over to her place. He wanted to talk to her about what Manny had said about the rogue's signature; plus, he wanted to return the rift device and schematics. He was more than willing to lock them up in his gun safe, but she hadn't said she wanted him to keep them yet.

He knew Tori usually didn't go to bed until close to midnight, so he wasn't worried about waking her. But when she didn't answer, his concern for her grew. He banged on the door with his fist.

"Yeah, yeah, I'm coming," he heard Randall yell. In another couple of seconds the door swung open and Tori's brother stood there with his hand on the knob and a scowl on his face. His hair was wet and he was wrapped in a navy-blue robe. He must have just gotten out of the shower. "What the..." His gaze hardened. "What the hell is wrong with you? Do you know what time it is?"

"I do, actually." Dante didn't like Tori's brother. At their introduction, the guy had been a jerk, and Dante didn't see much change now. Granted, he'd shown up on their doorstep late at night, but from what he understood, Randall was out late most nights anyway. "Is Tori around? She's not answering her phone," he said by way of explanation.

"She's sleeping."

Dante frowned. "Is she all right?"

"What's it to you?" Randall crossed his arms.

Dante tightened his jaw. While he was sure it would be highly satisfying to plant his fist in this little prick's jaw, he was equally sure Tori wouldn't appreciate it. He was also sure he wouldn't be leaving the rift device and schematics here tonight. "We're friends. I'm concerned."

"Right. Friends." Randall didn't seem too keen on the idea. "She's fine."

At first Dante didn't give a damn whether Randall wanted him to be friends with Tori. But then he figured one of them had to be the grown-up here, for Tori's sake. He'd make an effort to connect with her brother. Pasting what he hoped came across as an interested expression on his face, he asked, "So, how'd the council meet and greet go?"

Randall just stared at him.

"I've never been to one, obviously," Dante said. "I was just curious about it."

"Yeah, humans don't get invited to those. Just prets." Randall gave a careless shrug. The fingers of one hand began drumming against his thigh. "I didn't go."

"Really?" Dante knew enough about these things to know they were a big deal as far as the council was concerned. A really big deal, yet Tori's brother hadn't bothered to go. "Why?"

"Wasn't interested in meeting the council." The look on Randall's face suggested he was confused and irritated at Dante's probing. "Anyway, what's it to you? You're not my keeper."

Oh, yeah. Tori's brother was a douche bag and not scoring any points here. "I imagine your not showing up isn't going to make things any easier on your sister." At Randall's low growl, Dante held up one hand and said, "Look, man, I was just trying to get to know you a little, that's all."

"Yeah, well, *man*, I'm not interested in that, either." His sneer was pronounced. "I'll let Tori know you stopped by."

"Thanks. Ask her to call me, will you?"

Without responding, Randall closed the door with a solid *click*.

All Dante wanted to do was remind her about having dinner at his place the next night. He hoped her little punk of a brother would give her the message, though Dante suspected he wouldn't.

The next morning, his belly full of eggs, bacon, and toast, he drove to the station. His cell phone rang, and as he pulled it free from its holder his heart jumped at the thought that Tori might be calling. When he saw the main dispatch number on the display, he squelched his disappointment, his greeting less than enthusiastic.

"We've got a DB over on Fifth Avenue by the horse fountain," the dispatcher told him. "First uniform on scene said it looks like a werewolf attack."

"Got it. I'm on my way." Dante made a U-turn at the next intersection and headed toward the crime scene. He drove up Marshall Way and pulled to a stop next to a marked unit that was parked sideways, blocking off the roundabout where the horse fountain was the centerpiece.

He lifted his chin in greeting to the uniformed officer standing sentry at the perimeter. "Joe," he said as the man lifted the yellow tape for Dante to duck beneath.

"Dante." The officer thumbed over his shoulder. "It's a real mess over there."

"Any witnesses?"

"Nope. It's pretty quiet around here. Some of the coffee shops and restaurants have been open for business for about an hour. If anyone was here when this went down, they're not talking."

"Figures, not that I can blame them. I imagine seeing a werewolf attacking someone is a scary thing." Even from where he stood, Dante could see evidence markers all over the scene. He walked over and stood at the edge of the crime scene, a small bricked area with a few round concrete picnic tables and large planters with yellow flowers in them. George, the council ME, was bent over the victim, and several criminalists were at work, taking pictures and collecting data.

Dante went over to a tech who was busy sketching the scene. Dante watched as he accurately represented the scene on graph paper while studiously ignoring the cop peering over his shoulder.

Someone walked up and stood next to Dante. He glanced sideways and saw the werewolf liaison from quadrant four standing there. "What brings you to my crime scene, Ash?" Dante asked.

"From the description, this sounds like it's my guy. So dispatch sent me instead of Tori." He raked dark blond hair off his forehead. "Crap. Even from here this looks bad."

Dante was glad Tori was getting some time off but he

missed not being able to talk through the case with her as they walked the scene.

The ME glanced up from the body suddenly and motioned them over. They both took care where they placed their feet as they joined him. The closer to the body they got, the stronger the smell of bleach and ammonia became. "You smell that?" Dante asked Ash.

"Yeah, I do." He huffed a sigh. "Damn it."

Dante hunkered down and looked at the body, or what was left of it. It was a man, his head turned to one side, the neck clearly broken. His clothing lay in tatters around him, and blood smeared nearly every inch of his skin. The torso was ripped open, a gaping, bloody hole where organs should have been. This reminded Dante of one of the early scenes in his career on the Special Case squad, about a year ago. He looked over at the ME. "Please don't tell me the suspect ate part of this poor guy."

Ash squatted down and gave a few sniffs, wrinkling his nose before standing back up.

"I can't say, because that would involve supposition on my part," George replied, as persnickety as ever. He took off his latex gloves and dropped them near the body, then grabbed a small cylindrical container from his shirt pocket and pulled off the cap. He shook a toothpick out and stuck it between his teeth, then replaced the container in his pocket. "What I *can* tell you," he said with teeth clenched around the small wooden stick, "is that all the internal organs are gone. They were ripped out, not cut, and from the amount of blood in the thoracic and abdominal cavities, I'd say the victim was still alive when this all started."

God. The poor bastard had been eaten alive? Dante

shared a look with Ash. "If this is the same rogue that's been turning people," Dante said, "why would he kill this guy instead of turning him?"

"He's succumbed to bloodlust," Ash murmured. "Shit."

Dante glanced from the werewolf liaison to the ME and back again. "Bloodlust?"

Ash drew in a deep breath. "It's a fine line we draw, those of us—like shapeshifters and vampires—who have a taste for humans. If we deny ourselves too long, we can go into a frenzy when we finally do get a bite. Or if we've been indulging too much, it basically shuts down our body's response to satiety."

"Leptin levels drop and ghrelin levels rise," George added. "The release of cholecys..." He trailed off and sent Dante a chagrined look. "Sorry. Geek speak. Let's just say that our brain doesn't tell our stomachs that we're full. So we feel hungry all the time."

Ash looked at the carnage. "Not just hungry. Ravenous. So we kill again. And again, the taste for humans becomes an addiction we can't fight. We don't *want* to fight." He rubbed his chin and met Dante's eyes. "I've been close to that condition, man, and it's a hard thing to turn away from. The sense of power you get, taking someone's life, is a heady feeling. I can pretty much guarantee that all our guy can think about now is when he's going to get his next meal, when he's going to feel that way again."

This was bad. Very bad. "So we have a starving werewolf on the loose? Great." Dante stood and glanced around. He itched to investigate further to see if the killer had left his signature. "What's your TOD, doc?"

"I put time of death around two, three hours ago, just before sunrise."

Dante shot Ash a surprised look. "That's kinda pushing it, isn't it?"

Ash shrugged. "It was still dark, plus there was a full moon out last night." He paused, his face darkening. "Aw, hell. I hope that doesn't mean we have more than one vic."

Dante turned to the ME. "Were there any other victims?"

"Not that we're aware of," the ME said. "The senior tech said so far there's no evidence of anyone else on scene, but then again, there's little evidence that the attacker was here, either."

"Except for this guy," Dante said with a dry look at the victim.

"Yeah, except for that," George replied. "As usual, he used bleach and ammonia." He gestured toward Ash, who was wiping his nose with a plain white handkerchief. "I know it bugs you that you can't pick up on his scent."

"Hell, I won't be able to smell anything for at least a day." Ash took in the crime scene. "Is it okay if I take a look around, doc?"

"Yeah, I'm done here." The ME motioned for the morgue attendants to come forward. Looking at Dante, he said, "They'll take the body back to the city morgue, where your ME can have a look at it. I'll get my report over to him ASAP."

"Thanks, George." Dante moved out of the way and walked the scene with Ash. At the southwest edge he stopped and knelt down to look at something curious.

"What is it?" Ash hunkered down as well.

Dante pointed to a row of dead leaves lined up on the bricks beneath one of the large planters. "Look at that."

"Six in a row, just like my other scenes." His phone rang and he stood and pulled it out of the back pocket of his jeans. "Asher." He paused, listening to whoever was on the other end of the call. "Yeah, I'm here right now."

Dante stood and watched Ash's face.

The werewolf liaison's "What?" was shocked and hard-voiced. He listened with a clenched jaw. "I'll be there as soon as I wrap up here. Give me half an hour or so." He shoved his phone back into his pocket and told Dante, "There's another victim up in the north quad. Rivera's on scene now."

"Two in one night? He's escalating."

"No kidding." Ash shook his head. "I shoulda known he wasn't finished. He was simply storing energy."

"Or that break really fed his addiction." Dante walked Ash to their parked cars. "He started going into withdrawal, and so last night was a...feeding frenzy." It almost made him sick to his stomach to phrase it that way, seeing as how the "food" had been some poor bastard's inner workings. And there were plenty of unknowing humans in this town who could be this monster's next meal. They needed to stop whoever was doing this and fast.

"Damn it." Ash huffed a sigh. "Rivera said the killing up north happened about seven hours ago."

"So...dinner and then breakfast?" Dante asked.

"I guess." Ash paused by Dante's truck. "Let me know if you find out anything else, all right?"

"You got it." Dante watched the werewolf liaison walk to his flashy red-with-black-racing-stripes muscle car.

Dante had his own sporty car he wanted to buy. Maybe he'd finally get one when they put this case to bed.

He climbed up behind the wheel and started his truck. The diesel engine rumbled to life, and Dante backed up several feet before making a U-turn and driving away. He'd made it about halfway to the station when his cell rang. He answered with a terse, "MacMillan."

"Hey." It was Tori. She sounded alert, her voice bright and energetic. The extra sleep had clearly done her some good. "Rand told me you asked me to call when I woke up, so...here I am, calling."

Well, what do you know? Her brother had actually delivered the message. "How're you feelin'?"

"I'm fine. Those meet and greets really take it out of me. I don't know why. But I'm not planning on doing much of anything today." She paused, then asked, "Did you want something in particular, or did you just want to chat?"

"Oh, we have plenty to chat about, believe me," he said. "But not over the phone. What I wanted was to remind you about dinner tonight at my place. Steaks on the grill, and maybe a ride if the horses will tolerate having a werewolf around."

"You had me at steak." She laughed, a soft trill of sound that went in his ears and shot straight to his groin. "Should I bring anything?" she asked.

"Hell, no. You're my guest." He made a turn onto the street where the station was located. "How does six sound?"

"Six is great. I'll see you then."

"Oh, and I still have the thing, so we can work on it again."

"Okay." Her tone softened as she said, "I'll see you tonight."

That sultry voice did it to him every time. His cock stiffened. He could come up with no other response except a quiet, "See you later."

Mind on the job, MacMillan. Otherwise they'd never make it to the food or the device.

Chapter Fourteen

By late afternoon Tori had had enough of lazing around. She puttered around in the yard, making sure the flowers had enough water and pulling a few stray weeds out of the graveled landscaping. Then she went inside to get cleaned up for her evening at Dante's.

It was silly how excited she was about going to his house. She had to leave in an hour, and she felt like a schoolgirl with her very first crush. Her insides trembled, her mind skittered from one thought to another, not allowing her to fully land on anything specific. Even though she had been to his house before, this time seemed more like a date and less like work. Maybe a cold shower would clear her head.

After a couple of seconds of cold water beating down on her, Tori decided cold showers were overrated. She turned the faucet to hot and finished up. As she was cinching her robe around her waist, the smell of Italian spices drew her to the front of the house. She walked past the guest bathroom, and the smell of ammonia made her stop. She peered in and saw the toilet bowl brush resting in the toilet. Hmph. Rand had cleaned? She went into the kitchen, rubbing her wet hair with a towel, and almost ran into her brother. He'd been on his way out when she'd gotten up this morning, stopping briefly to tell her Dante had come by late last night, then he had headed out. He'd gotten back only about half an hour ago.

" 'Ello," he said as he easily sidestepped her, holding a cup of tea. "How'd the yard work go?"

"Fine. It's not like it was hard or anything." She draped the damp towel over one shoulder and stared at him. "You, ah, cleaned the bathroom?"

He stared at her. "I thought I'd do some chores around here. Is that all right?"

"Sure. Yes, absolutely." It was her own damned suspicious nature that made her equate ammonia with the rogue werewolf. "Where were you last night?"

He set his cup on the island and turned toward the stove. Donning a pair of oven mitts, he opened up the oven door. "What do you mean?" His voice gave away nothing of what he was thinking, and she picked up no unusual emotional scents from him, either.

"I mean you weren't at the newcomer meet and greet." Tori drew in a breath and determined not to let him distract her with that absolutely yummy looking pan of lasagna. "It's a requirement for all preternaturals new to a city to attend one of those, not just to meet the council members, but also the local liaisons."

"But I already know the local liaison," Rand said with a small smile.

"Sorry, buddy. That doesn't count." She couldn't resist taking another sniff or two of the lasagna he lifted out of the oven. "You don't want to get me in trouble with my bosses, do you?"

He snorted. "They can't hold you responsible for me.

It's not like I'm your kid. Anyway, this stupid meet and greet is only required in the cities where the councils are located. If I lived down in Tucson or over in Yuma I wouldn't have to do this."

"That's because it doesn't make sense to have people travel from all over the surrounding areas to come to their regional council. But it does make sense for the council to get a feel for the prets who live in their town." She stared at him as he put the pan of lasagna on top of the stove and removed a foil bag of garlic bread, then closed the oven door.

He pulled off the mitts and set them on the counter. "Whatever. It's a waste of time."

"That may be true," Tori replied, and God knew she didn't disagree. "But it doesn't make any difference." She took a step closer to him and rested one hand on his forearm. "Since you didn't show up, the council is going to think you're trying to hide something from them."

"Well, I'm not." Her brother slid his arm out from under her grasp. "I'm not going to jump through hoops like a good little doggie simply because they tell me to." His irritation hit her nostrils on a wave of burned rubber.

"Rand—"

"No!" He sighed and briefly touched her shoulder. The scorched smell lessened. "Look, I understand that as one of their liaisons you have a job to do. Just this once, can't you leave the job behind, for me, and just be my sister?"

She bit back a sigh. He was right, though it was hard, distancing herself from work. It was so much a part of who she was now. How could she attest to her brother's whereabouts, when even she had no idea where he'd been? "I'll try," she told him. "I hope you know that if they ask me about where you were, I'm going to have to tell them you chose not to come." She hoped it wouldn't come to that. She didn't want to have to choose between her job and her family. She liked what she did and couldn't imagine not being a liaison.

"That's fine. You do what you have to do."

"So…" She tried to be as nonchalant as possible, but she was afraid she wasn't going to be successful. "What'd you do last night?"

"Not much. I sat around and watched TV mostly." Rand opened a cabinet and pulled out a couple of plates.

Tori watched him closely. "You didn't go out at all?"

"No." He took two forks from the silverware drawer and placed them on the plates. "Let's eat."

She pressed her lips together. Without coming right out and asking him if he had been turning people into werewolves without permission, she had nowhere else to go with this line of questioning. With Rand being so agreeable, she didn't want to spoil the mood, which she was probably about to do, anyway.

"What is it?" He glanced at her as he set the plates on the counter. "You don't like lasagna?"

"I love lasagna. It's just…" She met his eyes. "I'm going over to Dante's for dinner tonight. I need to leave in about forty-five minutes. But, you know what? I'll call him and cancel." She turned and started out of the kitchen. "It'll just be you and me tonight."

"No, don't cancel." Rand slid open the utensil drawer and drew out a spatula. "Go have dinner with your cop friend. I have plans tonight, too."

"Are you sure?" Tori hated the idea of missing an opportunity with her brother, especially when he seemed so open with her. "I'd really like to spend some time with you. I can have dinner with Dante some other time."

He looked up at her. "No, really. It's okay." For the first time since he'd shown up on her doorstep, he seemed calm. Almost serene. "It's not like I'm getting ready to leave town or anything. We'll catch up tomorrow. Go. Have fun."

He seemed to have gotten over his snit about Dante. She was glad, but wondered what had brought about this sudden change of heart. "I thought you didn't like Dante."

"Can I say that I'm happy with the idea of you being with a human? No, I can't." His gaze, candid and open, landed on her. "He seems a decent enough sort. I mean, he's a cop, so he can't be all that bad, right? And he did check up on you last night when you weren't answering your phone, so at least he's looking out for you."

"Right." She lingered a few moments, watching him dish up half the lasagna onto his plate. She halfway expected him to hit her up for some money, he was being so nice. "Okay, then, I guess I'll see you later." She turned and went into her bedroom to get dressed.

She was wrapping a hair band around her still-damp braid when Rand yelled, "I'm leaving now."

"All right. See you later," she called out. She grabbed a thin, short-sleeved blouse and shrugged into it, flipping her braid to the outside, and tugged the jacket down over her fanny pack. Once she was ready, Tori headed out the door.

On the way, she stopped at a store and picked up a bouquet of flowers—some carnations, a few bright daisies, and some babies' breath—for Dante's sister. When she pulled up in front of his house, she glanced toward the

corral. A big Appaloosa, a buckskin, and a cute little
burro stared at her car, all three with tails swishing, brushing persistent flies from their hindquarters. Tori grabbed
the flowers, opened the door, and got out. The horses
threw their heads back, their eyes showing white. The
burro drew himself up, standing stiff-legged and looking
wary. It wasn't unusual for livestock to react this way
upon spotting a werewolf.

The front door opened and Dante walked out. His full
lips lifted in a smile. "Hey." He walked up to her and
leaned over to press a kiss against her cheek. Taking a step
back, he put his hands on her shoulders and looked down
at her. "You look great. You must've needed a day off."

She raised her eyebrows. "Are you saying I looked
haggard?" She propped her free hand on her hip and
waited to see how he'd get out of this one.

"Not at all. You're always gorgeous. You're just even
more gorgeous today."

She grinned.

"Those for me?" He glanced down at the flowers. "You
shouldn't have. Really," he said, humor dancing in his
eyes.

"They're for your sister." Her smile widened at the relief that spread across his face.

"Oh. Good." Dante looked over at the horses that were
neighing low in their throats and stomping their hooves
restlessly. The burro still had his eye on Tori. "What's up
with them, I wonder? They're acting like there's a cougar
about ready to pounce."

"I'm sure it's me." Tori lifted her face and took a couple of sniffs. "I don't smell a cougar or even a coyote.
Of course, if I'm upwind of something I wouldn't be

able to pick up the scent." She watched the horses for a few seconds. "I've been around horses before, and after a few minutes, when they see I'm not getting any closer to them, they usually calm down, but these guys...they're still scared. They're acting almost as if they're surrounded by predators." She glanced around the area but didn't see anything lurking behind the scrub brush and cacti.

"I'd hoped we could take a short ride after dinner," Dante said. "But I can see that's not gonna happen. I guess they need to get used to you first."

"Sorry," Tori said. He shot a look at her and she shrugged. "I'm a predator, and they sense it." She couldn't mask her disappointment. She had looked forward to going for a ride. She shot a sidelong glance at him. Maybe she could just save the horses and ride a cowboy instead. She'd have to see how the evening went.

"Come on in," he said, cupping her elbow. "Meet my sister."

Tori let Dante guide her into the house. As soon as she walked in she smelled grilled meat, onions, and the fresh scent of rosemary mixed with an orange and vanilla fragrance from a lit candle in the foyer.

The dining room table was set with midnight-blue-colored plates trimmed in brown, glasses—both wine and water—and silverware.

A dark-haired woman by the stove wiped her hands on a dishtowel and came forward with hands outstretched. "Tori! How nice it is to meet you."

Tori shook her hand as Dante said, "This is my sister, Liliana."

"Please, call me Lily. Everyone does." Lily released Tori's hand.

"Lily." Tori held out the flowers. "Thanks for having me in your home."

Lily smiled and took the bouquet. "Thank you, they're beautiful." She pulled a vase from the cabinet beneath the sink. After filling it partway with water, she put the flowers in it, arranging them until she had it just so, and carried them to the dining room. She placed them in the center of the table and then went back to the stove. "I should be thanking you, anyway. With you coming over, Dante finally got all his computer crap off the dining room table."

Tori grinned at Dante's abashed look. "What can I help you with?" she asked and walked farther into the kitchen. Looking at the other woman, she could understand why Dante was still so concerned about her. She was too slender, probably at least twenty pounds underweight, and the paleness of her skin bore mute testament to the stress she'd been under. Despite her appearance, she seemed happy, and Dante said the cancer was completely gone, so that was most important. The rest of it, well, Lily just needed time. And if the cancer was gone, she had it.

"No, you're our guest. You're not going to help prepare the meal." She looked at Dante. "Didn't you say the two of you had some work to do? Why don't you get busy on that? I'll let you know when dinner's ready."

"You're sure?" Dante walked over to his sister and peered into the pan on the stove. "I'm sure we can—"

"You'll make more of a mess, is what you'll do." She grinned and made a shooing motion with her hands. "Go on, get. I'll call you when it's time to eat."

"All right." He glanced at Tori. "Come on, then. We've been given our marching orders."

Tori hesitated. It seemed rude to go off and leave all the work for Lily to do. "You're sure?"

Lily's laugh was as cheery as wind chimes. "I'm sure. Go."

"Come on," Dante said again.

Tori went with him down the hallway and into a home office. More distressed pine in this room in the shape of a complete wall of bookcases crammed full of books of all sizes, and a large desk in one corner. Various pieces and parts of computers lined another wall. She pointed to them and asked, "This is what you had on the dining room table?"

"Yeah, well, I haven't had a lot of time lately to work on it. I'm buildin' my own computer," he added.

"Wow." She'd known he was a gadget guy, and he'd seemed to know his way around the device the last time they'd looked at it, but she'd had no idea he was such a…"You're just a geek underneath all that manliness, aren't you?"

He grinned and tipped an imaginary hat. "Yes, ma'am, I am." He moved papers and files off his desk and pulled over another chair. "Before we get to work on the rift device, let's talk shop." He looked at her, his expression serious. "Did Ash call you about the attack this morning?"

She frowned. "No, what attack?"

"This one happened by the horse fountain at Fifth and Marshall."

"Are you sure?"

He nodded. "Left a row of six dead leaves by one of the planters. It was his second attack last night." He paused, his face grim. "He *ate* part of the guy, Tori. All of his internal organs were gone. Ripped out."

"Oh, God." This wasn't good. Crap like that would only enflame an already tense situation with humans. It would make them even more afraid of preternaturals and much more willing to do reckless and desperate things to protect themselves.

"There was another killing, prior to ours, that happened earlier up north. I'm sure Ash will be in touch to fill you in," Dante added. "Or you can go ahead and call him."

"That's okay. He'll call me when he has more info." God, she prayed the rogue wasn't her brother. If it was, and she'd stayed silent...she'd have two people's deaths on her hands. "Let's take another look at the rift device, shall we?"

"Sure thing." He left the room and returned in a couple of minutes with the device and schematics in hand. "I had them locked in my gun safe," he said. "I would've given 'em to you last night, but I didn't want to wake you. Not that your brother would've let me," he added dryly. He handed her the device. "Here. Hold this a sec."

She noticed the difference in the size and shape of their hands—hers slim and dainty, his wide and large.

She watched those hands as he pulled a small screwdriver from one of the side drawers of his desk. When he held out his hand, she put the device in it and watched as he took the casing off. She tried to focus on anything other than his long, strong fingers. But all she wanted was the feel of those hands all over her body.

Tori forced her attention onto the rift device. As before, she stared down at a small motherboard with a mini-processor and USB port.

He traced some fine wires with his finger and pointed

to the USB port. "This gets hooked up to a…" He spread out the schematics and bent closer to the rendering. "I'll be damned."

"What?" Tori bent over and looked, too, but nothing made much sense to her.

"They've constructed a Wien bridge oscillator." He glanced at her, his face only a few inches away. "It's a type of electronic oscillator—an instrument for producing a voltage of a required frequency—that generates a very low distortion sine wave. This oscillator is built around four resistors and two capacitors and can generate a large range of frequencies." His gaze dropped to her mouth. His eyes darkened and his lips parted, but then he seemed to collect himself and he shook his head. He looked back down at the schematics. "With something like this they could dial up whatever frequency they wanted and amplify it."

"So they make the output of this"—she pointed to the device—"stronger?"

"That's my educated guess, yes." Dante straightened. "But how does that tie into the rift?" He blew out a breath and tucked his fingers into the back pocket of his jeans. "Okay, so walk me through how the rift works. The comet goes by and temporarily opens a rift, a hole, between the two dimensions."

"Picture it like sliding down a zipper," Tori explained. "The opening at the top gets wider the farther down you unzip. Entities spill into this dimension all along the opening, more of them toward the top and middle as it widens." Using her forefinger and middle finger in the shape of a V, she drew double lines across the desk, bringing her fingers together to complete the shape. "Then as the comet gets farther away from Earth, it…it's like the release of the effects of gravity snaps the zipper tab back the other way, closing it."

Dante gave a low whistle. "Man, can you imagine what it'd be like if the rift wasn't temporary? Or if it at least stayed open longer?"

They looked at each other, a look of horror on both of their faces. He must have been thinking the same thing.

"And this Wien bridge thing…could it have that effect?" she asked.

He frowned. "No, there's no way something this size could keep the rift open longer."

She looked at the schematics. "What if…" She looked back at him. "Could someone use this to model a larger device?"

He shared a look of alarm with her. "It's possible. Shit. If they do that, the human race will be in a lot of trouble."

Chapter Fifteen

Then he just sat there, this sheepish look on his little face, while eggs and flour pooled on the floor all around him." Lily laughed until she had to reach up to wipe tears from her eyes. "Oh, my God. It was so funny."

"Mom didn't think so."

Dante's dry comment set Lily off again.

Tori couldn't stop smiling at the interaction between the two. She and Rand had never been close like this. Maybe it was the age difference between them, maybe it was the way they'd been raised. She didn't know, but watching Dante and Lily made her miss things she'd never had. "What did she do?" she asked.

"What could she do? I was ten and just trying to help." He shrugged. "I misjudged how much I could carry."

"Hmm. That might explain something," Tori murmured with a sideways glance at him. "You had early training on not taking on more than you can handle."

"These days it's not a question of if I can handle it, but whether or not I have the time to give it my undivided attention." He brought the cup of water to his lips. Over the rim of the glass his dark eyes snagged and held hers. "Because *this* particular project I'm getting into seems like it might be rather time consuming."

She smiled, slowly, and leaned forward. "And worth every second, I promise." She stroked her fingers up the stem of her wineglass.

Lily laughed. "Oh, brother, has she got your number." She stood and began clearing the table. She paused, holding the bowl with leftover green beans in her hands, and let out a long, loud yawn. "Sorry," she said when it was over.

"Why don't you go lie down?" Dante came and took the bowl out of her hands. "We'll clean up."

"No, I can do—"

"Don't be silly." Tori stacked plates and forks and carried them to the sink. "You cooked, so it's only right that we clean."

Lily was clearly torn between being a proper hostess and being bone tired. Finally the fatigue won, because she said, "Okay. Have Dante make you a margarita. There's still some left over from last night. His are the best."

Tori smiled. "I'll do that." She picked up the platter that had held the steaks. Tori's had been rare, and neither Dante nor Lily had seemed fazed by the blood running from the meat. "Dinner was delicious. Thank you."

"You're welcome. I enjoy cooking. And with you here, it actually forced my brother to slow down long enough to sit and eat a real meal instead of just grabbing something on the run." She winked at Dante and then left the kitchen.

"Great, now I have *two* women ganging up on me," he muttered.

"Oh, you're man enough to take it." Tori bumped his

hip with hers and pulled open the dishwasher door.

As if they'd been doing so for years, they began loading the machine in unison. Tori finished putting silverware in the basket and, while Dante grabbed soap from under the sink, she pulled an antibacterial wipe free from its container and started wiping down the countertops.

Dante added soap to the dishwasher tray, then closed and latched the door. He flipped the dial to normal wash and turned toward Tori. She'd taken off her heels a few minutes ago and was giving a few last swipes to the countertop, her hips swaying with her movements.

"Come on," he said. "Let's grab the margaritas and head out onto the patio."

She glanced at him. "Okay." She grabbed the glasses while he removed the pitcher from the refrigerator. "Should I get Lily?" she asked.

"No, let her rest." Dante knew his sister tired easily, and preparing dinner had taken a lot out of her. "We can always make more."

They went outside and sat on a glider at one end of the patio. The misters kept the air cool enough that it was bearable to be outside in the heat. Though the sun had begun making its descent, it was still hot outside. "This is nice," she commented, holding the glasses while Dante poured the drinks.

"It is. I put the misters in a couple of summers ago. I wanted to enjoy the scenery without suffering heat stroke." He set the pitcher on a small glass table beside the swing and sat down, starting the glider swinging gently. He turned toward her and took his glass, holding it up in a toast. "Cheers."

She clicked her glass against his. "Cheers." She took a sip. "Mmm, delicious."

Dante stretched one arm along the back of the glider and rested the other on his thigh, balancing his glass to keep his margarita from spilling. As the sun set and dusk bloomed, a few outdoor lamps he had lining the winding walkway turned on, bathing the backyard in a soft yellow glow. After a hard day at work, sitting out here for a few minutes to center himself never failed to calm him.

Until now. He was too aware of the woman next to him. Her light perfume scented the air around him, her warmth pulling him closer. He tried to look at her without staring, but it was impossible. Her bare feet sported shiny purple toenail polish. Her light-blue blouse paired with a soft peach scoop-necked top and filmy blue skirt accented her delicious curves. She looked downright edible.

He cleared his throat. "How's your brother doing?"

"He's good." She frowned and shifted on the glider to face him, one leg bent. "Actually, I'm a little worried." She paused. "I don't know, Dante. He says he wants to catch up, to stay around so we can get to know each other again, and then he acts like he couldn't care less." She took a sip of her drink. "But then he goes and does something sweet like making dinner for me. Lasagna." She seemed almost guilty as she added, "I almost canceled tonight."

"Tori, I know how important family is to you." Dante put his drink on the side table and twisted toward her. "You *should* have called and canceled." Though the cynic in him whispered that Randall wanted something and that was why he was being so sweet. "I would've understood."

She waved one hand. "He wouldn't let me. It's okay."

Her smile was genuine. "He's going to stay in town, so we have time."

"Yeah, well, you're both immortal, so you definitely have plenty of time."

A shadow of sadness passed over her face. "Living forever isn't all it's cracked up to be." She pressed her lips together and looked down at her lap. "You make human friends and watch them grow old and die. And when you make wrong choices, the consequences never go away. At least as a human, death is the final forgiveness." She raised her eyes. "You're so lucky to have Lily. She's lucky to have *you.*"

"She's been through a lot," he said. "It's just the two of us now, so we look out for each other." He wrapped his arm around on her shoulder, feeling both strength and frailty beneath his palm. "Kind of like you and Rand."

That slender shoulder lifted in a shrug. "I don't know how much he looks out for me, but I do look out for him." She sighed. "He missed a mandatory meeting last night, and pretty much expects me to make everything all right. Like I have a magic wand or something."

"Hmph. Well, I guess that's what older sisters are for." He paused and stared at her. "You are older, aren't you? I mean, it's hard to tell, 'cause he acts like he's about fourteen."

"I'm older. He's just..." She shook her head. "He's always been a little...breakable. Coming through the rift and turning into a werewolf hasn't done him any favors."

Dante pondered that for a moment. "I'd think having superhuman strength, hearing, vision, and all that would give a boost in ego."

"For some it does." Tori's tongue swept out to leave

her lips wet. "For others, like Rand, it only highlights the deficiencies they won't, or can't, let go of. They focus only on the fact that if it weren't for the wolf in them they wouldn't have all those things you mentioned. Rather than seeing all they have gained, they feel as if they are the weak, ineffectual person they've always believed themselves to be."

"I guess I can understand that." He rubbed his thumb against her collarbone. "Is it just you and Randall? Or do you have other family here?"

She looked down at her lap. "I'm so glad to have him with me. You can't imagine what it's been like being alone for so long."

That didn't exactly answer his question. He put a hand under her chin and raised her face to his. "Tori? Do you have other family here?"

She hesitated, then looked up with moist green eyes. "Rand is the only brother I have. I've been alone for so long."

Dante made a mental note that she still hadn't really answered his question, but he let it go for now. He needed to reassure her. "You're not alone anymore, sweetheart." For the first time since he'd known her he saw uncertainty in her eyes. His heart skipped a beat. He'd done that to her with his damned vacillating. Not anymore. He took the drink from her hand and placed it beside his, then faced her again. "I promise you, Victoria, you're not alone," he whispered and slanted his mouth over hers.

He started out gentle, but when her lips parted and her tongue swept over his, gentleness gave way to rough hunger. He groaned and cupped his hands around her head, the tips of his fingers resting against her thick braid.

Her hair was like silk, the lips beneath his even softer, making him wonder if she'd be this damned smooth all over.

Tilting her head, he slid his tongue along the seam of her mouth and then thrust inside. She made a low, eager sound, her hands sliding around to clutch his back.

Dante held her head still and deepened the kiss. Her mouth was sweet, with a hint of lime and tequila. He leaned back, resting against the arm of the glider, and spread his legs, drawing her on top of him. Her sweet weight settled between the V of his thighs, pressing against his growing erection.

Tori pulled back, just a few inches, and whispered, "I see *someone's* got time for me." She stroked her fingers across his fly, making his hips lift in response. "He's got better sense than you," she said.

"Yeah, well, I don't usually let my cock do my thinkin' for me." He nibbled along her jaw line until he reached her ear, giving the lobe a slight nip. "But here... now...seems like a good time to start." His mouth slid to the softness of Tori's throat, tasting the saltiness of her skin over the pounding of her pulse.

"Dante..." Her voice had that sultry, throaty quality that always revved his engine.

He kissed her again, tongue sweeping the dark cavern of her mouth. She tasted sweet and rich, like dark chocolate. When she pulled his tongue deeper, suckling him gently, eagerly, he groaned and tugged her hips closer to his.

She pumped against him, a slow, steady undulation, a dance of desire that made his cock as stiff as a pike. Slender hands clutched at his back, kneading the hard muscles.

He'd never felt hunger like this before. Raw. Demanding and pulsating with a life of its own. He heard his name again, sounding far away. The rattle of the patio door impacted his awareness just as he heard Lily's "Dante, I'm going...Oh." A slight pause, then another, louder, "Oh." She gave a sigh. "God, this is so not something I wanted to walk in on. Reminds me of that time with you and Suzie Weisterman when you were in the tenth grade."

"Damn it, Lily." Dante lifted Tori off him. He crossed one leg over the other and rested his ankle on top of the opposite knee. Hunching his shoulders, he curled his hands over his shins and tried to hide his erection. Tori moved back to her side of the glider, looking a little embarrassed and mightily amused.

"Don't 'damn it, Lily' me," his sister muttered. In the illumination of the patio lights he could see red flags of color streaking across her cheeks. "If you two want to get it on, why don't you take it inside? Like, in your bedroom. Behind closed doors." She put her hands on her hips. "You'd think you'd have learned after Suzie."

"Oh, dear God..." Dante hung his head. His little sister hadn't lost any of her ability to embarrass the hell out of him.

Tori laughed, clearly delighted with his discomfort. "Why don't you sit with us for a while?" she said to Lily.

He shot her an *Are-you-kidding?* look, which she completely ignored.

Thankfully, Lily turned down the invitation. "I'd love to, but I just came out to tell you that I'm just going to go on to bed. And I also wanted to thank you for cleaning up the kitchen. I appreciate it."

"It was my pleasure." Tori got off the glider and went

over to his sister. "I'm so glad to have met you, Lily. If you ever need anything, even an ear to rant to about whatever boneheaded thing your brother has done..."

"Hey!" Dante frowned. "I don't do boneheaded things."

"...call me." She pointed over her shoulder toward Dante. "He has my number." She gave Lily a quick hug and then retook her seat on the glider. "Guys do all sorts of crazy things that drive the women in their lives nuts. I know your brother is no different."

"Boy, you're right there," Lily said.

"Hey!" Dante crossed his arms. "I can hear you, you know."

Both women laughed. Lily gave a slight wave and went back into the house.

Dante sat there, trying to get over his embarrassment.

"I have to tell you," Tori began, "I really like your sister. She's sweet. And I admire the way she's dealt with the double whammy life has thrown at her. It can't have been easy, going through a divorce while fighting cancer." She placed a hand on his thigh. "I'm sure it helped her to know she had you to lean on." Approval filled her tone.

Her touch fired up his libido again, but her words upped his embarrassment. He didn't like being complimented on something that he'd really had no choice in. "I only did what was right," he said. "What was I supposed to do? Let her struggle on her own?"

"Of course not, but even family can be cold-hearted when it comes to people in need."

He wondered for a moment if she knew the reaction her brother had had last night when Dante stopped by. Randall had been less than sympathetic about causing her trouble. Talk about cold-hearted.

She squeezed his thigh. "I think it says a lot about you, about the kind of man you are, that you wanted her to stay here. I applaud you for that." Her hand slid up his thigh and halted just short of the mark.

Every thought fled Dante's mind like water swirling down a drain. All but one: He had to get this woman in his bed. Now. "You know," he drawled, "I think Lily had the right idea." When Tori appeared confused, he added, "About going to bed, I mean."

Now she looked disappointed. "Oh."

He leaned toward her. "There are other things to do in bed besides sleep."

Her smile was slow and wickedly sensual. "If Lily's trying to sleep..."

He shook his head. "Split floor plan. Our rooms are on opposite ends of the house." He stood and held out one hand. When she took it, he pulled her to her feet and into his arms. "Are you sure about this?" He wanted to give her a chance to change her mind before things got too hot.

She looped her arms around his shoulders, warm fingers sifting through the hair at the nape of his neck. "I'm sure. I've been sure for a while now." She scraped her fingernails lightly across his skull, setting up fireworks in his groin. "What about you? Are you sure about this?"

His direct gaze never faltered. "Life's too short, and I'm sure I don't want to pass up the opportunity to be with you. And if it ends up meaning our time together is limited...well, I'll take what I can get. A few months or years is better than decades without you. So, yeah, I'm damned sure." Dante swept Tori into his arms and strode into the house, pausing to flip the lock on the patio door before heading to his bedroom.

He placed her gently on the bed and stared down at her a moment. What she did to him...He wasn't a believer in love at first sight, though he'd certainly been attracted to her from the moment he'd seen her. The more he was around Tori, the more he was interested in her, admired her. She was his friend, soon to be his lover. Yet, more than that, she was the woman of his soul.

Dear God, he wanted her like he'd wanted no other. Possessiveness—raw, sharp, and primitive as hell—surged inside him with astonishing fervor. He came down on top of her, bracing his weight on his forearms, and crashed his mouth onto hers. Her soft, sweet scent wrapped around his senses.

With a groan he pulled her up, helped her shrug out of her jacket, then pulled the silky blouse over her head. As she lay back down, bare, pink-tipped breasts quivered with her quickened breathing. He buried his face between them, feeling her heart thudding against his skin.

He'd been an idiot to fight this for so long.

Tori squirmed beneath him, her hands coming up to fist in his hair. She directed his face toward her right breast.

"Just what I like," he murmured and swiped his tongue over the velvety tip. "A woman who knows what she wants." He licked the nipple again, watching it go red and hard before his eyes. As he closed his mouth over it, her breath hitched in her throat and then eased from her in a long moan. He paid homage to her, suckling each nipple, wringing cries from her, making her arch against the bed.

"Dante..."

He raised his head and stared down at her. She had the prettiest breasts, plump, pale, and soft. Her nipples were a contrast, tight and red, wet from his mouth. He moved his gaze to her face, seeing her full lips parted, her eyes flecked with amber arousal.

That reminder of her inner werewolf should have given him pause, but it didn't. What it did do was ramp his arousal even higher. His cock, thick and heavy, strained against his jeans and pulsed with each heavy heartbeat.

He wanted to be buried deep inside her. With a growl of impatience he managed to get the side zipper of her skirt undone, and then he lifted her and yanked the skirt off. It was quickly followed by lacy peach-colored panties.

Soon, she was completely bare to his gaze. "God, you're beautiful."

"I'd like to be able to return the compliment," she murmured. She rose up on one elbow and ran a hand from his shoulder down to his wrist. "But you're still dressed."

Dante took care of that little problem in two seconds. He reached into the top drawer of his bedside table and pulled out a condom, and took care of that in about one second flat. Then he was on top of Tori, gently easing himself between her soft thighs. He braced himself on his forearms and brushed strands of hair away from her face. "God, you're so lovely, inside and out. You're a feast to a starving man."

"I've never felt this way before. I feel like...I need you like I need air to breathe."

Emotion clogged his throat. He clasped her hand and held it against his cheek. "I feel the same way. Whatever I have to do to make this work, I will." Releasing her hand, he bent his head and pressed his mouth to hers. This time his kiss was soft. Reverent.

He licked a path down her throat, lingering in the sensitive bend of her neck. He stroked a hand through the folds of her sex, letting his thumb circle her swollen nub.

Shivering, she thrust her legs apart farther. "Now, Dante. I want you inside me."

She was slick and hot. Ready. He slid one finger into her sheath, teasing her, teasing himself. With a short snarl she flipped him onto his back and straddled his hips. She took him in a slow, devastating descent that robbed him of breath. Of his mind. He arched, his heels digging into the mattress, the move pushing him even deeper.

She planted her hands on his shoulders, bracing herself as she lifted her hips up and down in a rhythm that threatened to shatter him. She took...everything. And he...

He was finally willing to let go and love her.

Chapter Sixteen

Several hours later, Tori awoke in a sweat. It took her a second to figure out where she was, but once she remembered, she knew right away the reason she was so warm. She had a hot, naked man pressed against her back. Dante's soft, even breathing told her he was asleep. His right arm was draped over her, a welcome weight. His hand cupped her breast, and his left thigh rested between her legs.

She carefully slid off the bed and padded into the bathroom. Once she'd finished, she crawled back into bed with him, lying on her side so she could look at his face subdued in the light of dawn. In repose his face was softer. Even though he carried himself with such a carefree attitude, he was anything but. He worried about his sister. He worked hard on his career. He was concerned that he'd somehow do wrong by Tori. He really was a kind man, a genuinely nice guy, though sometimes he let the bad boy show. Most important, he made her laugh. That combination was impossible to resist. And as a lover…

My God. He was incredible. She'd felt cherished, as if she were the only woman in his world. That was a heady feeling.

She reached up and brushed a fringe of hair off his forehead. Lying here in the still hours of early morning, with only the light of the moon illuminating their small island of solitude, it was easy to push aside the anxieties of the day. She could look at this man for the rest of her life.

Her gaze traveled down the strong column of his neck, across the sharp ridge of his collarbones, over the light dusting of hair that sprinkled his pecs. She rose up on one elbow to get a better look at him.

"Like what you see?" Dante's voice was husky, whether from sleep or arousal, she didn't know. Maybe a combination of both.

"Very much." Tori stroked her fingers up and down his stomach. "I'll need to leave soon. I have to go home and get ready for work."

"Well, then, give me a minute and we can get a head start." He slid off the bed and went into the bathroom. After a few seconds she heard the toilet flush and then he was back, scooping her up into his arms.

Not expecting the move, she gave a startled squeak and grabbed his shoulders. "What are you doing?"

His grin was pure devilry with the promise of more sensual wickedness. "Takin' a shower with my lady," he said as he walked into the bathroom. He set her feet on the plush rug in front of the shower and held her close to his heart while he turned on the water and held his hand under the stream, waiting for it to warm up.

The glass-enclosed shower was big enough for two, with an adjustable shower head and a small built-in bench at one end. Anti-slip strips were evenly placed on the tile floor.

He stepped into the stall, helping her in, and pulled the glass door closed behind them.

"You know I could've managed to walk from the bedroom into the bathroom under my own power," she said, watching water splash off his broad shoulders and trickle down his chest.

"Hmm. No doubt. You're the strongest woman I know, both physically and mentally." There was such caring, such love in his voice it brought tears to her eyes. "However, you deserve to be carried every now and then."

Not even a strong woman like her was proof against that kind of sweetness. She pulled his face down for a long, slow kiss. When they broke apart, they both were breathing heavily.

Tori put shower gel in her palm, inhaling the spicy, manly scent, and ran her soapy hands over Dante's massive shoulders. She marveled at the differences in their bodies. He was so big, so broad, muscles flexing and releasing as the two of them moved against each other, touching, seeking. Finding. His hot erection stroked against her belly, making her go soft and slick between her legs.

He reached out and squirted a dab of shower gel into his wide palm and then rubbed his hands together to create lather. "Let me," he murmured. He ran his hands all over her, washing her with exquisite care. He brought her nipples to hard buds, using his mouth after the water rinsed the soap away.

She sighed and undulated against him, feeling the velvety soft head of his cock rubbing against her stomach. He ran his hands under her breasts, between her thighs, making her legs threaten to stop supporting her weight.

His hands trailed down to her legs and then he went on one knee and washed her feet, first the right one and then the left.

As he set her left foot on the shower floor, he knelt on the tile before her, looking up at her with hot, dark eyes. Water flowed over his shoulders, running in rivulets down his chest. Their gazes locked and his mouth went to her belly, pressing against her skin before his tongue dipped into the tiny hole. Lightning zinged to her core.

As he kissed his way over her hip, she braced her back against the wall, shivering at the coolness of the tile on her back, and widened her stance. He blazed a trail to her inner thigh, pausing there to nip her lightly with his teeth.

She gasped and arched against him. To make more room for him, she lifted one leg and draped it over his brawny shoulder. "Please," she said, her voice raspy with need.

He nuzzled her thigh, the stubble on his jaw rasping against her skin. His tongue licked through her folds with one sure stroke, ending with a jab against her swollen clit. She gasped and moaned, arching into him even more. His fingers sank into her hips as he held her still, his head buried between her thighs as he got down to serious work. Lapping and sucking and thrusting until she slid down onto the bench, unable to support her own weight. He stroked two fingers into her sheath, his tongue sucking and flicking at the top of her sex.

Tori came hard, her keening wail rising above the sound of the pounding water. When she was finally spent, she collapsed against the tile, panting and staring at him with eyes she knew had to contain some of the wildness she felt inside.

He pulled his hand back and brought it to his mouth, tasting her. Looking at her from beneath dark brows, he said, "I love it when your eyes go amber like that," his voice rough and low.

She saw his erection, hard and ruddy, and knew he needed release. Knew that she needed him right then and couldn't wait another moment. Reaching out, she urged him to sit on the corner bench and knelt between his legs. She took him in her hand, marveling at the strength of him, the vulnerability he was loath to admit.

Using more shower gel to lubricate her hands, she began to stroke him. The sight of his blunt head sliding through the ring of her fingers, the tip ruddy and weeping, made her hot all over. His chest rose and fell as his breathing accelerated, his lips parting with his rising pleasure.

"You're such a beautiful man," she murmured, squeezing the fingers of her right hand a little tighter around his length. She reached her left hand between his thighs and grasped his sac. She focused her attention on bringing him to completion.

"Ah, God, I don't think I'm gonna last much longer..."

He was so sensual, so open in front of her, powerful and vulnerable at the same time. The house could have caught on fire and she'd have remained transfixed by this sight.

"I'm going to..." He threw his head back, the cords of his neck straining, his hands clenching and unclenching on his thighs. His hips punched up, driving his flesh deeper into her fist.

"Come on, Dante," she said. She wanted this to last forever. "Come for me."

As if her voice was all the trigger he needed, his orgasm roiled through him, spilling onto her hands and breasts. He bucked and moaned, his flesh straining through her fingers until finally he was still.

He met her gaze before leaning forward, snagging her chin with one hand, and kissing her. Then he stood and drew her to her feet, turning her into the water to wash away the evidence of his release.

After their shower, they dried each other off, hands lingering, bodies touching. Dante pulled a new toothbrush from the medicine cabinet. "An extra one I got the last time I went to the dentist," he said. "You can use it if you'd like. After some breakfast, of course."

He wrapped a deep-green towel around his lean hips and went into the bedroom, returning with a soft, well-worn T-shirt. "This might be better than just a towel."

She smiled and slipped it over her head. The seams on the shoulders went halfway down her upper arms, and the bottom hem reached her midthigh. "You must buy extra long," she mused.

"I do." He looked at her, eyes black with desire. He glanced down, drawing her gaze to his groin where the towel had begun to rise over a growing bump. "Damn. I'm like a teenager around you." His grin was a white flash against tanned cheeks. "Not complainin', mind you."

Breakfast consisted of cereal and coffee. Though Dante offered to cook something, Tori declined. She hadn't had any raw meat in a few days, and her wolf was snarling its displeasure. She didn't think Dante was quite ready to see her scarfing down uncooked hamburger meat just yet, so she'd wait until she got home.

By the time she was dressed and ready to leave, Dante

had also gotten dressed in blue jeans and the T-shirt she'd discarded. His big feet were encased in cowboy boots.

"That's kind of casual for work, isn't it?" she asked. "Not that I'm complaining. I like cowboys."

He grinned. "I've gotta take care of the horses before I go in. The more I do, the less there is for Lily to do. She needs her rest."

Tori gave him a hug. "You're such a good man," she whispered, leaning up to press a kiss to his lean cheek.

She knew he'd shrug off her compliment, which he did with a scowl and muttered, "It's nothing."

She shook her head and pulled away. Hefting her fanny pack in one hand, she looked at him. "What do we do with this?"

"You finally ready to admit it's not safe at your house?"

"I admitted that to myself a while ago," she said with a frown. "That would be why I'm wearing it twenty-four seven."

"Hmm." Dante held out his hand, and she gave him the pack. He slid open the zipper and pulled out the rift device. "I'll put this in my gun safe. You keep the schematics—I think it's a good idea that we keep them separate."

"That way if someone gets one of these, we still have the other one. Hopefully." She took the bag from him and fitted it around her waist. "And you're confident Lily won't be in any danger?"

"Your brother doesn't know I have it, right? Hopefully he has no idea what it is." He put the device in the gun safe and made sure it was secure. "I think Lily will be fine." He opened the top drawer of his dresser and pulled out a thin, flat cell phone. He held it out to her.

"What's this?" she asked, taking it from his hand.

"It's an old cell phone I haven't gotten around to recycling. Put that in your little pack there," he answered, motioning toward her back. "It might fool someone since it's the same size and shape as the device."

"Good thinking." She put the phone inside her fanny pack.

He took her hand and walked with her outside to her car, giving her a searing kiss before letting her go. "Call me when you get a minute," he whispered against her lips.

"You got it." Tori glanced toward the house and then back at him. "Please tell Lily I said good-bye, and thank her again for a lovely dinner."

He nodded. "Drive safe."

"I will." She went on tiptoe and pressed a kiss against the corner of his mouth. "God, you are too tempting," she said as she held those sexy lips against her own. Taking a breath, she whispered, "I'll talk to you later." She got in the car and started the engine.

As she made her way down the drive, she saw Dante lift a hand in farewell before he headed toward the stable.

Pulling into her driveway ten minutes later, she let herself into the house and listened for Rand. When she didn't hear anything, Tori headed down the hallway, pausing at his bedroom, before rapping softly on the door. When there was no response, she pushed it open, but he wasn't there. She glanced at his bedside clock. It was just before 7:00 A.M.

Where the hell was he?

It wasn't like he had to get her permission to stay out all night but she couldn't help but worry about him. She'd fallen asleep at Dante's and hadn't called to let him know she wouldn't be home. Checking her phone and finding no messages, he apparently hadn't been too worried about her well-being, which saddened her.

She went back into the kitchen and tamed her inner wolf with a couple handfuls of raw hamburger meat. Just as she was rinsing the last bite down with a glass of water, her cell rang. She set the glass on the counter and put the phone to her ear. "Hello?"

"Good morning, Tori." Tobias's voice came clear and strong through the receiver. "I hope I didn't wake you."

"Uh, no. I've been up awhile," she said. But it couldn't be good that he was calling her so early in the morning. "What's going on?"

"I was wondering if you could swing by the house for a few minutes. I'd like to get an update."

"I need to change clothes first, but I should be able to be there in about fifteen minutes."

"See you then." He ended the call.

Tori went into her bedroom and tossed her phone on the bed. She took off her clothes and redressed, this time in a T-shirt and jeans. She fastened the fanny pack around her waist and shrugged into a denim-colored blouse, leaving it hanging open like a jacket. She slipped her phone into the back pocket of her jeans. After she put on her shoes and strapped on her gun, she stopped in the kitchen to jot down a quick note for her brother. Using a Snoopy magnet, she stuck the note to the fridge, then headed out to her car again.

Tobias opened his front door before she even pulled her car to a stop. As she approached, he put a finger to his lips. "Let's try and keep it down, all right? Nix is still asleep."

"No, I'm not." Nix appeared at his side, complete with rumpled penguin pajamas and bed head. Her eyes were bloodshot and a hint of fangs peeped over her bottom lip. "Hey, Tori."

"Hey." Tori went into the house and followed Tobias and Nix into the kitchen.

"Can I pour you some coffee?" Nix asked as she reached for the pot.

"No, thanks." Tori watched as the other woman poured herself a cup. "Um, you're still drinking coffee?" Tori asked.

"I am half demon." Nix shrugged. "I like coffee."

Tori gave a nod.

"Can I get you some breakfast?" Tobias asked. "Since I got you out here so early?"

"I already had breakfast, thanks." She glanced at the two vampires standing in front of her. "But, uh, if you need to..."

Tobias shook his head. "I already fed."

"I haven't," Nix muttered.

Her gaze fixed on Tori so long that Tori started to get a little anxious. Perhaps Nix was wondering if a little were-wolf would go down smooth and hot this morning.

"Oh, stop looking so nervous," Nix said. "I don't eat friends."

"I wouldn't let her, anyway." Tobias arched a brow at his wife.

"Like you could stop me if I really wanted to go after her." She paused and then thrust out her lower lip. "Never mind. You could wipe the floor with me with just your pinkie."

Tori laughed. When they both looked at her, she said,

"I just remembered a bumper sticker I saw a few weeks ago. 'Friends don't let friends eat friends.'" When neither of them smiled, she muttered, "I guess you had to be there."

At that Nix grinned. She started to say something and then stopped, lifting her face and sniffing. "What's that smell..." More sniffs. Her gaze shot to Tori. "You were with Dante last night. Or this morning." A sly look crossed her face. "Maybe both?"

Tori only stared at her.

"I recognize the scent of his shower gel."

Tobias scowled.

Nix patted him on the shoulder. "I recognize the *scent*, fang boy. That's all."

"Let's go in the living room," Tobias said. When they were all seated, he and Nix on the plump sofa and Tori in an armchair across from them, he crossed his legs and looked at Tori. "So, where are we with the rift device?"

She told him that she and Dante had decided the device would be safer locked up at his place, and that she had the schematics. She also filled him in on their suspicions. "On its own, this is used for communications through an artificially created rift. An infinitesimal tear between the two dimensions, one big enough for radio waves to travel through. Dante thinks, and I agree, that this thing could be built on a larger scale." She looked from Tobias to Nix. "That would be bad."

Nix frowned. "I'm not a radio expert or a computer geek, so you'll need to explain the bad."

"The rift that opens with the comet either could be made larger or could be held open longer than normal." A thought struck her cold. "Maybe..."

After a few seconds Tobias said, "You do realize you didn't finish that sentence out loud?"

"If on a small scale, the device can form a tear between the dimensions without a comet in sight, what if on a larger scale..." She couldn't finish the thought.

Nix had no such problem. "A larger device could open a rift all on its own." Her eyes were wide. "This is worse than I thought."

Tobias drummed his fingers on his knee. "I've been asking around, discreetly, trying to find out who on the council is aware of the device. So far I haven't had any luck." His stormy gaze met Tori's. "We need to find Natchook and put a stop to this."

Her heart thumped. "Natchook? Why?"

Tobias studied her a few moments. "I didn't tell you this because..." He shrugged. "Natchook is the one I took the device from, after he tried to kill Nix."

Her heart thumped again, this time with guilt.

"What was that?" Nix leaned forward.

Tori lifted her brows and tried to act nonchalantly. "What was what?"

"Your pupils dilated and the blood flow to your face increased momentarily." Her lips curved downward. "What are you feeling guilty about?"

Tori grinned. "Jeez, turn a woman into a vampire and she gets crazy skills." When neither vampire laughed, Tori sobered. Damn it. She knew eventually she'd have to come clean about this, but she'd wanted to do it when she brought Stefan in. She didn't want it to happen like this, making it seem like she'd been harboring him.

She heaved a sigh. "I've seen Natchook."

Tobias went very still. Nix hopped to her feet with a "What!"

There was no easy way to lead into this. "He's going by the name Stefan Liuz." As Tobias's face began to darken, his pupils expanding to obliterate the gray of his irises, she hastened to add, "I've only seen him once, I swear. At the Devil's Domain about a week ago. I wanted to be the one to bring him in instead of letting you hunt him down." She spread her hands in a silent plea for understanding. "I didn't want you to kill him."

"Do I have to remind you that he murdered the leader of my planet?" Tobias rose to his feet, a terrible stillness about him that only a vampire could have. "Judgment was pronounced. A verdict was rendered."

"But we all got a second chance after the rift. All of us. Doesn't he deserve that, too?"

Tobias didn't answer her.

Nix put her hands on her hips. "I'm confused. How is it that you're a werewolf but your cousin is a vampire?"

"Parents from different planets." Tobias said.

Tori nodded. God, she felt like a crumb right now, seeing the disapproving and disappointed looks on her friends' faces. "Apparently his mother's genes were stronger than his father's."

"How do I find him?" Tobias leveled a harsh glare on her.

"I don't know. Really, I don't. He said he'd be in touch with me, and I haven't heard from him since then." She stood. "Tobias, please understand. He's family. I've been alone for so long, it seemed like a miracle that my brother and cousin came back into my life."

"Hold on a second." Tobias's gaze hardened even further. "Your brother is in town? He didn't come to the meeting."

"I know. I've already talked to him about that. He was supposed to and...blew it off. I'll get him to the next one." She swallowed. "I wasn't hiding him. Or Stefan. I just wanted my cousin to get a fair hearing for his crimes. I didn't know he was behind the rift device." She stared at Nix. "I didn't know he was the one who tried to kill you. I swear."

Nix shook her head and crossed her arms, turning to stride to the window and look outside.

Finally, Tobias blew out a breath. "Okay. I can't say I'm happy about this, but I understand." He glanced at his wife, and Tori knew he was thinking about how alone he'd been before he and Nix had gotten back together. His stern eyes returned to Tori. "If he contacts you, call me immediately. *Immediately*," he ordered.

She pressed her lips together and nodded. "I will." She inhaled slowly. "Is there any way you can..." She trailed off at the unforgiving look on his face. "Never mind. I'm sorry," she said.

After a couple of seconds, Tobias rubbed the back of his neck. "Forget about it. Just let me know when you hear from him."

She could tell he was still angry, but there wasn't a lot he could do. Stefan hadn't reached out to her since that first chance meeting, and she didn't have his contact info. When she drove away a few minutes later, she'd never felt more helpless in her entire life.

It was moments like this that made her wonder why she did what she did. If she wasn't a council liaison it wouldn't have been such a big deal that her cousin was

Natchook. It wouldn't be such an enormous thing to have a brother who might be the rogue werewolf. All she'd ever wanted was family. Why did she have to get saddled with the Munsters?

Chapter Seventeen

So none of the combatants from the grocery store are our rogue up in quad four?" Captain Scott perched one buttock on the edge of Dante's desk and folded his arms over his chest.

Dante shook his head. "The council liaisons have conducted the interviews with the vamps and werewolves involved, and they're satisfied with their alibis for the other nights in question." He picked up a folder that had the completed report and handed it to his boss. "You can read it for yourself if you'd like."

Scott thumbed through it, the scowl on his face deepening. After a few seconds he tossed the file back onto Dante's desk. "Do you believe 'em?"

Dante rocked back in his chair. "Believe who?"

"The liaisons."

"Of course." Dante knew Tori was truthful and wouldn't go along with any kind of cover-up. "Why would they lie?"

Scott's brows beetled. "I can't believe one of my best detectives would be that naïve. People lie all the time, MacMillan, sometimes for no reason at all."

Dante shook his head. "I know people lie. I'm just not

sure what they'd gain in this particular case. They don't want rogues runnin' around attacking people any more than we do."

"Are you sure about that?" Scott leaned forward, resting his forearm on his thigh. "The more of them there are, the more power they have."

Dante couldn't tell his captain about the rift device, and the very real threat that many more preternaturals might be joining them at the next Influx in December than anticipated. As if that wasn't enough to deal with, there was still someone turning people.

Scott's brows crinkled. "Hell, we don't know for sure how many EDs are on this planet, do we? Not every ED reports in with their regional council. There could be twice as many as we think. Hell, they could already outnumber us."

"It's impossible to tell for certain," Dante murmured. He wasn't thrilled with the idea of being at the bottom of the food chain on a planet full of vampires, shapeshifters, and other creatures that go bump in the night. The reality was they didn't know how many prets lived on Earth. Hell, they didn't even know exactly how many were in Scottsdale, let alone the entire planet.

"That's why I'm supporting Senator Martin's Preternatural Registration Act." Scott shook his head. "I ain't turning into a minority without a fight."

Dante brought his chair up straight. Humans had been living with preternaturals for a very long time; they just hadn't known until it became common knowledge. "You'd support legislation that would require prets to register with their local government and be fitted with a microchip?"

"It would allow them to be identified as an ED and list what type they are. *And* it could keep pertinent medical information as well," he said, as if that made the whole idea acceptable. "Maybe someday..." His voice lowered. "That microchip might also be a GPS. Hell, we do it with dogs."

Dante shook his head. "People will never go for that." *He'd* never support something like that. It would be like accepting that prets were no more than animals. And he knew for damn sure that Tori was much more than a wolf.

"Why not?"

"If we start putting GPS and RFID chips inside prets, how long will it be before someone starts thinking it'd be a good thing to do with humans?" He leaned to one side, resting his forearm on the desk. "That's why California and a couple other states passed laws prohibiting the forced implant of microchips into humans."

"Exactly." Scott pointed a finger for emphasis. "I don't have a problem about not allowing it for humans. But we're not talking about humans, are we? We're talking about EDs."

"Sounds like Nazism all over again to me." Dante crossed one leg over the other. "As long as you're not preternatural, you have nothing to worry about, right? Then someone decides that a certain race, religion, or political view is just as undesirable as prets. Where will it stop?"

"You're overthinking this, MacMillan. Humans have nothing to worry about if the PRA goes into law."

"And when the rift happens and you suddenly find that you've become a werewolf? What then?" Dante stared at his captain. "Will you willingly join the others and line up to be injected with a microchip?"

Scott stood up. "If it's the law, I will."

"That's my point." Dante leaned forward. "It shouldn't be the law, especially not here, in this country. We were founded on the ideal that all people are created equal."

Suddenly, one of the other detectives signaled Captain Scott. "Well, I guess that all depends on your definition of 'people,'" his boss said as he straightened. "We'll just have to agree to disagree on this one, MacMillan." He walked away to talk to the other man.

Dante huffed a sigh. This Preternatural Registration Act was a slippery slope. While he was uneasy about the uncertainty of the numbers of prets in their midst, he would never support forced microchipping.

He glanced at his watch. Almost six P.M. It had been a quiet day as far as new cases, which allowed him to get caught up on paperwork. He hadn't heard from Tori at all, aside from a quick text to say hello. He wondered if something was wrong. Perhaps he'd missed a cue that she was unhappy with how things had gone between them. Then he told himself to stop being such a girl about it. If she hadn't called, it probably meant she was busy and nothing more.

He knew that if he didn't hear from her soon, he was going to call her, damn it. He stood and grabbed his suit jacket from the back of the chair. "See ya tomorrow," he said to the detective at the desk next to his.

"Have a good one," the man responded without looking up from his keyboard.

Dante left the building, the humidity slapping him in the face. God, he'd be glad when summer was over and they went back to more temperate weather. He unlocked his truck and climbed behind the wheel. Once he got it started he flipped the air conditioning to high and buckled himself in. He was partway home when his phone rang. He reached into his back pocket and brought the cell to his ear. "MacMillan."

"It's Tori." She sounded a little tired but that voice...it was enough to make his body tighten with anticipation.

"Hey, sweetheart." He exited the 101 loop freeway and made a right onto Shea Boulevard. "How'd your day go?"

"Fine." She didn't sound so sure. "I'm actually still working, but I need to talk to you. Do you want to meet me at the Devil's Domain tonight for drinks?"

"Sure. Would you rather go someplace for dinner?" He flipped his right turn signal and drove onto his street. "Or you can come over to my place." Where there was plenty of food and a king-sized bed.

"I already ate something," she replied. "I really need to be around people tonight. Pick up some energy from the crowd. Is that okay?"

"Honey, whatever you need is fine by me." Dante could tell something was bothering her. "Tell me what's wrong."

Her sigh was heavy with dejection. "It's more than one thing, but to start...I don't know where Rand is. His bed wasn't slept in, and he hasn't returned any of my calls." She sighed again. "I'm worried about him."

Dante figured her douche bag of a brother could take care of himself, but he didn't like hearing the worry in Tori's voice. "He's probably out with friends."

"He's been here only a couple of weeks. He doesn't have any friends, at least none that he's talked about." She cleared her throat. "Anyway, we can talk about it tonight."

"All right. When do you want to meet?"

"Can you make it in an hour?"

He pulled into his driveway and in another few seconds stopped the truck in front of the house. An hour would give him time for a shower, a fresh change of clothes, and a bite to eat. "I'll see you around seven-thirty."

At seven-fifteen Dante pulled into the parking lot of the club, feeling human again after a cool shower and a quick hamburger and fries. Lily had tried to get him to eat a salad. Instead, he'd put some lettuce and a slice of tomato on his burger. His sister had not been impressed with his efforts at compromise.

He didn't see Tori's car when he shut off the ignition and climbed down from behind the wheel. He'd taken a few steps when he heard something off to his left. A *click-clack* that wasn't quite the heel of a shoe, but more like... He paused to listen. The sound stopped as well. He started walking again and the sound began once more.

In his years as a cop he'd learned to trust his gut, and right now it was telling him he was in trouble. He slowly reached beneath his jacket and thumbed the safety snap on his holster. He kept his breathing slow and even, and focused on his surroundings.

There were a dozen or so people at the front door waiting to get in. Another car pulled into the lot and parked a few aisles over from the one he was walking down. And the *click-clack* of what sounded like dog claws stayed with him.

Dante drew his gun slowly, keeping his hand under his jacket, and clicked off the safety. His only warning was a low, wet-sounding growl. He whirled, bringing his gun up. A snapping, snarling wolf, amber eyes glowing, gray fur standing upright at its scruff was already airborne. Dante went down beneath its weight, grunting when his body met the asphalt. He discharged his weapon. Once. Twice. Three times. Shouts and screams filled his ears. In the struggle, his hand got slammed to the pavement, and he lost his grip on the gun. It skittered out of reach. He fastened his fingers in the wolf's fur at its neck, trying to keep those snapping jaws from clamping down on his face.

The wolf—werewolf!—looked at him with intelligent hatred glowing in its eyes. The damned thing knew who he was. This wasn't a random attack. It shifted its weight, rocking back, dislodging Dante's grip for a moment.

And that moment was all it took.

Sharp teeth clamped onto Dante's shoulder, cutting through layers of clothing to bite through flesh. Pain slashed deep. Dante yelled and balled up his fists to hit the wolf on the side of its head. The animal merely growled and tightened its jaws.

Dante groaned. Agony radiated from his shoulder downward. Bright spots floated at the edge of his vision. God, he couldn't black out now. This thing would eat him alive. Literally.

He began losing feeling in his right arm. He brought up his left fist and punched the werewolf's nose. It yipped and growled, but didn't loosen its hold. Dante struck it again, as hard as he could. He felt the wolf's hold loosen, just a bit, and he struggled to get his feet between him and this furry bastard. Another punch to the werewolf's nose shoved its head back.

Dante curled his fingers into the fur and the wolf's neck again, doing his best to hold it at bay. Just when he thought he was going to lose that battle, the wolf was knocked off him by another, smaller wolf. Dante rolled to his feet, darted over, and grabbed up his gun in his left hand and trained it on the two snarling animals in front of him.

The smaller wolf, mostly black with smatterings of brown, showed its teeth as a low, vicious-sounding growl rolled up from its chest. The gray wolf tried to stand its ground, but after a few more seconds its tail drooped between its legs and it scampered away.

The remaining wolf lifted its muzzle and sniffed the air, then turned toward Dante. He broadened his stance and kept his weapon trained on the animal.

The wolf sat on its haunches and gave a low whine, its amber gaze trained on Dante. A slight swish of its tail got his mind working. "Tori?" he asked.

Dante holstered his weapon, glad the department had had the foresight to budget for silver bullets. He'd stop complaining about not having a car provided by the city as long as they kept spending money on silver ammunition. His right shoulder was on fire. He winced in pain and put a hand to the wound, feeling hot, sticky blood coat his palm. "You should probably get outta here," he told the wolf.

She nodded and disappeared between two cars.

"Hey, man, are you okay?" A couple of burly guys ran up to him. "We called the cops."

"I am a cop, but thanks. The more the merrier." Dante leaned one hip against the nearest car. It was that or fall on his face. Attacked by a werewolf and saved by another one. All in a night's work.

"You should come inside," one of the men said. "In case that thing comes back." He paused and then asked, "You sure you're all right, man? You're bleedin'."

"I'm good, thanks." Dante was confident that Tori had chased the other wolf off, and he also needed to make sure the scene was preserved. He'd get medical help later. There was nothing that could be done for him now. If the werewolf had released any of its essence into Dante's bloodstream, Dante was looking at spending these final few hours as a human. He pulled his ID from his back pocket and showed it to them. "I need to make sure nothing gets disturbed." He looked at the men. "Would you guys be willing to stand up at that end and keep people from coming this way until the police get here?"

"Glad to do it." They walked off, talking animatedly, their voices excited at what they'd witnessed.

Dante changed position to park his rear on the hood of the car. In another minute or so he heard Tori call his name.

"Are you all right?" she asked, heading his way. She was dressed in a filmy blue dress that seemed to float around her calves as she hurried toward him. Her nostrils flared and she hurried her pace. "You're bleeding!"

"I'm fine." He looked a little closer. Seeing the sway of her breasts, he realized she didn't have a bra on.

She must have seen where his gaze went, because she muttered, "I didn't have time to put all my clothes back on."

In just a few seconds she stood beside him and placed a hand against his cheek. "My God. When I saw him on top of you..." Her indrawn breath was shaky. "He could have killed you."

Tori drew another trembling breath and gently pulled Dante's shirt and jacket away from his shoulder. The wound wasn't as bad as it could have been; it had already stopped bleeding. But his flesh was mangled and would need stitches.

There were all kinds of scents here: fear and aggression, relief and dismay, the coppery tang of blood. And Rand, of course. Her brother's smell was all over Dante.

Her brother had attacked her lover. Why would he do that? He'd seemed to come to terms with her relationship, so why attack Dante? And why now?

She took Dante's hands in hers and lifted them, turning them over and seeing a raw scrape on the back of his left hand. "You'll need to get checked out," she murmured, looking at small bits of dirt and asphalt in the wound. "Dante..." She stared into his eyes, unsure of how to tell him her brother was his attacker.

He squeezed her fingers. "I'm all right, honey." Leaning down, he placed a soft kiss on her lips, a caress that only made her want more. "I'm sorry about this. I know you needed to talk."

He'd nearly been mauled by her brother and he was apologizing? She couldn't stand it. "Dante, I have to tell you..."

A council crime scene van pulled into the parking lot along with two police cars and an unmarked unit. The plainclothes detective got out of the vehicle and leaned his arm on the upper edge of the door. "Hey, MacMillan, how'd you get here so fast?"

"He's the victim, man." A guy standing at the end of the row of cars spoke up.

The detective's brows rose. "Is that a fact?" He looked at Dante. "You gonna start goin' furry on us?"

"No." Dante scowled.

Tori didn't blame him. His co-worker looked like he was about to crack up laughing. It wouldn't be so funny if it had been his ass under the snapping jaws of a werewolf. And it was entirely possible he *could* turn. Though she'd be surprised if Rand had wanted to turn Dante into a werewolf. No, she was pretty sure he meant to kill him.

The uniformed officers joined the detective, standing with hands on their guns like they expected Dante to shift into a werewolf at any minute.

"I'm not gonna go furry," Dante said.

"Good…that's good." The detective looked at the uniformed officers. "Call for an ambulance and collect witness statements, starting with those two." He motioned to the two men at the end of the row.

The officers moved off. The detective waved toward the crime scene technicians. "It's all yours, boys."

Dante sighed and gingerly rotated his shoulder, stopping with a wince. "It looks like the rogue has moved his act to our quadrant. This is his second attack."

She was all too aware of that, and the fact that her brother had gone from turning people to killing them…eating them. What the hell had gone wrong? She'd have to tell the council that he'd attacked Dante. That would point them toward him as the rogue as well, but it couldn't be helped. She'd given him the benefit of the doubt, and that was going to come back and bite her in the ass. "It could have been another werewolf," she offered somewhat lamely.

He shot her a look full of disbelief. "Now that'd be a coincidence, wouldn't it? We have two rogue werewolves?"

He sounded like Ash. She drew in a deep breath and slowly exhaled. "No, you're right, of course. Dante—"

"Excuse me." One of the criminalists stopped beside Dante. "Detective MacMillan, how many times did you discharge your weapon?"

"Three times."

The tech nodded. "That's how many shell casings I've got." He looked around the scene. "The werewolf came at you from where?"

Dante pointed to his left. "I'm not sure which set of cars it came between. I just know that when I turned it was already airborne."

"All right. We'll figure it out." His face creased in a smile. "The good news about this is that the bastard didn't have a chance to do his usual cleanup." He looked at Tori. "We've got 'im."

Oh, God. Oh, God!

"All right, I think Detective Andrews wants your statement." The criminalist moved back toward the area where the shell casings were and began taking pictures.

"Tori, if you don't want to stick around, you don't have to." Dante cupped her cheek. "This might take a while."

"No, I want to." She walked with him to the detective.

As soon as they reached him, Dante's phone rang. He pulled it out and looked at the display. "It's Lily," he said and answered it. "Lily? What's up?"

Whatever she said caused him to stiffen, his face going hard and determined. "Lock yourself in the bedroom. I'll be there in ten minutes." He looked at Detective Andrews. "Call for backup and send them to my house. Someone's trying to break in, and my sister's home alone."

Chapter Eighteen

Dante headed toward his truck, Tori right beside him. The drive to his house was accomplished in tense silence, mostly because of his erratic driving. He cut corners, jumped over the curbs, and ran red lights. He had his lights flashing and the siren wailing, which helped move traffic out of the way. He was trying to be so strong yet she knew he was in pain when she saw him wince, particularly anytime he lifted his right shoulder. She bit her tongue, trying to curb her desire to tell him he needed to be seen by a doctor, because she knew what his answer would be. What *her* answer would be. Not until they knew Lily was safe.

With his mind on his sister, Tori didn't think now was the time to tell him that her brother was the one who'd attacked him. She'd wait until they checked on Lily and Dante had his wound seen to, then she'd confess.

And probably lose him. That thought drove her heart to her throat, but he deserved to hear the truth from her before finding out from someone else. As soon as they safeguarded Lily, Tori would go to council headquarters and make her report. If she was lucky she'd only lose her job. She hadn't committed a fatal mistake, but she could very well be spending some time locked in silver. Now she was glad Barry hadn't taken her up on her offer, since she might be right where he was soon.

Dante roared the truck up his driveway and brought it to an abrupt stop in front of the house. He slammed it into park before it had completely stopped, making the heavy vehicle shudder back and forth. Leaving the keys in the ignition, he was out of the thing while it still rocked.

Tori followed him. She could hear sirens in the distance and knew that backup was close, but...Damn. The front door was ajar. They couldn't wait.

She went inside with Dante, who'd drawn his weapon. She drew in a breath and filtered through the various aromas. The strongest one was that of her brother. His scent was prevalent because his blood was on the scene—she could detect that bittersweet coppery tinge in the air.

Oh. Dear. God. What the hell had he done?

As they made their way toward the bedrooms, Tori kept an ear out for any unusual sounds, but the only thing she heard from inside were halting moans coming from the bedroom on the right. The door was slightly ajar. "Dante," she whispered. When he looked at her, she tipped her chin toward the room.

His jaw firmed, he eased the door open with his foot and entered. After a few seconds, he holstered his Glock and knelt beside his sister. "Hey, there," he whispered, stroking her hair away from the bruises covering her face. Her left eye was swollen shut and her bottom lip was split.

Tori remained in the doorway. Rand's scent was overwhelming, telling her that this was where the attack took place. "Give me your phone," she said quietly. "I left mine in my car." When he handed her his cell, she dialed 911 and requested an ambulance. After finishing the call, she stayed put so she wouldn't disturb the scene. She was going to catch hell as it was when it became known that her brother was the one responsible for the attacks. She didn't want to also be accused of contaminating a crime scene, either deliberately or through thoughtless action.

And what about Dante? She wanted to comfort him while he in turn cared for his sister. But with guilt weighing her down, she just...couldn't.

She looked at Lily, lying still on the floor, struggling to stay conscious. Dante continued to talk to her, trying to keep her focused on him. Blood streaked her bare legs, and Tori could see at least two bite marks high on the outside of Lily's upper-right thigh. Another bite had left a ragged, bloody wound on her left shoulder. Her white tank top was splotched with red, and the amount of blood at her midsection made Tori think Rand had also bitten her stomach. Had he been trying to kill her, torturing her before he made the fatal bite at her throat? Or had she and Dante interrupted him before he could start...eating?

Dante put his fingers on Lily's wrist. "Her pulse is steady, thank God."

"That's good." Tori took a couple of steps toward the bed and grabbed the comforter. "Here, put this over her. She's going into shock."

He spread the cover over his sister. "She's not gonna be happy there's blood all over her bedspread. It'll be ruined."

"Small price to pay." Tori clenched her fists as her anger at her brother grew. How dare he come to Lily's home, bringing all this viciousness with him? Not only had he ruined complete strangers' lives and probably cost Tori her job, but he'd attacked an innocent like Dante's sister. Lily's life would never be the same.

When Tori told him it was her brother behind the attacks, Dante would be furious, and rightly so. Most likely he'd wish he'd never met her. Never went to bed with her.

"Tori." Dante pointed to his sister's vanity. "Look at her perfume and makeup."

Tori glanced at where he indicated. Two bottles of perfume, a bottle of foundation, a tube of mascara, and two containers of eye shadow were lined up in a row. Six items perfectly aligned.

"Lily's neat," Dante said, "but she's not that neat." He stared at Tori. "This doesn't make sense. Why would the rogue start attacking people in their homes? All of his attacks up to now have been in public." He looked down at his sister. "Of all people, why would he come after my sister?"

Tori had to tell him. "Dante…" She closed her eyes briefly. How was she supposed to tell the man she loved that her brother, whom she also loved, had tried to murder his sister?

"What is it?" He lightly ran his hand over the top of Lily's head, then looked past Tori. "Damn it! Where's that goddamned ambulance?"

A few seconds later she could tell the cops had arrived. It was too soon for the ambulance. "I'll go get them," she said. She went out to the front yard, her thoughts roiling, trying to figure out how to confess to Dante. Two police cars had pulled in behind Dante's truck.

She pulled her badge from the small pocket in the side of her dress. As the cops got out of their vehicles and approached her, she held up her ID. "The scene's secure," she told them, giving both men time to inspect her credentials before she put it away. "The suspect's long gone. We'll need to get CSSU out here, though. Call them."

"Yes, ma'am," one of the officers said and bent his head to the radio mounted at his shoulder.

Tori pulled out Dante's cell phone and dialed the council dispatch. When the call connected, she told the dispatcher, "We need to roll out crime scene specialists to Detective MacMillan's place. And call Ash. His rogue has attacked again."

"Damn." The werebear dispatcher blued the air with more robust swear words. "This scrub's giving us a bad rep."

"We already have a bad rep, Merle," Tori said dryly.

"Is MacMillan okay?" Merle asked. "He's all right for a human," he added as if to explain away his concern.

"He's been bitten. So was his sister." Guilt swarmed her. If she'd spoken up before about Rand's possible involvement, would Dante's sister have been spared this attack?

"Damn," Merle said again. "They gonna turn?"

Tori sighed and pinched the bridge of her nose against a tension headache that was beginning to build. "I don't know. Dante's mobile and seems fine except for some pain from the bite. His sister's pulse is steady, and the wounds that I could see have already stopped bleeding."

"Well, guess we'll know within a few hours."

If they didn't turn, Dante would be fine, but Lily would maybe have to face another battle with cancer. Tori didn't know the statistics, but she'd known a few women whose breast cancer had recurred. And it had been fatal.

"I've asked the cops to have CSSU come, too," she told Merle. "But we really should have our people on scene."

"Gotcha. I'll roll them out as soon as I hang up."

"Thanks." Tori ended the call. She was just turning to go back into the house when she heard more sirens. A minute later an ambulance rolled to a stop behind the cop cars. A man and a woman hopped out of the ambulance, grabbing their medical kits and a gurney. Tori motioned to the two and said, "This way. We have a human with multiple werewolf bites to her left leg, right shoulder, and I think her midsection." As they headed back to the bedroom, she continued, "She's fading in and out of consciousness, but her pulse is steady."

The medics entered the bedroom and Tori stopped in the doorway again. Dante moved out of the way and stood by while they knelt beside Lily. The woman pulled the comforter off her so they could assess her condition and then wrapped a blood pressure cuff around her upper left arm.

The other EMT lifted Lily's top to expose her midriff. "This doesn't look too bad," he said. "Not as bad as some I've seen." He looked at Dante, his gaze focused on his shoulder. "We should get you to the hospital, too."

Dante nodded. "You better believe I'm coming with you."

"Of course, sir." The medics carefully lifted Lily onto the gurney, before wheeling it out of the house.

Tori fell into step beside Dante. "I'll meet you at the hospital."

He nodded and climbed into the ambulance after his sister. All his attention was focused on her.

Tori watched the vehicle drive off and then turned to the cops on scene. "Secure the house and wait for the crime scene techs. I'll make sure a detective gets out here to run the investigation."

They nodded.

She hurried to Dante's truck and drove away, her thoughts whirling. One thought was prevalent—she had to tell Dante that her brother was the one who'd attacked him and Lily.

She broke all sorts of laws getting to the hospital in time to see them unload Lily from the back of the ambulance. Tori sprinted to the emergency entrance and followed them inside.

The medical personnel took his sister into an examining room. Another nurse asked Dante to follow her. Before he could go, Tori grabbed his hand. There wasn't ever going to be a good time to tell him what she had to, so here went nothing.

"Dante, I have to tell you something," she said, her voice soft. "There's no easy way to say it." She took a deep breath and in a rush blurted, "My brother's the rogue. He attacked you and Lily."

Dante twisted to look at her. "What?"

"I think—I *know*—Rand's the rogue. He did that." She gestured toward his shoulder and then the room his sister was in.

Dante's mouth formed a grim line. "You set me up?"

"What!" Shocked surprise made her stomach knot. How in the hell had he made that leap? Oh...she'd been the one to ask him to meet her there. "No! Of course not. I would never—"

"Never what? Never hide a secret about your family?"

Now was not the time to tell him about Stefan, she could see. "I'm sorry. It's just...I smelled him in the parking lot and as soon as I entered the house. Then the way Lily's makeup was arranged, and the six bits of pebbles or debris left at all the other scenes made me think of him. He has OCD, and he's fixated on the number six." As Dante continued to stare at her, astonishment and growing rage on his face, she said, "I didn't want to believe it, so I told myself I was making something out of nothing. I didn't think Rand would ever do something like this. He has. He did."

"You can't know for sure that it's your brother." That was the cop in him talking, not the brother. The cop that was trained to never jump to conclusions, even if there was a multitude of supporting evidence. But he didn't know what she knew.

"I do." She pressed her trembling lips together. "Dante, I could smell him. He's all over your house." She glanced at his sister. "All over Lily." She met his eyes again. "I smelled him on you at the club. He did this. I am so sorry."

His gaze, fixed on Tori, filled with growing horror and anger. "For God's sake, why the hell didn't you say somethin' to me before now? Before he attacked my sister! Attacked me!" A look of disgust entered his eyes. "Why didn't you do your damned job?"

"He's my brother! Sometimes you have to look out for family."

He shook his head. "Family isn't always a matter of blood, you know."

"I'm sorry," she said again. She knew it was her fault his sister was in the hospital. If she'd spoken up about her suspicions, this probably could have been averted. "Try to understand," she pleaded quietly.

He shook his head. "Excuse me, while I look out for *my* family." He walked away from her to stare down the hallway, his gaze hard, mouth grim. Then he put his attention on his sister. As the nurse touched his arm, urging him to an exam room of his own, he moved farther away and Tori knew she'd lost him.

With a sigh, she got to her feet and walked out of the hospital. She had to head to council headquarters and confess her sins. She tried like hell to ignore the fact that she might have lost the one man she truly loved.

Dante's exam didn't take long. A phlebotomist drew some blood and a doctor patched him up, telling him the test results would be done in a few hours and they'd know whether or not he would turn. Dante barely listened. Whatever happened to him was immaterial. Lily was the important one.

He had to sit in the waiting room while the doctors stabilized her and got her to a private room. Dante held her hand while she drifted in and out of sleep. Now that his initial worry for her had lessened, he had time to think about what all of this meant for him.

He'd been bitten by a werewolf, meaning he could become one. Did he want to be a werewolf? That was the sixty-four thousand dollar question.

Part of him said no. Not just no, but Hell, no! Yet another part of him, the part that understood his sister would probably turn, the part that knew he was in love with one, whispered it might not be such a bad thing.

Tori was immortal. He was not. If he stayed human, at

best they had thirty or forty years together. Those years would see him aging, getting sick, or fighting off disease while she would stay as young and vibrant as she was today. He didn't want that for her, to be in a relationship with a doddering old man.

He gave a low snort. They didn't have a future, no matter what his feelings were. Or had been. She'd withheld information that resulted in Lily lying in this hospital bed. Dante would keep his humanity if he had a choice, thank you very much.

Staring at his sister's bruised face, he whispered, "You're gonna be all right, honey."

She blinked sleepily, her head lolling against the pillow. "Dante?"

"I'm right here." He gently squeezed her fingers. "Right here." He wouldn't tell her about his own attack. She needed to focus on getting better, not expend energy worrying about him.

She licked her lips. "Not...Tori's fault."

"Shh." He stroked his thumb over her fragile wrist. "Don't try to talk."

"This..." She swallowed. "Important."

He knew how stubborn she was. It was one of the things that had gotten her through the last several months. "Okay. What is it?"

"Don't blame Tori." Her eyes pleaded with him. "She was protecting...her brother."

"At your expense." Dante couldn't—*wouldn't*—forgive that.

Lily shook her head. "No. She didn't know...he would...come after me."

"Still—"

"Dante, no." She struggled to sit upright.

He put his hands on her shoulders and pushed her gently back down. "Lily, don't."

She collapsed onto the bed with a sigh. "You love her. She loves you." She took a deep breath. "If you suspected me of a crime, would you tell someone as soon as you suspected?" Her voice was stronger now, steady. "Or would you wait until you knew for sure?"

"I wouldn't wait if I thought people's lives would be in danger." He stared at his hand holding hers. "She should have told me."

"And that's the problem, isn't it?" His sister sent him an arch look.

"What is?"

"That she didn't tell *you*."

"We're partners," Dante said in defense. "Colleagues." That was a more accurate term than "partner."

"You're more than that and you know it." Lily closed her eyes. "Don't let this come between you, Dante. I'm all right."

He studied her, his heart finally beginning to relax from the galloping pace it had been keeping since he'd found her lying on the floor of her bedroom. "I can see that."

Her eyes opened. "I feel a little strange."

He frowned. "Is something wrong? Should I call a nurse?"

"N-no," Lily said slowly. "But I feel different." Wonder filled her voice. "I feel strong. Really strong. For the first time in a long time."

Dante tightened his hand around hers. He knew what this meant. His sister was now a werewolf.

His jaw tightened. Damn Tori and damn her brother. It was a good thing she didn't have any other family members here. Who knew what kind of havoc they'd wreak?

And what did this mean for him and her? Was there even a him and her? He knew he loved her, but he wasn't sure what kind of future they could have together after this.

Two hours later the doctor who'd patched him up came into Lily's room. In deference to the sleeping woman, he whispered, "We have the results of your test. All negative." He gave an encouraging smile. "You won't turn into a werewolf."

Dante murmured his thanks and stared with unseeing eyes at the hospital bed. This was what he'd wanted, wasn't it? To remain human? But now, hearing it stated in definitive terms, his heart sank.

His only family in this world—his sister and his lover—would live forever. All too soon he'd be just a blip on their memories.

Chapter Nineteen

Tori paced the hallway outside the main council chamber. When she'd called Tobias and told him about her brother, he'd ordered her to report in immediately. To say he hadn't been pleased would have been a massive understatement. She'd arrived at the council building almost three hours ago and had been kept waiting. That was never a good sign.

She figured they were trying to determine what to do with her. She heaved a sigh. She'd be silvered for sure, she knew it. And it was no less than she deserved. She'd really mucked this one up.

Finally, the door swung open and one of the guards, a werecat named Jeff, came out. "They'll see you now," he said. He was blond haired and had a husky build, not at all like most other cat shifters, who were lithe and sinewy.

As she walked forward she asked softly, "Who's in there?"

"Caladh, Tobias, and Vida." His voice sounded almost apologetic.

She blew out a breath. Caladh and Tobias she was fine with, but Vida Undset...Oh, boy. The werewolf membe of the council had come through the last rift in 1939, so she wasn't that old, but boy was she formidable.

Tori walked into the chamber, forcing herself to keep a confident stride even though she was quaking on the inside. She came to a halt a few feet from the large mahogany table behind which sat the three council members. She bowed her head and waited.

"This is most distressing, Victoria." Caladh's voice was low and rough with disappointment. "We had higher expectations of you."

She looked up. "I know, my lord."

"If you suspected your brother, you should have come forward immediately, not waited until people died. Until a police officer and his sister were attacked." Caladh shook his head. "Most distressing."

She looked at Tobias and then Vida. Both wore the same censure on their faces. "Do we know for certain if either of them have been turned?" she asked. It was killing Tori, that she could have prevented it by simply doing her job.

The three councilors looked at her in silence for several long moments, then Caladh said, "The young lady has been turned. Detective MacMillan has not."

Tori pressed her lips together to keep them from trembling. Two lives forever changed. Dante would never forgive her.

"When did you first suspect your brother of these crimes?" Vida asked. Her posture erect, the woman clasped her hands and rested them on top of the table.

Tori drew a bracing breath. "Not until Ash told me about items being arranged in rows of six. I couldn't believe that my brother would do something so...so heinous, and I talked myself out of it." She wet her dry lips. "I can only say that my love for my family clouded my judgment, and beg for the council's understanding."

"So this is why you did not tell Tobias about his nemesis being in town?" Vida's eyes fixed on Tori.

Tori glanced at Tobias, whose gaze remained steady on her. So Tobias had told them about her relationship to Stefan. She'd expected it, really, but somehow it was still a surprise to get it thrown back in her face.

"Even knowing that Tobias has a formal writ," Vida went on, "you delayed in telling him that Natchook is here."

"Yes." Tori clenched her fists to hide the trembling of her fingers. "Until Rand showed up two weeks ago, I had been alone in this world for almost a hundred and fifty years."

"We have all been alone here, Victoria." Caladh leaned back in his chair. "Tobias and I have both been here since 1793. We have no family here. In the last two hundred years we have made friends who became our family. Why could you not have done the same?"

"I did, but I also knew my brother was here. How could I not long to have him with me?" They had to understand. They had to.

Tobias folded his arms over his chest. His gaze held sympathy warring with chastisement. "And Stefan?"

This one she knew she was going to lose. "Many...most of the prets who come through the rift were criminals in the other dimension. It's just a few, relatively speaking, who were considered to be political dissidents or religious heretics. Everyone who comes through the rift is given a second chance. Crimes they committe prior to their Influx are forgiven." She spread her hands. "Why not Stefan's?"

Tobias stood and slapped one hand flat on the table. "Your cousin used the rift to escape justice. Had he not, he would have stood trial and been found guilty. And while other murders would have resulted in a rift sentence, the penalty for assassinating a political figure—especially the leader of an entire planet—was death." His nostrils flared. "Natchook . . . *Stefan* has been on borrowed time the moment he came through the rift. And it's up." He sat back down, no less intimidating. "Where. Is. He?"

"I don't know. I swear." When they all wore identical expressions of skepticism, she repeated, "I don't know."

"Phone number, then." This from Caladh.

She shook her head. "I didn't get it from him."

"Oh, come on." Vida's eyes narrowed. "You honestly expect us to believe that you saw a cousin you haven't seen since before your Influx and you didn't even get his phone number?"

Tori took a breath and held it for a few moments, trying to hold onto her cool. She knew how this looked. And she didn't like looking like an idiot, especially in front of her bosses. She exhaled through pursed lips and then said, "I saw him by accident for all of sixty seconds at the Devil's Domain. I barely had the chance to say hello before he ducked into the back rooms where I'm not allowed to go," she added as if they didn't know.

"Got hungry, did he?" Tobias asked.

Tori pressed her lips together. "I think, looking back on it, he saw Dante and didn't want to be recognized." She shot Tobias a look. There wasn't much else she could say without opening things up for questions that might lead to the rift device. And at this point, neither of them knew if Caladh or Vida were aware of it. She could only acknowledge that she was aware Stefan was the one who had attacked and turned Nix into a vampire, nothing more.

Tobias seemed to realize he was treading on quicksand, for he leaned back in his chair with a low grunt and kept quiet.

"Getting back to the most pressing matter at hand," Caladh said as he rested his forearms on the table. "Do you know where your brother is at least?"

"I don't." Tori knew she wasn't scoring any points here. "But I give you my word, if I find him I will bring him in." She couldn't cut him any more slack. Not now, not after he'd killed people. Not after he'd attacked Dante and Lily.

"I'm sure you understand why we don't trust your word." Vida's tone was as dry as cemetery dust. "You have failed us, Victoria. In no small way."

Tori glanced at the three councilors. The sadness in Caladh's eyes held her.

"Go home," he told her. "We will contact the rest of the council and determine the punishment fitting of such dereliction of duty." His voice softer, he said, "While I personally can understand your inaction, even your desire to believe the best of your brother, I cannot excuse the fact that because you did not speak up, lives have been forever altered. Lives have been lost." He looked over her shoulder at the security guard standing by the chamber doors. "Jeff, you and Conal go with her."

So they were placing Tori under house arrest, sending her home with a werecat and a fey warrior. It wasn't like she had even thought about running, but they were going to make sure she didn't.

Caladh turned a stern gaze on her. "If you hear from your brother..."

"I'll let you know."

"You'd better." This came from Vida.

They dismissed her, and she turned and walked out of the chamber with her head held as high as she could. She knew she'd screwed up, but what else could she have done? She didn't have concrete evidence that Rand had gone rogue. A hunch wasn't enough to turn in her only brother. As soon as she'd had definitive proof, she had come forward.

Only it had been too late to keep Lily from being hurt. Damn it. She should have said something sooner. Whatever punishment the council decided to lay on her, she deserved it.

"Hang on a minute," Jeff said. He went to the security desk, picked up the telephone receiver, and punched in a number. When it was picked up on the other end, he said, "You and I have guard duty." He listened for a moment, then muttered, "Tori Joseph." He glanced at her. "I'll explain it later. Just get up here. We need to go." He hung up the phone and walked back to her. "At least they didn't tell me to chain you up," he said softly, a slight smile tilting one side of his mouth.

Just then Vida came out of the chamber holding a silver bangle.

Tori drew in a breath and extended her arm. The werewolf councilor fastened the bangle around her wrist, using a small key to lock it in place. She pocketed the key and went back into the chamber.

"You were saying?" Tori asked, trying to ignore the slight discomfort she felt from the silver against her skin. At least it was no longer a full moon. She didn't want to go through that again.

Though she should prepare herself. That might be what the council decided was warranted.

"Sorry." Jeff appeared as uncomfortable with the situation as Tori was.

She heard the door to the basement open and looked to see Conal Riordan headed their way. The fey warrior was about six five or six, broad shouldered, lean hipped, with a loose stride that would put a cowboy to shame. He wore a gun strapped to his thigh. Dark hair brushed his shoulders, and green eyes held irritation as they fell on Tori. "I was winning," he muttered. "Aces over eights."

"That's the dead man's hand," Jeff said. "It's probably best we interrupted the poker game."

"Hey, just 'cause Wild Bill Hickok was shot in the back while holding that hand doesn't mean everyone who draws those cards is going to die." Con scowled at Jeff as he stopped beside them. "Are we ready?"

Tori sighed. She wasn't scoring points with anyone today. "Let's go, boys," she murmured. They exited the building and she stopped beside her Mini Cooper. "How do we want to do this?"

Con took one look at the vehicle and scowled. "You ride with her. I'll drive my car."

Yeah, she figured he'd have a hard time folding that big body into her Mini. Without a word, Jeff got in the passenger seat. Tori seated herself behind the wheel and started the car, waiting until she saw Con pull his cherry-red Camaro behind her. She pulled out and drove home, making sure not to lose Con at any traffic lights.

Once at home, she parked the Mini in the carport and headed inside, Jeff and Con right behind her. As soon as she unlocked the front door and pushed it open, she knew something was wrong. So did her bodyguards. Con immediately shoved her behind him. "Stay with her," he said.

Obviously not talking to her.

Rand was home—she could smell him. There was also another person's scent, one she hadn't smelled in over a week. Stefan. He'd been here, too.

She could also smell blood. Someone had been wounded. Rand? She put her weight on one foot and then the other, anxious to get inside to check on her brother.

In a few seconds, Con called out, "Tori, you should get back here."

She ran to her brother's bedroom and found him on the floor. Con was already on the phone talking to dispatch. She vaguely heard him order an ambulance and a security force.

Tori knelt beside Rand. His green eyes were glazed with pain. Blood stained the right side of his shirt. She unbuttoned it and carefully lifted the material away from him. A bullet wound between his fourth and fifth ribs still oozed blood. Now she knew which one of them had been hurt.

"Damned cop had silver bullets," Rand muttered from between clenched teeth. "Last shot caught me in the side." He gave a short laugh that ended in a moan. "That hurts. Bullet's still in me."

She looked up at Con.

"Ambulance should be here in a few minutes," he said.

Turning her gaze back to her brother, she asked, "You attacked Lily with a bullet in your side?" At the thought of Dante's sister lying on the floor, bleeding from several bites, anger flooded her anew. Rand was damned lucky he was hurt, or he'd have gotten it from her.

He gave a weak nod. "I thought if I shifted to human and back to wolf again it would push the bullet out, but I think it made things worse." He coughed and then groaned.

"Why, Rand? Why did you attack Dante? Even worse, why would you attack his sister?"

Rand's lips tightened. "The cop had it coming. He was taking you away from me. As for the girl…" He coughed, blood mixed with spittle coating his mouth. "She was in the way. I followed you that night, you know. When you went there for dinner and spent the night with him. I saw him put the device into his gun safe the next morning. I knew Stefan would be pleased if I were to return it to him." He looked highly satisfied with himself. "Plus, I wanted to make the cop suffer. He shot me."

"You attacked him!" Part of Tori wanted to shush him, keep him from talking about the rift device in front of the two guards, but the larger part of her didn't care. She needed answers, because she didn't understand his reasoning. Had he lost his grip on reality? "They're my friends, Rand. I can't believe you would…" She reached out and grabbed a jacket off the end of his bed and draped it over him. "I don't understand any of this. Why did you do it?"

"I never meant…I didn't want to betray you," Rand whispered. "That's why the other attacks happened outside of your jurisdiction. I didn't want to jeopardize your job."

"Oh, give me a freaking break." Tori was torn between being worried for him and just being plain mad. "Admit it. You didn't want me to catch on to what you were up to. Besides, the last attack where you killed someone took place in my quadrant."

"I lost control. I got a taste for flesh. For blood." He coughed and winced. "Stefan said..." He bit his lip and then met her eyes. "He said that I could prove my worth to those in the group who didn't have faith in me. He said I could join him. I could be one of his lieutenants if I turned people." He drew in a breath and then winced. "I needed something to believe. Someone to believe."

"Rand, there are all kinds of things you could have chosen to believe in, like honor, courage, and virtue, which mean more than money and power. That money and power mean nothing if you've sacrificed your integrity for them. And, maybe most important, that good *always* wins over evil. Always." She stared down at him. Lifting a hand, she stroked the hair at his temple. "Those are things worth believing in, aren't they?"

"Maybe." His breath rattled in his throat. "What if I needed more? I've never been strong like you. Independent, not caring what other people think of you. *I* care. I wanted to have someone, just one person, look at me and say, 'There goes a man who's made a difference.'"

"Instead, you've helped increase the tension between humanity and the rest of us. You've probably cost me my job." She held up her wrist to show him the silver wrapped around it. "And you hurt people I care about."

He didn't seem fazed by her accusation or by her current predicament. He ran his tongue over his dry lips. "But in the end the cop and his sister are fine, aren't they?

I mean, they didn't die. And you, you're good at a lot of things. You'll be able to get another job. Me, on the other hand…Stefan's been in touch with people in the other dimension. Additional holding cells are being built and criminals of all species are ready to be stripped of their bodies so they can start new lives here on Earth. There'll be even more of us."

"New lives? Or will they just keep doing what they've been doing, only in a new place?" She could hardly believe what she was hearing. How had all of this been going on under her nose and she'd had no clue?

"Stefan told me I would be a leader when the next Influx happened." His eyes held pleading. "There isn't a whole lot I'm good at. But making people like us…" His eyes took on the shine of fanaticism. "That was something I could do." Pride joined the madness. "And I was good at it, wasn't I? None of you had a clue who the rogue was." A slight smile curled his lips, before his eyes fluttered then closed, and he slumped in her arms.

Her heart stuttered, but then she saw his chest moving. She blew out a sigh of relief. Even though he'd done terrible things, she didn't want him to die, though that outcome would most likely come about once the council rendered their verdict. He was still her brother, and she loved him.

"We know who the rogue is now, don't we?" she whispered, fighting back tears. "So in the end you weren't good at that, either."

She sat with her unconscious brother, two burly bodyguards standing behind her, and waited for the ambulance.

Chapter Twenty

The next morning, Dante woke from a restless sleep with a crick in his neck from sitting in a chair at Lily's bedside. Seeing that she still slept, he rose as quietly as he could and stretched, biting back a groan as stiff muscles protested the movement. He stared at his sister. The bruises on her face were gone, the split lip healed. She looked as if nothing had happened.

Except she had been forever changed. And he, he would go on as before. Human, with a finite life span. The knowledge had eaten away at him ever since the doctor had confirmed Lily's transition just after midnight, though Dante and Lily had both known it before then. His sister had taken the news better than he had, and in the light of day, he had to admit it could have been worse.

She could be dead. At least now she'd be around a long, long time.

He used the bathroom and then washed his hands. He splashed cold water on his face and rinsed his mouth out. When he came out of the lavatory, Lily was awake. "Good mornin'," he said, sitting on the mattress beside her. "How're you feelin'?"

Her smile was more carefree than he'd seen it in a long

while. "I feel great." Her smile faded. "But you look like crap. Have you been here all night?"

"Thanks. And, yeah, I have." He took her hand in his. "I couldn't go home until I knew you were gonna be all right."

"I'm gonna be fine, Dante. I can feel it." She turned her head to stare out the window. "It's terrifying and wonderful at the same time." She looked at him, her eyes dark and wide. "It's a little creepy to be honest, but I know I'll be okay."

"Do you...feel different?" He couldn't contain his curiosity. Not too long ago he'd thought perhaps he'd be going through this same thing, after all.

She tilted her head to one side, considering, then her gaze met his again. "Everything looks brighter. Smells are crisper, and my sense of touch..." She turned her hand over to grip his. "It's almost like I can feel the ridges in your fingertips."

"That particular sense will fade soon."

Dante turned toward the voice from the doorway. It was Ash.

"You'll keep your enhanced sense of smell and vision, and wait until you eat something for the first time..." The werewolf liaison gave a brief smile. "Your sense of taste, well, you'll be amazed." He looked at Dante. "Can I talk to you for a minute? In private?"

"Sure." Dante glanced at Lily. With a squeeze of her fingers, he said, "I'll be right back."

"I'll be here," she said with a smile.

He went with Ash down to the end of the hallway. "What's up?" Dante asked.

"I want to talk to you about a couple of things." Ash

leaned one shoulder against the wall. "First off, how's your sister?"

Dante lifted one shoulder in a shrug. "Physically she's fine. The wounds are gone and she's in no pain. Emotionally, she seems to be adjusting surprisingly well."

"It happens that way sometimes. It'll hit her a little later and she'll have second thoughts." Ash held Dante's gaze. "We'll make sure she's all right, man. You can count on that."

"I know you will." Dante pushed aside the thought that the best person to help his sister was Tori. He'd have to figure out later where she fit into his life, if anywhere. Right now he was too angry with her.

"Okay, next thing." Ash took a breath and blew it out between pursed lips. "I realize you and I don't know each other all that well, and if I'm really stepping out of line, you let me know." His eyes met Dante's. "As you can imagine, Tori's in real trouble here."

"She should be." Anger that Dante had managed to bury beneath worry for his sister roared to the surface. "If she'd come forward about Randall, my sister wouldn't be in there." He pointed back toward Lily's room.

"Maybe." Ash bent one leg, crossing his ankles. "I understand why she didn't. Can't you? She had no proof, just an initial reaction to facts." He shook his head. "If the situation were reversed, would you have done it differently?"

"If I suspected that my sister might be out there killing people? Hell, yeah." Dante paused. First of all, he knew he would have dismissed any initial suspicions he might have had because he knew his sister. Not that she wasn't capable of murder—under the right circumstances, he firmly believed anyone was capable—but he didn't think she'd go around murdering random people.

Second, someone would have had to have produced some mighty strong evidence for him to have accepted what his gut was telling him and his heart was denying.

He pushed that all back and looked at Ash. "I'm having a hard time getting past the fact that Tori suspected her brother, didn't tell me, and now my sister's a freaking werewolf."

"You could look at it this way," Ash said. "Now you don't have to worry about her ever getting sick with some sort of disease."

As far as Dante was aware, Ash didn't know about Lily's bout with cancer, but he had a valid point. Dante looked down the hallway. On one level, he recognized that the attack had, in the long term, saved his sister's life.

That didn't change the fact that Tori had suspected her brother yet didn't say anything to anyone.

Could he have told on Lily? He didn't know. "It was a tough situation for Tori to be in," he finally responded.

"Yeah." Ash straightened away from the wall. "Look, ordinarily the quadrant liaison where the victim lives would handle this part, but since that's Tori and she's caught up in all of this, the council's asked me to debrief your sister."

Dante hooked his thumbs over his belt. "What's that entail?"

"Just asking her about what happened, getting details of the attack, and walking her through what her life is going to be like from now on." He rubbed a hand over his chin. "She'll need to come to several orientations, and her first full-moon shift will have to be supervised."

When Dante sent him a confused frown, Ash added, "The first full-moon shift is confusing and painful, and the hunger is…" He shook his head. "Left unsupervised, a new werewolf could cut a swath of carnage through town that would demand appropriate retribution." He pursed his lips. "Being a preternatural doesn't mean you can't be killed. It just takes a bit more to get the job done."

Dante nodded. "Let me talk to her for a minute."

"Sure thing." Ash paused, then said in a rough voice, "There's just one more thing."

"What?"

"Randall Langston was brought in around midnight. He's in a room the next floor up."

"In the secure wing." Dante clenched his jaw. The bastard who'd attacked his sister had been one floor up this whole time?

Ash nodded. "He came out of surgery about an hour ago. Seems someone plugged him with a silver bullet."

"Hmph. Only one hit?" Dante braced his palm against the wall. "Guess I need to get to the practice range."

"Yes, well." The werewolf liaison gave a small grin. "You don't have to worry about him anymore. He won't be able to get to your sister while she's in here. And in a few weeks he won't be anybody's problem anymore."

"What do you mean?"

"Preternatural justice is swift. And deadly. He turned people without authorization and killed innocents. His life is forfeit."

God. Poor Tori. Dante couldn't help but feel sorry for her. To find her brother only to lose him again, irrevocably this time… He shook his head.

"Yeah," Ash said softly. "It sucks to be Tori right about

now." His eyes were dark with compassion. "You might want to cut her some slack."

Dante looked at him but said nothing.

The werewolf liaison shrugged. He pointed toward the nurses' station. "I'll be over there, getting to know the ladies." He ambled off, hands in his front pockets.

Dante went back into his sister's room. She'd turned on the TV and looked away from the news program when he walked in. She peered over his shoulder. "Where's the other guy?"

"The other guy is Ash. Uh..." He racked his brain for the liaison's full name. "Bartholomew Asher, but he goes by Ash."

"That's good. He looks more like an Ash than a Bart." She tilted her head to glance through the doorway and then looked at Dante again. "Is he comin' back?" Interest brightened her eyes.

His werewolf sister had the hots for another werewolf. Dante knew it was going to take a while for him to wrap his head around this. He was just glad Lily seemed to be adjusting so quickly. "Ash is a liaison to the council. He's a—"

"Werewolf. Yeah, I could tell. There's a wild, kinda foresty smell to him."

"Foresty?"

"It's a word," she muttered.

"Not much of one." He grinned at her juvenile response of sticking her tongue out at him. "Mom always said that if you kept doing that your face would get stuck that way."

She poked her tongue out at him again.

He sobered and sat on the edge of the bed. "Ash is going to talk to you about what happened. You up for that?"

"A lot of it's hazy," she said. "I'm okay to answer his questions."

"He's also gonna talk to you about what things're gonna be like for you going forward." He met her eyes. "Are you up for *that*?"

She sat up. Dante grabbed the pillows and put them behind her back. "Thanks," she said. As he sat down, she grabbed his hand. "This is kinda scary, you know? Yet…exciting at the same time." Sudden tears swam in her eyes. "Dante, I won't ever get sick again. Ever."

He squeezed her fingers. "I know, honey. And for that I'm glad."

"But?" When he didn't say anything, she added, "There sounded like there was a 'but' with that."

"She kept the truth from me."

Lily frowned at him, knowing exactly what he was talking about. "She did not," his sister said. "She didn't share her suspicions with you. She's like you in a lot of respects, Dante. She takes facts and feelings and mulls them over before she makes a deduction. First conclusions are discarded unless there's hard evidence to support them." She stared at him. "Tell me you wouldn't have done the same."

That thought stayed with him as he drove home ten minutes later. He'd left his sister with Ash, confident the werewolf liaison would be able to help her more than he could at the moment. As he turned onto his street, he went back over the events of the last couple of weeks and reflected on how close he and Tori had become. The love they'd shared. He knew she'd missed having family around, knew she'd been a little envious of the relationship he and Lily had. So he understood her desire to be reunited with her brother and her willingness to believe the best of him.

Dante couldn't imagine being estranged from Lily for a week, let alone over a hundred years.

He pulled into his driveway and stopped the truck in front of the house. He needed to take care of the horses and get a shower and some food. He also had to sort through the feelings rolling around inside him. There was hurt that Tori hadn't trusted him. Anger at her deception.

Love and understanding. And, admittedly, disappointment that he was now the odd man out.

He blew out a breath and turned off the engine. Maybe he could make more sense out of this once he talked to Tori. He climbed out of the truck and went straight to the stables. Both horses nickered a greeting, and Sugarplum set up a loud braying. "I know, boys. You're all hungry. Sorry I'm late with the feed."

He got the horses fed and went into the house. Shucking his clothing, he took a shower. It was only when he started getting dressed that he noticed the top drawer of his dresser was slightly open. Towel fastened around his waist, he walked over and pulled the drawer the rest of the way open.

His stomach dropped. The door to his gun safe was askew. He lifted it, knowing what he'd find. Or, rather, not find. Sure enough, the rift device was gone.

He closed his eyes. Son of a bitch. Had Lily been attacked because she was his sister, or because she was in the wrong place at the wrong time?

Just how much culpability did he share with Tori?

He blew out a breath and grabbed his phone from atop

the dresser. He had to let Tobias know the device was gone.

Tori cradled a cup of coffee at the dining room table. Jeff and Con were both in the living room where they could see her yet still allow a little privacy. She stared down into her mug. Her thoughts tumbled over each other but centered on the two men in her life: her brother and her lover.

She knew Rand would be put to death. He had made other prets without sanction by the council. That carried a heavy penalty. *The* penalty. It was painful, but she finally admitted to herself that the man known as Randall Langston was nothing like the sweet brother she remembered from before the rift. There was nothing more she could do for him.

Then there was Dante. He might be able to eventually forgive her for not telling him about her suspicions concerning her brother, but once she told him that Natchook was also related to her, that she'd known he was around and hadn't said anything, well...that might be harder for him to overlook.

She sighed. It was remarkable how quickly someone's life—*her* life—could go from the top of the world to the lowest abyss of hell. Once again she was all alone in the world.

The doorbell rang. She stood out of habit, and with a warning glance at her Con said, "I've got it."

As he opened the door, a fresh, woodsy scent wafted her way. Dante. He was here. Her heart leaped out of her chest. She sat back down. She wasn't ready to face him. Not yet and definitely not here, with witnesses. She stood up again. She should tell him to go. She sat. No, that wouldn't be right. Whatever he had to say to her, she needed to let him say it. It was the least she could do.

"You have a visitor," Con said as he walked past her. She heard him say to Jeff, "Let's give them a minute," and watched her two guards head to the back of the house.

"But..." Jeff started to protest.

"She's not going anywhere," Con growled. "Move."

Tori turned her head to look at Dante. She mustered a smile that quickly faded in light of his grim countenance. "How's Lily?" she asked quietly.

"She's fine, all things considered." His lips thinned. "Damn it, Tori. Why didn't you say anything before last night?"

She closed her eyes. "I should have, I know." Opening them, she stared at him. "I didn't want to admit my own brother could be behind the attacks. I never dreamed he'd go after you and Lily. Never!"

"Did he say why he did it?"

"He followed me the night I had dinner at your place."

"The night we made love." His voice was husky.

She couldn't find her voice. She gave a short nod and cleared her throat. "That's why the horses were spooked more than they should have been. Remember, I told you they acted like they were surrounded by predators."

"To them, they were," he said. His dark gaze remained on her.

"Rand stayed all night. That morning, when you put the, uh, *thing* in your gun safe, he saw you do it." She drew in a deep breath. "Plus, he wanted you to suffer for shooting him. If I'd thought he would go after Lily to get to it, I would never have agreed to let you keep it there. I would have turned him in if I'd thought that. You have to believe me."

He studied her a moment, then gave a brief nod. "Okay. I do believe that. And I share some culpability in this, because I suggested we store it at my house." He rubbed a hand across his mouth and chin. "To be honest, if I'd been in your shoes I probably would have done the same thing, because I'd do just about anything for Lily." He sighed. Pulling out a chair, he sat down. "My sister's a werewolf now, Tori."

"I know." She leaned forward a little. "It's not always such a bad thing. She won't get sick, ever again." While she would never have suggested that Lily ensure her cancer didn't come back by turning into a werewolf, the fact that the cancer no longer had a feeding ground had to count for something.

He folded his arms and rested against the back of the chair. He looked so closed off. "Ash told me what's gonna happen to your brother," he said. "I'm sorry. Not sorry that he's gonna be punished for what he's done, to be honest. But that you're gonna lose him."

"Thanks." She looked down at her hands. "There's something else I need to tell you." She went into her brief meeting with Stefan and the relationship between them.

Dante went stiff. "Son of a... Have you told me the truth in anything?"

"I guess not." She looked at him. "And I'm sorry for that. But I'm telling you the truth now when I say that I love you."

His expression didn't change. She had no idea what he was thinking.

"If I'd been braver," she whispered, "I would have told

you the truth...all of it." This was the hardest thing she'd ever done, but she didn't break eye contact with him. He needed to see the honesty in her gaze.

"Does Tobias know?" His eyes were as hard as the line of his mouth. "About Natchook being in town?"

"He does now." She blinked back tears. Dante hadn't responded to her declaration of love. Her fear had come true.

She'd lost him.

At that realization, Tori dropped her gaze and stared down at her hands, fingers white with pressure as she clasped them to hide the trembling. "I was...naïve. Mistaken. Stupid. Whatever you want to call it. I just wanted my family back, and I thought Stefan deserved the second chance every pret gets by coming through the rift."

"Even knowing what he did to Nix? Knowing that he would have killed Tobias if he'd gotten the chance?" Disbelief rasped Dante's voice. "Knowing that he's the one behind the rift device?"

She jerked her gaze to him. "I didn't know that. I just found out from Tobias yesterday."

"And now that you do?"

"Of course he needs to be stopped." Her stomach churned. Surely he didn't believe she could think otherwise? Then again, what else was he supposed to believe? She'd given her brother the benefit of the doubt and he ended up being a rogue killer. Her cousin was already a murderer.

She'd wanted her family with her. Now she wondered why.

"As soon as Tobias told me what Stefan...Natchook was up to, I told him that I saw him about a week ago.

And before you ask, I don't know where he is, I swear." Tori stood and started to pace. "I know you don't have any reason to believe me, Dante, but I'm telling you the truth. I am sorry that my decisions caused Lily to get hurt. Sorrier than you'll ever know." She lost steam and plopped back down in her chair.

"You already said you were sorry for that." He blew out a sigh. "And I accept your apology." He rubbed a hand across the back of his neck. "So . . . where do we go from here?"

"What do you mean?" Her heart took up residence in her throat.

"I want to trust you, Tori. I'm usually a good judge of character, and I think this secretiveness is not your usual style."

"It's not." Her pulse rate picked up speed. Was he going where she thought he was going with this? Oh, God, she hoped so.

Dante stared at her. This was the woman he loved. That she was also a werewolf and he wasn't complicated things, sure. That she was the sister of the werewolf who turned his sister complicated things even more. When he'd thought he might turn, he hadn't exactly been thrilled with the idea. Now that he knew otherwise, though, it left him feeling . . . hollow.

Alone.

When it came down to it, he loved Tori. It was as much his fault as hers that Lily had been put in a position of danger.

The question was, was he ready to take the risk of building a life with her? More important, could he face a life without her, however short, relatively speaking, that life might be?

The answer was easy. No.

He stood and drew her to her feet. "I love you," he said, and watched her face go white. "Is that such a bad thing?"

"I think maybe I just hallucinated for a second." Her bright eyes searched his. "Say that again. Please."

He cupped her face in his palms. "I. Love. You." He pressed his mouth to hers for a long, lingering kiss. When the caress ended, he rested his forehead against hers. "I don't know where this road is gonna take us, but I do know that I want to travel it with you."

As a crazy as hell, horrifying yet wonderful thought struck him, he paused, drawing back to stare down into her face.

"What?" she finally asked when he remained silent.

"You could turn me."

She blinked. Disbelief warred with hopeful speculation in her eyes. "What?" she repeated.

"I don't want the next thirty or forty years with you. That's not enough. Not nearly enough, sweetheart. I want forever." He pressed a kiss to the corner of her mouth. "Turn me."

"I...can't." She stroked soft fingers down his cheek. "Dante, you can't really want this. You're just upset. Concerned about Lily—"

"You're damn right I am." He gripped her hand in his and held it against his face. "But I'm also serious about this. When I thought, back at the hospital before the test results came in, that I might turn into a werewolf..." He shook his head and placed a kiss on her palm. "I'll admit

I wasn't too happy about it. But when the results came back negative, I was disappointed. No, more than that. I was devastated." He swallowed, hard. "I don't want to be alone, Tori."

"You'll never be alone." Her arms wrapped around his waist as she buried her face in his neck. He felt moisture against his skin and pushed her back so he could see her. Sure enough, her eyes glittered with tears.

"Hey, hey." He swiped his thumbs under her eyes. "None of that now."

"It's just..." Her lips pressed together. "I thought I'd lost you. I never thought you would forgive me."

"You're human, sweetheart." He gave a crooked grin. "Well, nearly human, anyway. You make mistakes. I do, too. When I think of how much time I wasted fighting my feelings for you..." He shook his head. "The thought of not having you in my life is unbearable."

"Dante..." She drew his head down and kissed him, her soft lips moving under his, parting, taking. Giving.

Someone cleared his throat, and they parted to see the two guards. "Sorry to interrupt," the dark-haired one said. He held up his cell phone. "Just got the call. You're to go back to the council for your sentencing."

Dante frowned. "Sentencing? What the hell is he talking about?" he asked Tori.

She held up her right wrist and for the first time he noticed a band of silver around it. "They wanted to make sure I didn't attempt to shift so I could escape." Her slender shoulders lifted in a shrug. "I withheld information. I'm to be punished."

"Tobias told me to let you know it's not serious. He's sure the council will go with a thirty-day suspension from duties. Minus any silver…enhancements." He gave her a wry grin.

Tori took a deep breath and released it in a quick exhalation. "Thanks for letting me know, Con."

The guard nodded. "We need to go."

"Would you give us a minute?" Dante asked. When the guard didn't move, he added, "Please."

The man gave an aggrieved sigh but motioned his colleague to go to the back of the house again.

Dante took hold of Tori's shoulders. He had to tell her about the rift device before she heard about it from Tobias. Otherwise, she might think Dante had kept information from her to get even. "I need to tell you this before we head out."

"We?"

"There's no way in hell I'm not going with you."

Her smile was tremulous. "They probably won't let you in." Her tongue swept out to wet her full lips. "And I have to get permission to turn you. Even then they may not grant you entrance."

"Then I'll wait outside."

Her soft palm stroked his cheek. "I love you." Her eyes searched his. "What did you need to tell me?"

He took her hand in his, wrapping his fingers around hers. Keeping his voice to a whisper, he said, "The device is gone."

She gave a brief nod. "I know. Rand told me last night."

"I didn't notice it until this morning when I got home from the hospital. I figured your brother had taken it. It would have been too much of a coincidence for it to go missing at the same time as Lily's attack and it *not* be him."

"He gave it to Stefan." In a low voice, she told him how she'd smelled her cousin's scent at the house upon arriving home last night. And what Rand had confessed to her. "At least we still have the schematics."

"Now Stefan may have what he needs for his plan to succeed." Dante's dark eyes held hers. "And we have no idea where he went, or what his next move is."

She tightened her hand on his. "This isn't over, not by a long shot."

"Nope." He tipped her chin up. "But whatever's gonna happen, we'll face it together."

"I like the sound of that," she whispered. "And whatever happens with my job, I'll help you and Tobias stop Stefan. I swear."

As she went up on her toes to kiss his mouth, Dante knew their life wouldn't be an easy one. He had faith that the good times would outweigh the bad. As long as they had each other, they could face whatever the world—this one or one from another dimension—threw their way.

Tori stood in silence, hands clasped behind her back, and waited for someone on the council to speak. All thirteen members were gathered, wearing their flowing white robes. Stern faces gave away nothing of what they were thinking. She took a deep breath but couldn't sort through any emotions. Her gaze went from one to the next, ending with Tobias on the end. One edge of his mouth tipped up and she took that as a sign of encouragement. Even though Con had told her the punishment was going to be fairly light, someone could have changed their minds. And to add to her nervousness, she was going to ask them to allow her to turn Dante. She knew she should wait until they weren't so angry with her, but she couldn't help her anxiousness.

Finally, the council president spoke. "Liaison Joseph, you are standing before this council due to gross negligence of your duties. Your inaction resulted in several deaths and unsanctioned turnings by your brother. Do you have anything to say before we pronounce sentence?"

Tori swallowed. "I..." What could she say that would make any of them feel lenient toward her that she hadn't already said? She refused to beg. "No, my lord Arias."

A glint appeared in Deoul's eyes. He seemed pleased by her response. With a slight nod, he glanced around at the other councilors before meeting her gaze again. "It has been determined that you will be suspended from active duty for no less than thirty days."

She hardly dared relax yet. Going without pay for thirty days would be rough, but she could do it.

"However," Deoul went on, "you will not be placed in silver." At the slight smile of relief she couldn't contain, he raised his brows. "Not all of us were convinced of the wisdom of forgoing that punishment."

She straightened her lips, trying to look suitably chastised. She still had a favor to ask, so now was not the time to antagonize anyone. "I thank the council for their mercy."

"Hmm." Deoul looked at his co-members. "Does anyone have anything to add?" When the other councilors remained silent, Deoul said to Tori, "You may go."

She didn't budge.

He raised his eyebrows. "You have something more?"

"Yes, please."

He waved a hand. "Proceed."

Tori drew a bracing breath. "I beg the council's indulgence...I ask for permission to turn Dante MacMillan."

Stunned silence filled the room before councilors began talking, some louder than others. She glanced at Tobias and saw he was sitting still, his gaze on hers, waiting for the furor to die down.

Deoul got to his feet and braced his palms against the table. "You would request this favor after all you've allowed to happen?"

"I would." She had to talk over the hubbub of voices. "I don't ask it for me. I don't ask it for me," she repeated when they'd quieted again. "I ask this favor for Detective MacMillan."

"How does Dante feel about it?" Tobias leaned forward in his chair, eyes as placid as his voice had been.

"It was his idea."

That shut them up.

"Really?" Caladh also leaned forward, his dark eyes filled with curiosity. "Why does he want to become a werewolf?"

In that moment Tori decided to leave any reference to herself out of it. If they thought he wanted to be like her *because* of her, they might well use that to punish her. "So he can be with his sister. She's the only family he has, and he doesn't want to grow old and eventually die, leaving her alone."

"As a werewolf, she has a new family now, yes?" This from Vida. "She has us. Her pack."

"With all due respect, madam councilwoman, it's not the same thing." Tori knew that all too well. "She's his flesh and blood."

"If I may," Tobias said and stood. "Detective MacMillan would be an excellent asset to the council and to the preternatural community at large. We should consider this."

"Agreed." Caladh leaned back in his chair.

The other councilors murmured their agreement.

Deoul looked at Tori. "Go home. We will advise you of our decision within the next forty-eight hours."

Tori knew, whatever they decided, she'd stand by her man, as corny as that sounded. She'd see to it that Dante wasn't alone.

Epilogue

Rain fell in heavy sheets, bringing much needed water to the drought-stricken Sonoran Desert. Two wolves ran side by side through the downpour and then stopped beneath a mesquite tree. Muscles and sinew rippled beneath skin and fur. Bones shifted and realigned, reforming themselves. Wet fur receded, leaving behind only tanned skin as the wolves became human.

Became man and woman.

Tori took several shuddering breaths and fought her way back from the mind of the wolf. Her body ached, and as the last of the wolf retreated inside, it gave her one final slash of pain. She took another deep breath and looked at the man next to her. "Well?" she asked, her voice raspy. "Was it what you expected?"

Dante's eyes still held the amber glow of the wolf. "So much more. My God." He cupped her chin in his hand and slanted his mouth over hers. She leaned into the kiss, going down onto her knees to wrap her arms around his neck. She raked her fingers through his wet hair, dragging her nails lightly across his scalp. He drew back and stared down at her. "The sense of freedom, of belonging..."

"Belonging to..." she prompted.

"Everything." He planted another kiss on her lips, this one brief and hard, a promise of things to come. "Let's get dressed and get home," he said, reaching behind him for the plastic bag that held their clothing. He handed over her jeans, T-shirt, and underwear and they dressed, awkwardly bent over beneath the branches of the tree. Then a barefooted dash through the downpour brought them to his heavy-duty pickup truck.

As he drove from the trailhead back toward the main road, he reached over and took her hand, strong, warm fingers wrapped around hers. "So are you ever gonna tell me what made the council change their minds?"

Initially, the council had denied the request. Then they'd backed down and told her she could turn him, but only if she promised to have nothing further to do with Dante. It would have devastated her, but she would have done it. She would have given him up if it meant he could have a long life with his sister.

In the end, Tobias had convinced the others that requiring that of her punished Dante as much as it hurt her. And so they'd done away with any sort of requirement attached to the turning.

"I already told you. You did. Your dedication to your job, your pursuit of the truth, your respect of preternaturals." She squeezed his hand. "All I did was ask. They agreed because it was you."

"Hmm." He looked like he didn't believe her, but that was because he didn't think he was all that special. Thankfully, the council had disagreed.

As did Tori. She thought Dante was pretty damn special. And now she had the rest of immortality to spend with him.

He was her love. He was her family. She'd been so hopeful with her brother and her cousin, and had her heart crushed by their cruel, immoral acts. Now she had a husband and a sister by marriage and, if fate was kind, in the future they'd add to the MacMillan clan.

She couldn't wait to see what the future held.

Sparks fly when a fae warrior and a demon bad boy cross paths.

When they learn they're working for opposing sides, can the fire between them survive?

Please turn this page for a preview of

Heart of the Demon.

Prologue

Zombies got a bad rap these days. At least that's what the drunk one kept telling Finn Evnissyen as he sat at the bar nursing his beer.

"I mean, come on. Do I look like I'm rotting?" The guy held out one arm and turned it so Finn could see the underside. The action sent a waft of ammonia covered up by too much cologne.

That small hint of ammonia told Finn that this guy had become a zombie within hours of death instead of days. Yeah, if he'd been dead longer than that he wouldn't be so pretty and would be much more odiferous.

The zombie flexed his arm again. "Nope," he muttered, answering his own question. "Skin's as clear as a baby's bottom."

Finn didn't give a rat's ass about the zombie's skin or baby bottoms. "Uh-huh," he grunted. He swiveled around on his stool to look out over the bar. It was just after three in the afternoon, and the bar already had a healthy clientele made up of various preternaturals and humans. Finn brought his glass to his lips and sipped while he checked out the other drinkers.

A couple of blue-collar looking guys, probably human,

sat at a back booth with pretzels and beers and their eyes glued to the large TV screen hanging on one wall. It looked like a pre-season game of the Arizona Cardinals and Green Bay Packers. Finn watched for a few minutes, trying to ignore the zombie still yammering in his ear.

There was a lone drinker at the end of the bar that caught Finn's eye. He leaned around zombie guy for a better look, and the loner hunched over his drink, obviously not wanting Finn to see him. Finn understood wanting to be alone with his drink, but he did want to know what kind of pret he was sharing a bar with. Doing his job as well as he did meant he'd made a few enemies. Hell, more than a few. So he wanted to make sure the guy trying to hide behind his drink wasn't a demon with a grudge.

Finn took a few sniffs of air and grimaced at the sickly-sweet smell emanating from the man next to him, a man who was still going on about zombies getting such negative press.

"Really, man." The zombie lifted his drink. "Just because we happen to like brains—"

"Mack!" Finn held up his hand to signal the bartender. Enough was enough. He slammed his glass onto the bar and scowled. He'd come here for a drink or three, not to strike up conversation with some random smelly dude. Since this guy wouldn't shut up, it was time to go. He slapped a few bills down on the bar and pushed off his stool.

"You gotta go?" The whiny zombie looked like he was about to cry. "We was just gettin' started."

"Yeah, well, somebody's disturbing my quiet." Finn shot the guy a look and headed toward the front of the bar.

He glanced behind him for another look at the man hiding behind his drink and saw he had leaned back and was watching Finn, a sneer curling his upper lip. Bloodshot eyes and a slight mottling of the left side of his face—not that noticeable unless you were looking for it—told Finn he was a hobgoblin. So...not a threat. Just surly.

As Finn pushed open the door, he slipped his sunglasses over his eyes. The humid monsoon air of a late Scottsdale afternoon slapped him in the face. God, it was so hot it felt like he'd just stepped into an oven. *Highway to Hell* began playing on his phone. He dragged it out of his pocket and answered with a terse, "What's up, Dad?"

"I need to see you. Now." Lucifer Demonicus got, as always, right to the point. "My office."

"I'm a little busy right now." He wasn't, but dear old dad didn't need to know that.

"My office. Ten minutes."

"Dad? Dad!" Finn realized his father had disconnected the call. "Damn it." He shoved his phone back into his pocket. He could blow off his dad, but if he did he had no doubt that the old devil would find him, or send some of his goons. "Damn it," he muttered again, and threw a leg over the seat of his motorcycle. One day he'd be free from his father's power to dictate his every move. As soon as he could find something to use as leverage, he'd be out from beneath the king of demons' tyranny.

Until then, though...With a scowl he started the motorcycle and pulled away from the curb. The sooner he got this over with, the better.

He headed his bike down Scottsdale Avenue toward the office building where the leader of demons in the region conducted his many businesses, legitimate and otherwise. He was just crafty enough not to get caught by the authorities. Finn had a lot to do with that as his father's enforcer. When a demon stepped too far out of line—and Lucifer was actually pretty lenient—Finn was the one sent to dispense justice. Which wasn't always quick, or painless.

Or neat.

But he got the job done because somehow in all the mess that was the preternatural community, being the son of the devil evidently meant he'd been born into indentured servitude.

Finn stopped at a traffic light and glanced at the car that pulled to a halt in the next lane. Flirty smiles on their faces, two of the most beautiful women he'd ever seen looked at him with invitation in their eyes. He didn't get even a single twitch of interest from his body. He blew out a sigh and looked at the light. When a demon could look at two succubi and feel nothing, something was wrong. Really, really wrong.

The light switched to green and he took off, nearly burning a swath of rubber in his hurry to get away from them. When he reached his father's office building Finn drove up onto the sidewalk and brought his bike to a stop by the front door. He heeled down the kick stand and swung his leg over the seat. As he went through the automatic doors he tipped his head at the security guys at the front desk. "Fellas," he greeted.

"You should move that before your father sees it." The guard gestured toward the motorcycle.

Finn merely grinned. If Lucifer had a problem with where he parked his ride, the old man could tell him to get lost. Finn would happily do so.

He took the elevator to the top floor, getting off at the penthouse suite. He crossed the inlaid wood foyer, his boots thumping over the expensive flooring, and went straight into his father's no-less than opulent office. "The master calleth?" he asked and flung himself down in one of the leather chairs across from Lucifer's desk.

"I did." Lucifer looked away from the bank of security monitors on the wall and leaned back in his chair. His dark eyes held Finn's. His youthful face, making him appear to be in his early forties when in reality he'd been on Earth for over seven thousand years, belied the fact that he had a son as old as Finn.

Not that Finn looked old. He wasn't vain, but he knew he looked good for his age, roughly thirty-five or so.

His father shook his head and gestured toward the monitors. "Don't think that parking your motorcycle right in front of the building is enough to cause me to release you from your...obligations."

"Obligations? Is that what my job is called?" Finn crossed his legs, resting one ankle on top of the opposite knee. He drummed his fingers on the arm of the chair. "How is it that just by virtue of being your son I'm automatically at your beck and call forever?" He held his father's dark gaze. "Seriously, I've been doing this for almost three thousand years. Don't you have another son you can foist this job on, make him miserable for a while?"

"Miserable. Really?" Lucifer frowned, the action barely causing wrinkles to form.

Finn folded his arms over his chest. "We've talked about this before. I want to do something more. I want to *e* something more."

"Is that so?" From the tone of Lucifer's voice, it was clear he didn't give a damn. "Well, no matter. I have another job for you."

No matter? Finn slouched in his chair. "And if I say no?"

"Don't turn it down before we've had a chance to tell you about it." Lucifer pressed a button on his desk and Finn heard the elevator start up.

"We?" Finn twisted around as the elevator doors pinged open. He frowned at the vampire who stepped into the foyer.

"Tobias, come in," Lucifer said, getting to his feet. The two men shook hands and the vampire took the chair next to Finn.

"What's this all about?" Finn asked as Lucifer sat back down.

A former liaison to the Council of Preternaturals, Tobias Caine was now a council member. He shifted in his seat to look at Finn. "We're looking at statistics taken over the years to determine the breakdown of preternaturals who come through the rift opened by the Moore-Creasy-Devon comet," Caine said. "It's apparent that out of all the pret clans, demons have the smallest representation."

"So?" Finn frowned. "There are fewer of us than other prets. We can hold our own."

"For how long?" Lucifer leaned his elbows on the desk. "Every seventy-three years, when the comet opens the rift between dimensions, fewer demons come through than any other preternatural. Century after century this occurs. In another few hundred years we could very well be nearly extinct."

"Can't we just procreate the old fashioned way?" Finn

wasn't sure what the fuss was all about. Preternaturals didn't just happen because they came through the rift and took over bodies of human hosts. "That's how I got here, after all."

"Demon women would have to be perpetually pregnant to make any headway," Caine said dryly.

"The only way preternaturals keep the community somewhat at peace is because there is a balance between all groups. As soon as one group becomes more powerful than the others, there will be a fight for control," Lucifer added.

"I've never been much of a big picture kind of guy," Finn said. "You might need to explain why you're acting like this is my problem."

"Because, *son*, it's my problem. Therefore, it's yours, too."

Finn blew out a sigh. Since this wasn't something that involved another demon directly, Finn's skills as an enforcer weren't being called upon. Which meant he could refuse it. "Sorry," he said, not meaning a bit of it. "Whatever it is you're wanting me to do, I'll pass." He wanted to get away from doing his father's bidding, not do more of it.

"You can't refuse to help, Finn." Lucifer crossed his arms and glowered at his son.

"Are you asking me to hunt down a demon who's been attacking humans or other prets?"

"Not exactly."

"Then I believe I can refuse. And I do."

"Look, I know you've never looked out for anyone but yourself, and you do a hell of a job at it, but we need you on this one," Caine said.

"You're such a sweet talker," Finn muttered. "I have one question: What's in it for me?"

Caine's scowl mirrored Lucifer's. He muttered a curse. "Cut the crap, Finn. You're not as much of a loner as you make out. Listen to your conscience." Caine pressed his lips together. "And if that doesn't work, I'll give you half a mill to do it."

"To do what, exactly?" It had to be something good for Caine to toss around that kind of money.

The vampire shared a glance with Lucifer, then said, "We want you to infiltrate a rogue group. We think they're planning... something for the next Influx."

The next influx of preternaturals through the rift was due in three months. That didn't give him a lot of time to go undercover.

"We figure your reputation will speak for itself," Caine added.

"The thing is..." Finn stretched his legs out in front of him and clasped his hands across his stomach. "I don't need the money. I've got plenty."

"Two million." This from Lucifer.

And it cut. Since when had Finn ever done anything he'd been asked to because of the paycheck? He might be a lot of things, but mercenary wasn't one of them. He clenched his jaw and shook his head. "I don't need the money," he repeated.

"Three million."

Finn folded his arms over his chest and thought about it. Oh, not about the money. He'd been truthful when he said he didn't need it. He had more money than he could spend in a hundred years. Or more. But there was something he'd been wanting, something that had been just out of his reach for so long…He really couldn't care less about what happened with the rift, but he would like to be his own man for once. Do what he wanted when he wanted instead of having to ask permission from his boss, who also happened to be his father and the leader of the demon enclave in the region.

He'd never felt like he'd measured up to Lucifer's expectations, and about five hundred years ago he'd given up trying. He did his job well because that was the kind of guy he was—you do the job you're hired to do regardless of the pay. And now he didn't care if good ol' dad was proud of him or not.

At least, that's what he told himself. And perhaps if he kept telling himself that eventually he'd believe it.

But for the chance to be his own boss…He'd been tossing around the idea of running a private security firm, one that would cater to the rich and powerful—both preternatural and human—and this might just be his chance.

"There's more to you asking for my help than my rep," he said, looking from his dad to Caine.

Lucifer cleared his throat, drawing Finn's gaze. "The chameleon abilities you got from your mother will prove useful."

Finn raised his eyebrows. "You told him?" he asked, amazed that his father would tell an outsider a closely guarded secret that not even all demons knew.

"I trust him."

Finn studied Caine. He didn't know him, not really. He'd had some dealings with Caine in the past, and the vampire struck him as…intense. Dedicated and single-minded in his pursuit of justice. And someone capable of taking secrets to his grave.

"As I understand it," the vampire said, "you can take on the abilities of any preternatural. So you can enhance your hearing to the level of a werewolf's, or your sense of smell, right?"

Finn nodded. "There's a little more to it than that, though. For a short period of time I can actually become that preternatural."

"Meaning..."

"If I mimic a werewolf, I can shift into a wolf. Or if I want to imitate a vampire..." He paused and got to his feet. "Here, let me show you."

It had been a while since Finn had impersonated a vamp. He studied Caine, took a deep breath to get his scent, then closed his eyes to concentrate on summoning his chameleon demon abilities. There was a burst of heat deep inside, then his body cooled down. His jaw began to ache and his canine teeth lengthened into fangs. When he opened his eyes, it was to see Caine staring at him in shock.

The vampire stood and walked over to him. "What the hell..." He stopped and drew in a deep breath. "Damn. You even smell like a vampire." He glanced at Lucifer. "This is definitely a skill we can use."

Lucifer gave a sly smile. "Indeed."

Finn let go of the pretense and became his normal self again. He dropped back down into his chair and exhaled. Since he was only part chameleon, he was unable to hold onto a deception as easily as a full-blooded chameleon could and even that little bit had taxed his energy. Not that he'd ever admit out loud that he was tired.

"Come on, Finn." Caine shoved his hands in his pockets. "We need you."

Finn thought about it a moment then, looking at his father, said, "I'll tell you what. You free me from my enforcer duties, and I'll do this."

"Done."

Finn's brow furrowed. He hadn't expected it to be that easy. It hadn't been when he'd asked before. He knew this was some serious shit for his father to so readily agree to his demand. "Fine." Finn looked at Caine. "Tell me what you want me to do."

Acknowledgments

Thank you to my family, friends, and fans. I couldn't do this without you!

Major thanks to Suzanne Moore, who lets me vent, rant, and otherwise make no sense, then gives me a drink, kicks me in the rear, and tells me to get back to work. I also need to thank my other critique partners, Roz Denny Fox and Alison Hentges. I'm only as good as you ladies make me.

A shout-out to my fabulous agent, Susan Ginsburg, and my editors, Latoya Smith and Selina McLemore. You humble me with your belief in me. And I have to give a high five to the art department at Grand Central for giving me yet another wonderful cover.

THE DISH

Where authors give you the inside scoop!

♥ ♥ ♥ ♥ ♥ ♥ ♥ ♥ ♥ ♥ ♥ ♥ ♥ ♥ ♥ ♥

From the desk of Cynthia Garner

Dear Reader,

You've now met several characters from my Warriors of the Rift series, and in SECRET OF THE WOLF you get to know Dante MacMillan and Victoria Joseph. Dante's a man with a lot of people depending on him, from his colleagues to his sister, who's just getting over chemotherapy treatments and an unexpected divorce—as well as three lovely four-legged friends named Big Ben, Studmuffin, and Sugardaddy.

Some of the real events that happened in the Phoenix area while I was writing this book included a huge dust storm called a haboob. The first one that blew through the area shut down Sky Harbor Airport. The monster was around 5,000 feet high when it slammed into Phoenix, but radar indicated it had reached heights of 10,000 feet prior to hitting the city. It was caused by the winds that come with our monsoon season, but instead of a rain storm the Phoenix area got a dust storm.

I think I'd rather have monsters in the form of werewolves and vampires, thank you very much. A 10,000-foot-high wall of dust is too apocalyptic for me. (Come to think of it, I may actually prefer a zombie apocalypse over a haboob. The one we had was very reminiscent of that one scene in *The Mummy*. Of course, if Brendan Fraser came along for the ride...)

While Dante and Tori didn't have to put up with monster dust storms, they did have to work with other monsters while they focused on a special project during their off-duty hours that brought them close in more ways than one.

As with *Kiss of the Vampire*, I have extras up on my website: a character interview with Tori, some pictures of Scottsdale where the story takes place, and a character tree showing the Council of Preternaturals and their hierarchy.

Look for the next installment, *Heart of the Demon*, coming soon! Finn Evnissyen may not be all he seems to be.

Happy Reading!

Cynthia Garner

cynthiagarnerbooks@gmail.com
http://cynthiagarnerbooks.com

♥ ♥ ♥ ♥ ♥ ♥ ♥ ♥ ♥ ♥ ♥ ♥ ♥ ♥ ♥ ♥

From the desk of Jill Shalvis

Dear Reader,

A few years ago, my family went camping. We brought our boat, and on the first day there, we launched it on the lake for the duration of our stay. My husband gave me my choice of driving the truck and trailer to the campsite or driving the boat across the lake to the dock. It was windy, and I'm a boat wuss, so I picked the truck. Halfway around the lake, I got the trailer stuck on a weird hairpin turn and had to be rescued by a forest ranger. He was big and tough and armed and overworked, and undoubtedly underpaid as well, but the man helped me out of a jam so my husband wouldn't kill me. Ever since then, I've wanted to write a forest ranger into one of my books as a hero.

Enter Matt Bowers. Big and tough and armed and overworked and underpaid. Like my real-life hero, he also stopped and helped a damsel in distress. Of course, Matt gets a lot more in the bargain than my poor beleaguered forest ranger ever got. Matt Bowers gets waitress Amy Michaels, beautiful, tough, jaded...and in desperate need of rescuing. She just doesn't know it yet.

Hope you enjoy watching these two warily circle each other on their path to true love. Like me, neither of them takes the easy way. I mean, what's the fun in that?

Our family had a great summer at that lake, and it's a great summer for me this year too with not one, but three Lucky Harbor novels. So if you enjoy AT LAST, don't miss sexy Special Ops soldier Ty Garrison in *Lucky in Love* and handsome doctor Josh Scott in *Forever and a Day*, coming in August.

Happy Reading—all summer long!

Jill Shalvis

http://www.jillshalvis.com

http://www.facebook.com/jillshalvis

♥ ♥ ♥ ♥ ♥ ♥ ♥ ♥ ♥ ♥ ♥ ♥ ♥ ♥ ♥

From the desk of Molly Cannon

Dear Reader,

There used to be a bar way out in the country where my husband and I would go with a bunch of our friends to dance on Saturday nights. We'd drive for miles and miles down these dark, unlit roads, and then in the distance we'd see the glow against the night sky from the pole lights in the parking lot. We'd pull in, the gravel crunching under our tires, and the place would be packed. After we found a place to park, we'd scramble out of our cars and head inside. The sound of country music and the smell of beer would hit us like a wave when we walked in the door. And the building—it was gigantic, a big, barn-like place—but we'd find a table and settle in for a night of two-stepping, drinking beer, and hanging out with our friends.

As I danced, I couldn't help but do a little people watching. The women would all be dressed to the nines in their dancing outfits, trying to catch someone's eye. The men would be on the prowl but doing their best to play it cool. I'd keep my eye on the blonde woman in the yellow dress: She'd come with one guy, but she danced with another one all night long. Or the tall, stern-looking cowboy at the bar who never took his eyes off the short, dark-haired girl in the pink shirt for a single second. She huddled up with a group of girlfriends, so I wondered if he'd ever work up the courage to ask her for a dance. There might be a couple arguing in one corner, and a couple kissing in another. It was always quite a show: love, lust, broken hearts, maybe some cheating, and a lot of hanky-panky—all played out to the quick-quick, slow-slow beat of a country song. That dance hall is gone now, and the countryside has been swallowed up by neighborhoods and paved roads with streetlights, but I haven't forgotten the nights I spent there.

So it's no accident that the first scene of my book AIN'T MISBEHAVING takes place in a parking lot. Not just any parking lot, but the parking lot outside of Lu Lu's, the local watering hole in Everson, Texas. When Marla Jean Bandy decides it's time to quit spending nights home alone after her divorce, when she decides it's time to bust out and have some fun, Lu Lu's is just the kind of place I thought she needed. Decked out in a tight red dress and her best cowboy boots, she's ready to get back out there and have a good time…until Jake Jacobsen, a childhood crush, shows up and tries to run interference. Marla Jean is about to find out that a parking lot on a Saturday night can be full of delicious possibilities.

I hope you enjoy AIN'T MISBEHAVING and have fun getting to know Marla Jean, Jake, and all the meddlesome, well-meaning folks in Everson, Texas.

Happy Reading!

Molly Cannon

www.mollycannon.com

Facebook.com

Twitter @cannonmolly

Find out more about Forever Romance!

Visit us at
www.hachettebookgroup.com/publishing_forever.aspx

Find us on Facebook
http://www.facebook.com/ForeverRomance

Follow us on Twitter
http://twitter.com/ForeverRomance

NEW AND UPCOMING TITLES

Each month we feature our new titles
and reader favorites.

CONTESTS AND GIVEAWAYS

We give away galleys, autographed copies,
and all kinds of exclusive items.

AUTHOR INFO

You'll find bios, articles, and links to personal websites
for all your favorite authors—and so much more.

GET SOCIAL

Connect with your favorite authors, editors, and
other Forever fans, and share what's important to you.

THE BUZZ

Sign up for our monthly romance newsletter,
and be the first to read all about it.